Rules of Darkness

A Post-Apocalyptic EMP Survival Thriller

D1736179

JACK HUNT

DIRECT RESPONSE PUBLISHING

Also By Jack Hunt

The Renegades
The Renegades 2: Aftermath
The Renegades 3: Fortress
The Renegades 4: Colony
The Renegades 5: United
Mavericks: Hunters Moon
Killing Time
State of Panic
State of Shock
State of Decay
Defiant
Phobia
Anxiety
Strain
Blackout
Darkest Hour
Final Impact
And Many More…

Dedication

For my family.

Prologue

What a pitiful sight. Andy Ford's eyes drifted across the fresh cluster of virgin faces seated in room 201 of city hall. He was beginning to have second thoughts on his offer to help the community of Whitefish, Montana. He figured there would be at least one jarhead — someone with a skill set that would make his job easier. Nope. These weren't preppers, warriors or even survivalists. They were average joes, wannabes and volunteers. In fact they were the only ones that sorry sack of shit Ted Hudgens could muster together. That was because anyone with a lick of sense had already left town, or barricaded themselves inside their home. Which at 8 a.m. was exactly where he should have been. He wouldn't have minded if he could have blamed someone for twisting his arm, but the irony was no one had convinced him to help. He made the choice of his own volition, well, the decision was partly guided by not wanting to have Corey show him up but still, he only had himself to blame.

Once again, his ego had got the better of him. Now if he'd just stayed silent in the last town hall meeting, he wouldn't be here sipping on dismal-tasting coffee and imagining his life was anything but this.

His shoulders sank under the weight of the responsibility.

Newbies.

Amateurs.

A complete disgrace to the flag.

But they weren't the only ones that made him shake his head. Andy cast a sideways glance at Hudgens who was introducing him. Standing there, red-faced, thumbs tucked into his waistband, belly sticking out, he was every bit the perfect representation of gluttony and self-indulgence. Hudgens was a hop, skip and a jump away from a heart attack. How he'd managed to land the position of mayor was a total mystery.

"It is my privilege to introduce to you, Andy Ford. Some of you already know him. For others, this will be a first. His track record speaks for itself. Andy's reputation precedes him. His skill set is unmatched. And his experience invaluable. It's because of these reasons and more that he's offered to help us…to help you, as we stare down the barrel at an uncertain future. Please give him your full attention, and on behalf of Whitefish, thank you for stepping up at this critical time."

Okay, he was kissing ass but that was because no one else would take the job. Hudgens took a seat to the right side of the room alongside Chief Bruce.

Outside the sound of heavy gunfire made the nervous ones in the group turn their heads toward the windows. A lot had changed in a month since the power across the nation had gone out. The harsh reality of their new world was now deeply ingrained. It hadn't taken long for them to burn their way through resources and supplies. After the fires and riots which devastated the town, the challenge to survive increased and with it came violence on a scale that only he had foreseen. Desperation was the new way of living and the prowling wolves of society were now on their doorstep — hungry and prepared to kill.

Andy sniffed hard, smoothed out his fatigues and stepped up to the front of the room. That morning he'd shaved off what little remained of his hair, and donned high-end tactical clothing that he had once sold in his army surplus store. On his hip was a SIG SAUER P320. He tossed the half-finished cup of mud masquerading as coffee into the trash and eyeballed the unfortunate group entrusted to him.

Another flurry of rounds caught their attention.

"Get used to it," he said following their nervous gaze. "It's not going to get any better. I'm not here to cherry coat this or hold your hand. I'm not your father, your leader or your minister. I have one job and that's to get you ready to replace those who have already given their lives to defend this town from looters and raiders. I'm not stupid, I know some of you are here to get the perks, for others you fancy yourself as a big hero, and the rest of you, you've convinced yourself you want to protect this town when really, it's the admiration you want. I don't care why you signed up. The few officers that are still operating don't care. And quite frankly, most of this town doesn't care. All I care about is that when I speak, you listen, when I teach, you pay attention and when I demonstrate, you do exactly what is asked without whining. Do I make myself clear?"

There were a few grunts, a couple of nods and the rest sat there blank faced. Andy knew that among the group there would be those who would test him. It was always the same when it came to teaching. While running countless prepper workshops he'd come across his fair share of people who showed up simply to throw their two cents into the ring. Those who came to learn he had no issues with, it was those who thought they knew it all.

"What are your credentials?" a guy piped up from the back before glancing at his buddy, a smile forming. He was mid-twenties, wearing a military-style jacket and cargo pants. His dark hair was shaved tight at the sides of his head, and he had a large amount on the top that was swept back with some shiny hair product.

"Excuse me?"

"Well the mayor said you have credentials. From what I can tell you haven't been through this experience any more than us. I mean if this was war and you had been through the heat of battle, I could understand, but from what I can tell, you are no different than us. What makes you qualified to teach? And what will we learn?"

There he was. There was always one.

"And you are?" Andy asked.

"Mike Fisher."

"What are your credentials, Mike?"

"That wasn't the question."

Andy stepped down off the small platform. "No, it wasn't. But in order to answer to your liking — as I'm sure you were planning on comparing the two — I need to know what you bring to the table?"

Mike squirmed in his seat looking more uncomfortable by the second as Andy made his way towards him. He swallowed hard. "I know how to shoot a rifle."

"Well that's pretty impressive. Short range? Long range?"

"Both," Mike replied.

"And what else?"

"I uh…" He looked at his two buddies sitting either side of him as if hoping they would back him up but they dropped their chins. "Look, does it matter?"

"Of course it does, otherwise you wouldn't have asked me what I plan to teach you."

"I just…I just think that we should know we're not wasting our time here."

"Wasting your time?"

"Yeah. I mean from what I hear, you ran an army surplus store but it was your brother who was in the army, not you."

Andy smiled. "Impressive. You've done a full background check. You're right. I didn't serve in the military. My brother Lou did but that doesn't mean squat. So, what else did you learn?"

"That your…"

As he tried to get the words out Andy walked behind and placed his hands on his shoulders. "Come on now. Don't be shy. What else did you find out about me?"

"That you are…"

Before he could finish, Andy wrapped his arm around his throat and yanked him back, pulling him to the ground. Those around him jumped up from their seats, a look of shock on their faces. His two buddies tried to come to his aid but Andy pulled his gun and aimed at them. "Back up!"

Hudgens looked dumbfounded. It didn't take long for Chief Bruce to rush over and try to intervene. "Let him go, Andy. What the hell are you doing?"

"Teaching lesson one. The element of surprise. Now

let me ask Mr. Fisher here, what he's learned. Well, Mr. Fisher?"

He struggled within his grasp, his face turned a deep red. Barely able to spit the words out, he replied, "Not to turn my back on the enemy. Never trust anyone," he said.

Andy released his grip. "Very good. Maybe there is hope for you." He got up and walked back to the front of the room as if nothing had happened. "Now in answer to your question about credentials. Tell me at the end if you learned anything. Now that we have that out of the way, let's continue, shall we?" he said turning towards a room full of shocked, if not slightly scared individuals.

Chapter 1

The raid was set for 9.a.m. Corey was outfitted in a full tactical police uniform and tucked into the back of his old man's green utility truck. There were four other vehicles on the ash-covered roads of Whitefish that morning, two of which were on loan from Kalispell, along with six additional officers. In the aftermath of the blackout, and the deaths of multiple officers, the Whitefish Police Department had been closely working with Flathead County, sharing resources and assisting each other. Still reeling from the death of Ella, Corey had taken a position with the local department if only to keep his mind occupied. According to Chief Bruce his military background was an asset.

Along with ten police officers Corey was on route to the intersection of 13th Street and US-93 after gaining intel on raiders that had struck their supply distribution van only days earlier. Of course it was a problem of its own making. For the first couple weeks, if anyone needed additional food, water or medical supplies, they had to go to the emergency operations center at the local school. There, locals were served on a case-by-case basis. This was fine for those who qualified but those who didn't were sent away empty-handed and instructed to fish and forage. This of course created a new set of challenges. The decision to turn people away wasn't done to be mean-spirited but to prevent the greedy from blowing through what little they had. It was a tough pill to swallow, but understandable in light of the circumstances. Most accepted this as the new reality and rolled with the change. Others? They refused to follow the rules.

Now, had the EOC supplies remained under the watchful eye of armed guards, there was a good chance they wouldn't be hunting raiders that morning. However, Hudgens had decided that those who couldn't come to the center due to health issues or age would have supplies dropped off at their residences. A simple task if the country hadn't gone to hell. A dangerous job in light of circumstances. The riots and fires had only increased the need. Sending out that van, even if it was guarded, was like dangling meat in front of lions. It was only a matter of time before someone took a bite. And they did. A group had risen and were responsible for a string of attacks that led to supplies being taken. The only thing they left behind was a symbol of a star. At first Hudgens didn't want to entertain the idea that one group might be responsible for a string of attacks throughout Whitefish but when officials of surrounding towns shared similar stories, and produced photographs of the same star sprayed on vans and walls, it could no longer be ignored.

Corey stared out the window as the truck kicked up dust. They drove past the charred remains of buildings toward their destination of Best Bet Casino. They wouldn't have given it a passing look on any other day as the need to protect the EOC and homes within the region, not places that once catered to gamblers.

"We're getting close," Ferris said over the two-way radio. "We'll wait for you to take up position before we move in." Corey wasn't holding the radio and Ferris wasn't in the same vehicle as him. Corey had purposely kept his distance since the incident at the hospital. Even though Ferris had told him through Chief Bruce that he had done everything in his power to ensure the safety of Ella, Corey didn't know what to believe. He couldn't exactly blame him for telling Gabriel where Corey was, as he'd threatened his family. Corey may have done the same thing. Still, he was torn up about it and preferred to avoid the topic. Instead he funneled his energy into working twelve to fourteen-hour shifts with zero days off. Under any other conditions he might have got pulled aside about his mental health but not now.

The truck rumbled past the casino and pulled into a large parking lot for Safeway. The brakes squealed as the driver eased off the gas and brought the vehicle to a halt. Within seconds four of them hopped out and ran at a crouch towards the building. There they were led in by the owner of the store and directed up to the roof where they would take up position with rifles. Ferris had organized it so that his team would swoop in and surround the small one-story brick casino and Corey and the other three would watch their backs from a distance. Corey didn't say a word to the other three officers as he crouched down near the edge of the building and got his rifle into position. He peered through the scope at the brick and mortar structure and waited. He wasn't in charge of the group. In fact he'd rejected the idea of helping but Chief Bruce thought it would be a good idea. He knew that was bullshit. His work in finding the inmates was the reason he'd brought him in. They assumed he would use the same expertise in locating those responsible in the recent string of attacks. But like he told them, it was luck. Nothing but luck. And in some ways, it wasn't even luck, it was a curse. Had he not killed Gabriel's brother, maybe, just maybe Ella would still be alive. Corey could have backed down from the offer to help the department but that would have meant moping around his father's cabin, and he was already getting on his last nerve. No, he'd figured his days would be spent patrolling the town, doing nothing but routine checks, but since the attacks on homes and supply trucks had increased he'd had his hands full trying to track those responsible.

"Corey. You good?" Reynolds asked. He gave him the thumbs-up before returning to looking through the scope. Over the radio he heard Reynolds give Ferris the okay. One by one the vehicles rolled in, swerving into different positions before the cops got out and took up position behind them. Due to the unknowns, and the high level of violence this group had used in their attacks, the choice to head in was ruled out. The safe way, the only way was to use communication, Ferris said. Corey had been in the room for the briefing. He and Ferris had exchanged a cold stare. Communication meant something very different to him. Still, he watched from the safety of the roof, directing his rifle at the windows of the building. At the first sign of trouble they were instructed to take out visible threats.

There was no movement.

Corey focused in on Ferris, his head was in the crosshair of his rifle. All it would take was one squeeze and he could take him out.

The thought had crossed his mind multiple times that morning. Some part of him thought that Ferris wasn't telling him the whole truth about the day Ella died. While he didn't believe Ferris was the kind of man that would have put Ella in harm's way, he knew how single-focused he could become, to the point of ignoring alternatives. It was possible that Ella had provided an alternative and he'd not listened. Had that got her killed? He would never know and that burned him.

With no radio inside the building or phone line, Ferris had to communicate using a megaphone. He pulled it from the trunk, and it let out a squeal as he turned it on. They'd been given a name for the man in charge of the group. Alexander Dreymon.

"Dreymon. This is the Whitefish Police Department. Come out of the building with your hands above your heads."

There was silence and no movement in the windows.

"Dreymon!"

Seconds turned into minutes before Ferris got on the radio and told Reynolds to keep a close eye as they moved in. Ferris raised a hand and indicated to the others to move in. Four of the cops ran at a crouch towards the main entrance. They were roughly fifteen feet from the main door when one of them yelled, "Grenade!"

It all occurred so fast.

The explosion, then rapid gunfire.

It was hard to tell whether bullets cut them down or the explosion but when the dust settled four officers were dead. Corey could hear yelling over the radio. Ferris had dropped down behind bullet-peppered vehicles along with three other officers. Corey got up and hustled over to Reynolds and snatched the radio out of his hand.

"Pull out. Now."

"What?" Ferris replied.

"Get those men out of there now."

"Listen up, Ford. Your job is to take them out."

"You'll get them killed. Get out of there now."

He knew the conversation wasn't about the men, but Ella. The truth was they had no idea how many were inside. The guy they'd flipped in Kalispell knew Dreymon headed up the group in Whitefish but he couldn't give an accurate number of those involved, and even if he could, there was no telling who was with him. For all they knew, the raiders could have been working in small cell groups throughout the town. That was how Corey would have done it.

Ferris stopped replying on the radio.

"Stubborn asshole," Corey said. "I'm going down to help."

"Hold your position, that's an order," Reynolds said.

"Fuck your order."

Corey ignored him, heading back down into the store and through a side exit. He burst out and hurried across to try and reach one of the officers that was still alive but trapped in between the vehicles and the casino. Ferris, Reynolds and the others engaged, tearing up the windows and walls of the casino as Corey zigzagged his way over to the cop on the ground, his name was Harris. He grabbed him by his vest and began dragging him out. The other cops were dead. In that moment he didn't think about getting shot and yet the odds of being killed were extremely high. He knew it was a bad move but how he felt about living had changed the day Ella and his unborn baby died. It was as if he was moving through life in slow motion, nothing more than a body going through routine. Death would have been freedom, bliss even. A sweet release from the hell that was now his life.

Crack, crack, crack!

The gunfire never let up for a second.

As he dragged Harris around a vehicle and into cover, Ferris came at him, all spit and fury. "What the hell are you playing at? You want to die?"

"Yes," Corey shot back without hesitation. Ferris shook his head, frowned and returned to the fight. There was no time for discussion nor did Corey stick around to explain, he had only one thing in mind and that was to breach that building. By the time Ferris looked to see where he was, he was already gone. Corey took two officers with him and circled the building. On the east side another officer was down, the other was taking cover behind a Jeep. They hurried over to provide support. "Listen up. I'm going in. Cover me?"

"Are you out of your mind?" The officer asked.

He didn't bother to answer that.

To them this must have seemed like pure madness. To him it was mild compared to the gunfights in Fallujah, Iraq. Over there they had no idea where insurgents were. A dash across an alley could mean a bullet in the back of the head. Here, he could see all around him. It was just a matter of timing, and with Ferris and the others not letting up, he knew the occupants were distracted. Still, as much of a death wish as he had since losing Ella, he wasn't planning on going in alone. He just needed to get close enough to throw in a few tear gas canisters. It was a matter of shaking up the building. Causing so much chaos that the occupants wouldn't know where to put their attention. If they couldn't get them to come out through communication, this was the alternative. He ran toward the building at an angle to avoid getting caught in the crossfire, and lobbed one through an open window. Then he scurried along the wall, pulled the pin on the next and did the same, this time breaking a window as he threw it. The sound of men shouting inside was the last thing he heard as he sprinted back to the cover of trucks and took up position.

As a line of coughing men came out, he heard Ferris shouting over the radio. "Do not shoot. I repeat. Do not shoot!"

It was the one and only order that Corey obeyed.

He wanted answers as much anyone else.

Moving in fast, officers barked commands to get the men to come closer. Once they were on the ground, and they felt it was safe to move in, they rushed in and handcuffed the individuals, hauling them away from the building. After, they were thrown against the side of a Jeep and told to get down on their knees. From thereon out the situation escalated fast. Officers outraged at the death of their colleagues rained down punches. Corey stood by as Ferris hurried over telling them to stop. He grilled the men with questions about who they were working for but they refused to say anything. Ferris walked up to one and took him by the hair and dragged him down to the ground. He pulled back his shirt to reveal a branded mark on one shoulder. He had Reynolds check another and he had the same. All of them were branded like cattle with the same symbol sprayed after raids.

It was a star.

"What is this?" Ferris asked.

"Morning Star," a long-haired individual with a pitted face muttered farther down the line.

Another one, chubby, with dark circles around his eyes, piped up. "Shut up, you fool."

"What is Morning Star?" Ferris repeated.

The long-haired guy smiled and looked over at Corey.

"Don't look at him. Look at me," Ferris barked.

"What is Morning Star?"

"You're asking the wrong question," another man said, his head hanging limp.

The chubby one again spoke up but this time he didn't scold any of the others, he simply gave a nod towards the building. "Enough with your questions. Take it and let us go."

"Take what? Let you go? My friend, you aren't going anywhere, not until I…"

Right then one of the other officers who'd been clearing the building came jogging over. He pulled up his mask. "Ferris. You should see this." He motioned towards the building. Ferris looked back at the chubby guy who they came to learn later was Dreymon. However, it wasn't him who was at the top of the chain. He was nothing but a pawn in a game where the rules were unknown. Ferris followed the officer, motioning for Corey to join him. They hurried towards the building and entered. Inside it was a mess. Bullets had torn up the walls, and the floor was littered with gun shells. Led through a series of corridors, they entered a main hall that was used for bingo. That was when their jaws dropped. Filling up the tables were boxes and boxes of canned and dry food. To the far end of the wall were piles of heavy firearms, military grade stuff. The kind of equipment that might have been used by the National Guard.

Ferris shot Corey a glance as they strolled around the room taking cans out of brown boxes and looking at them. It was a treasure trove of food, survival equipment and ammo. "The supply truck wasn't carrying this. Where the hell did they get this from?"

Ferris pulled out a rocket launcher. "Looks like they're set for starting a war."

"Or stopping one," Corey said. Ferris flashed him a look and set the weapon down.

"What is your deal?" Ferris asked.

"With?"

"I saw the way you charged in with no regard for your life. And all that bullshit back there when I asked if you wanted to die. Saying yes. I knew you were reckless back at McDonald Lake but this, this is off the deep end."

"You want to do this now?"

Ferris barked back at him. "I want to know that when I go into an operation, I'm not going to have my men die because one of them has a few screws loose."

Corey snorted and nodded, slowly looking around the room. "First, let's get something straight. I'm not one of your men. You work for Flathead; I work for Whitefish. And second…"

Before he could finish, Ferris cut him off. "You volunteer. You're not even a cop."

"And you are?" Corey scoffed. "Because I'm pretty sure cops don't give up an innocent to protect their own ass, or jeopardize the life of a pregnant woman."

"Ah, I see," Ferris said. "So that's what this is about. I told you what happened. It was out of my control."

"You were the only one in control of that situation. It was your operation!" Corey barked. "You were the one that led officers in, and you were the only one that returned."

"How many times are we going to hash this out? Huh?" Ferris shifted from one foot to the next. "You think I wanted those officers to die out there? Do you think I wanted your wife to die? I would have given my own life for her. And even now I wish it was me dead and not her."

"Yeah, maybe it should have been you," Corey said.

They exchanged an icy glare.

"You said you understood. Now, you don't? What is it, Corey? Because I think the chief ought to know if we are going to be working together."

Corey stared at him. Countless words went through his mind but nothing came out. It was rare for him to be at a loss for words but right then he was more liable to crack him one on the jaw than give him a snappy comeback. Ferris shook his head and walked away leaving Corey there. From inside he could hear Ferris shouting at the raiders.

"What is Morning Star? Is that some kind of fucked-up sect that you belong to? Some cute name you gave yourselves? Huh?"

Corey walked up to the door and leaned against it. A humid July breeze blew against his skin. He looked up into the blue sky where there wasn't even a cloud in sight.

"It's not what. It's who. You are asking the wrong question," the same guy spoke again, though he was quickly scolded by his buddy Dreymon. Ferris walked over to the man with buzzed hair and a ferocious-looking beard. Ferris got down close to his face and brought his service weapon under his chin to lift his eyes.

"Who?"

The guy grinned. "The one that will turn all this shit around."

"Is that so? Is he also the one that gave you that branding?"

"Nope." Corey stepped out into the warmth of the day and walked over to hear what he was saying.

"You work for him?" Ferris asked.

The guy nodded.

"He put you up to this? Raiding? Killing? Stealing?

Were you going to take all this to him?"

He didn't say anything so Ferris pushed the gun a little harder. "Where can I find this...Morning Star?" Ferris chuckled, shaking his head and casting a glance at those who had their guns trained on the men. A few officers were keeping watch on the perimeter. The man didn't answer him so Ferris grabbed him by the back of the head. "Are you hard of hearing? Where can I find your boss? Is he in Whitefish? Kalispell?"

The front of the man's pants darkened. Fearing for his life he peed himself. "In the national forest," he replied.

"Which one?"

There were two nearby, Kootenai and Glacier.

"I don't know."

"Don't bullshit me."

"He doesn't know. None of us do," the long-haired man said. "We collect what's needed and transport it to a secondary location where it's picked up and taken away."

"What secondary location?" Ferris demanded to know.

"Just northwest of Whitefish on 93 near Skyles Lake."

"Shut up, you idiot," Dreymon said.

Ferris pointed his gun at Dreymon. "Enough!" He paced back and forth tapping the Glock against the side of his leg. "And what's in it for you all?"

They said nothing.

"Do you not hear me?" he said, waving the gun around. "What kickback are you getting to do his bidding?"

"We don't go without," the long-haired man replied.

"Well now you do," Ferris said. He twirled his finger in the air. "Round 'em up. We're taking them in."

"Taking them in?" Reynolds asked. "Didn't you hear what Hudgens said? We don't have room. The jail cells are already at maximum capacity."

Ferris stopped walking. He stood there for what seemed like a minute observing the men. "Good point." In an instant, he turned and in one smooth motion fired a round into the head of Dreymon, then another into the next guy, and one more into the next until they had six dead bodies before them. All the other officers' jaws dropped except Corey's. For the longest time he'd had a feeling that Ferris was a hairline crack away from losing his shit. Now he'd just proven it. "Let's move out," he said, turning and looking at Corey as if expecting him to say something.

Chapter 2

"I'm telling you, it wouldn't be the first time a suit has screwed over the working man," Nate said, naked under a blanket running his hand through Erika's hair as they lay in the back of a semi-truck they'd found between Kalispell and Whitefish. At the far end of the truck Bailey was panting and basking in the sunshine. He and Erika had gone out with a group of four townsfolk that morning to search trucks and stalled vehicles along the highways and back roads for supplies. It had been an ongoing effort over the past four weeks. A great deal of focus was being placed on the acquisition of supplies even though fishing and hunting provided ample food. Truthfully, it was a matter of creature comforts. People didn't want to give up the old ways of thinking, the perks of living in a modern society. After a rather irate town hall meeting, Hudgens had caved in and told those in attendance if they wanted to venture out beyond the town to search, no one was going to stop them, but he couldn't be held responsible for any loss of life or injury as a result of run-ins with raiders. Raiders this, raiders that. Everything was about this damn group that was causing havoc throughout the county. They still hadn't seen them. In fact, Nate was beginning to think it was just a made-up story that Hudgens had concocted to explain why resources were running low. He had a sneaky suspicion that some of the higher-ups, the mayor, city council and members of the police department, were taking the lion's share of what remained while everyone else was left with smaller rations. "I think if we headed over to Hudgens' house we would probably find his garage packed to the ceiling with boxes of supplies. I don't trust that asshole."

"No, the chief wouldn't let that happen."

"Maybe he doesn't know about it. Or hell, maybe he's in on it," Nate said before sighing and changing the topic. "Anyway, when are you going to tell Tyler about us?" There had been a development over the past three weeks.

Since their near-death experience at the hands of that nutcase Denise; Erika and Nate had formed a close bond, one that became even closer after a night of heavy drinking. In all honesty he was taken aback and figured when Erika sobered up the next morning, she would regret that one-night stand but surprisingly she didn't. It wasn't long before they were taking advantage of free moments to sneak away and get their freak on.

Erika shrugged. "There's nothing to say. Tyler and I were never an item."

"But you dated him in Vegas."

"We went out for a meal, Nate. That's it."

"But he could have feelings for you."

"If he does, he hasn't made them known. Hell, we haven't seen him in three weeks. For all we know he might have decided to not come back. You heard what his old man said the other night."

"Ah, Andy's just bitter that his son went against his wishes." Nate pulled a face, looking out at the sky. Twenty minutes earlier they'd come across a semi truck among many other stalled vehicles. There was a momentary surge of excitement at the prospect of finding a cache of supplies, only to discover the back was open and someone had already beaten them to the punch. It was empty barring a few cardboard boxes. Trying to make the most of the moment, Nate put the moves on Erika in the back of the truck.

"Here?" She blurted out.

He shrugged. "Why not? It's as good a place as any."

"But the group will be waiting for us."

"They're five miles down the road. They're too busy. Besides, we won't be long."

"You won't. What about me?" She asked.

He grinned and wiggled his fingers in her face. "Let me work my magic."

That was all it took to convince her. They broke down some of the cardboard boxes and rolled out a blanket taken from the horse they'd arrived on. Next they peeled off each other's clothes and got tangled up under the cover. When it was over, they lay there at ease.

Since the power had gone out, Erika had become the only thing that was good about the event. There was no way in hell he could have scored a woman like that. She wouldn't have even given him a second glance had it not been for their shared experience below Denise's home. Getting close to death had changed something in both of them that night.

Nate grimaced. "I just feel awkward. I think we should tell him."

"And we will," Erika said tracing her finger over his chest. "I need to find the right time. With everything that's going on in town and with the raiders..."

Nate turned his chin and kissed the top of her head. "You think for a few hours we can not mention them? It seems it's all anyone talks about. I just want to forget that we're even in this predicament."

She rolled and looked up at him with those gorgeous green eyes of hers. "But we are."

He groaned. "I know that. I just don't need reminding every two seconds." He crawled out from under the covers exposing his naked ass and slipped back into his cargo pants. He looked at Erika who curled up in the blanket eyeing him.

"You want an espresso?"

She chuckled. "Yeah, and a latte, and a burger and..."

He smiled. "Suit yourself. You don't know what you're missing."

Erika frowned. "Espresso?"

"I'm serious. Wait here," he said, rushing to the far end of the semi and hopping out. Bailey lifted her head, and perked up her ears.

"Nate."

A few seconds late he reappeared holding a yellow contraption in his hand. "Wala!"

"What is that?"

"An espresso machine."

"Are you kidding me?"

It looked like an oversized pill or a closed travel mug. "It's a Wacaco Nanopresso. This thing is so damn cool. It's an espresso machine for those on the go." He acted all excited as he began taking it apart and showing her where everything went. "You throw your grinds in here, you add some hot water here, seal it up and begin pumping here. The pressure pushes it through and boom, sweet crema coffee."

Erika rested on her right elbow and looked it over. "Where did you get this from?"

"When we were scouring those storage units in Evergreen. I also picked up a few bags of coffee."

"No, I get that. But we were supposed to give anything we found to the EOC."

"Screw that. You think I'm handing over everything? We're the suckers out here doing all the scavenging, risking our neck. No, I'm taking a few things for myself."

"Uh huh." Erika smiled. "Only one problem. No hot water."

He tapped the side of his head. "I was planning on boiling some up. You see, I also got me one of these while I was down there." He pulled out of his jacket a torch lighter.

She snorted. "Don't let Andy catch you with that."

"Ah, who the hell has the time to start fires the way he wants? The guy is a caveman. Come on, let's go. Get that sweet ass of yours dressed. I'll make us some breakfast."

"Breakfast?"

"There's a river just through the trees. I'll catch some fish and brew us some coffee, and maybe we can chat about that place I mentioned to you."

Her smile quickly disappeared and she got up and slipped into her underpants.

"What is it?" Nate asked, seeing her mood change.

"About that. I was thinking we should hold off."

"Hold off? You like staying with Andy the Caveman?"

"No, but he's treated us well so far."

"Yeah, that's because he's made us his lap dogs. We're the ones cleaning the shit out of the stables, we're the ones bringing in eggs from the chicken pen, we're the ones milking those cows, and…"

Erika screwed up her eyes. "Nate. Just drop it."

Puzzled, he studied her.

"I thought you wanted us to spend more time together."

She pulled up her tight blue jeans and slipped into her untied boots. "I do. We are."

"But not living together."

"I…" she trailed off, looking as if she'd just swallowed a sour candy. "I just think we should take our time. You know, this is all new and…"

"You don't know if it's for you. Right, I get it," Nate said turning away and dropping down out of the semi.

"Nate. Come on! Don't be like that."

"Like what?" He replied over his shoulder.

"You know."

"I just suggested that we move into our own place. There are enough homes that aren't lived in right now. We could—"

"It's too soon," she said, cutting him off.

"Because you still have feelings for Tyler?"

She furrowed her brow. "No. Because it's too soon."

"Whatever." He waved her off as he headed back to

the horse and tucked the espresso maker into a pouch on the side. "We should probably get back and meet up with the others."

"What about catching some fish, breakfast, espresso?"

"I think I've lost my appetite," he said mounting the horse. He waited there for her as she collected her shirt, and eyed him with a scowl. The morning had started so well. He was actually beginning to think that there was a silver lining to the darkness they were in. But who was he kidding? She was just using him for what she wanted. He felt cheap. He felt… Okay, it wasn't a bad way to be used but still…everything had to be secret with her. She didn't want others knowing they were seeing each other. Like, as if anyone cared?

As Bailey jumped to the ground and trotted over, Erika climbed down and was about to get on the back of the horse when an eruption of a gun was heard in the distance. Nate's head swiveled. It was coming from where their group was. The road stretched before them; a chaotic mess of vehicles that had been abandoned. Erika mounted the saddle behind him and Nate snapped the reins, gave the horse a nudge and they took off heading back. An exchange of gunfire ensued. It was getting louder the closer they got. "C'mon, girl," Erika yelled to Bailey to keep up.

Nate craned his neck towards the south at the sound of all hell breaking loose. Blood pumped fast through his veins at the thought of what lay beyond the bend. Holding the reins in one hand, he reached down and unclipped the radio from his belt. "Matt. Come in, over!" he yelled but got no response. Erika patted Nate on the arm and leaned in so he could hear her over the strong wind whipping against their clothes.

"Drop me off before we reach the bend."

"Why?"

"Just do it!"

He brought the horse to a halt and Erika swung her leg and slipped down. She pulled an M4 carbine from a scabbard and darted into the tree line with Bailey. Right then a scratchy voice came over the radio. "We're under attack. I repeat." It wasn't Matt's voice but a woman known as Julia. She sounded as if she was hurt bad.

"We're coming," Nate said giving the horse a nudge and continuing on. As he rounded the bend, the rest of the road came into view. He yanked on the reins and dismounted. Bringing the horse over to the edge of the road, he tethered her to a tree and ran at a crouch over to the vehicles, taking up position at the rear of a truck with his AR-15. He cut the corner and peered through the scope trying to get a bead on their group. Nothing. He could see a group of four guys dressed in camo gear but they weren't with them. One had a thick beard and a shaved head, another was sporting a red bandanna, the third was wearing dark sunglasses, and the fourth had a green baseball cap. They were moving around vehicles checking for survivors. That's when Nate caught sight of Matt lying motionless on the ground, his gun a few inches from his hand. *Shit.* He unclipped his radio and tried to get in contact with Julia again. In a whisper he spoke through the radio. "Julia. It's Nate. Come in, over."

No reply.

He tried again but this time it wasn't Julia who answered, it was a gruff male voice. "I'm afraid your friend is unavailable right now."

Nate peered around the truck and saw the individual. It was the bald-headed guy. Nearby, Julia lay dead, a bullet through her head. Baldy raised a finger and without saying a word motioned to the others to head his way. Nate pulled back. His pulse sped up. His mouth went dry. *Okay. Okay. Stay calm. Don't lose your shit. You got this.* He exhaled hard and had closed his eyes for no more than three seconds when a slew of gunfire shook him up. At first he thought it was aimed at him as the sound came from the direction of the group. He dropped to his belly and looked beneath the truck trying to get a better view without sticking his head out into the line of fire. That's when he noticed three of the men were on the ground. *Erika?*

Another three round burst and the fourth man dropped.

That's when Erika emerged, Bailey walking beside her as she stepped onto the road. What the hell? Nate rose to his feet and rushed forward to find her crouched over one of their group checking to see if they were alive. She glanced at him as he jogged toward her. "How the…?"

"They're all dead," she said rising to her feet. "We need to collect what they've found and head back."

Nate looked around nervously. "You think they were raiders?"

She shrugged. "Who knows? Who cares?"

Nate went over to one of the attackers and pulled back his shirt to check the shoulder. Andy had told them that the raiders had some kind of branding on them. None of these men did. He gathered up their weapons. He filled up one of the saddle bags with several magazines. All the while he noticed Erika was just staring at Julia as if she was in some kind of trance state.

"Erika."

She ignored him, so he went over and reached for her arm. As he clasped it to pull her around, she brought up the Glock with the other hand so fast it scared him. Her face was stern. It was as if she was reacting on instincts to survive and didn't know who he was. "Whoa, whoa, it's me."

Rifle in one hand, Glock in the other, she blinked hard a few times then lowered the Glock and shook her head. "Sorry. I just..."

Erika took a few steps back and turned away.

Something was not right. The way she reacted.

Still, he let it slide.

Few words were exchanged between them on the journey home even though several times Nate tried to engage with her regarding what happened. She seemed lost in her thoughts. It was only when they made it to the outskirts of Whitefish did she respond when he said, "Back there. That wasn't like you."

She snorted. "Of course it was."

"I'm not talking about killing those men. After. It was like you saw me as a threat. You looked at me like you didn't know me."

"What are you talking about? I'm fine. I was just pumped up on adrenaline."

He nodded slowly but he wasn't buying it. It was the second time he'd noticed her act as if she was about to be attacked. "Look, we shouldn't mention that we were separated from the group," Erika said.

"Why?"

"It's better we just keep that whole thing in the back of the truck to ourselves."

"Because?"

"Because their families won't understand." Her chin dipped. "They'll blame us."

"They knew the risks," Nate added.

"Yeah, well..." she trailed off.

The horse trotted slowly up 93, and they took in the sight of what remained of Whitefish. Over the past four weeks, many more fires had started, homes had burned to the ground and the once picturesque mountain town now resembled a war zone. "We should really talk about what happened," Nate said.

"We just did."

"You know what I mean."

"I don't want to."

"Why is it when I bring up the incident of what happened in those woods you change the topic?"

"Uh, maybe because I don't want to remember."

"Did he do something to you? Jessie, I mean?"

"No."

"Zara?"

"Can we just drop it?" Erika said.

"But—"

"Enough!" she bellowed before groaning hard.

"Erika? What's the matter?"

"My head." She groaned hard and then…one second she was holding on to his hips, the next she slumped over and he barely caught her before she slipped off the horse. Bailey barked several times as Nate tried to bring the horse to a halt while trying to hold on to her.

As soon as the horse slowed, he swung his leg over and slipped off and brought Erika down to the ground. Her eyes had rolled back in her head and her body seemed to be going into convulsions. "Erika. Erika!"

Not wasting another second, Nate hoisted her back up, slumping her over like a saddle bag and then mounted the horse. He snapped the reins. "Move it!" he yelled at the horse, digging in his heels to get the mare to hurry. It didn't take him long to reach North Valley Hospital. By the time he made it there the convulsions had stopped but she was still unconscious. Since the assault at the hospital three weeks earlier, there were no windows, or even doors. Nate ducked as he rode the horse straight into the hospital lobby to the surprise of the security officer, and a cop who was manning the front desk.

"I need a doctor. Now!" he yelled as he slipped down and with their assistance put Erika on a stretcher. Nurses still volunteering their time moved into action wheeling her off down the corridor.

"What's her name?"

"Erika." Nate tried to follow but was told to stay back. "It's her head. She said it was her head," he shouted as he was held back. "It was her head," he said again in a quiet voice as an officer guided him away from the hallway.

"Come on, take a seat over there. I'll get you a coffee."

Still shaking he called Bailey over and they took a seat while Officer Rutland had the security guard get him a hot drink. Bailey whined so he ran his hand over the dog's head. "She'll be okay. Don't you worry."

The truth was he didn't know if she would. In all the time he was with her on the road from Vegas to Whitefish, she had never complained of headaches, nor had she had convulsions. There was nothing that would lead him to believe that this was some form of epilepsy, and yet it came across that way. The security guard returned and handed him a drink and he thanked him and waited for news.

An hour later, a doctor in white scrubs appeared and spoke with the security guard. He gestured to Nate and the doc came over. "Are you the spouse, friend or family member?"

"I'm..." he thought for a second about their intimacy

and connection, then replied. "A friend. Is she okay?"

He didn't outright say yes, neither did he say no.

"She's... Listen, we have to run some more tests but it appears she suffered some kind of brain trauma. Would you know about this?"

He thought for a second and then replied, "She did take a knock to the head back at..." Nate's mind went back to Denise, and Erika's first escape attempt. He remembered them bringing her in with a bloody gash.

Nate swallowed hard. "Can I see her?"

Chapter 3

Northwest of Libby, deep in the heart of the Kootenai National Forest, Tyler pulled the map and compass from his jacket and checked to see if he was close to the rendezvous point. It was like trying to find a needle in a haystack. The forest encompassed over 2.2 million acres and was nearly three times the size of Rhode Island. As a kid he'd spent many a day hiking and camping out inside the dense woodland and even his father admitted to getting lost in it. Beads of sweat rolled down the side of his face as he crouched at the foot of a Douglas fir, looking through a curtain of pines. Hours of hiking had taken its toll. His ankle was sore after twisting it on a rocky trail. A dull ache reminded him that no one, no matter how prepared, was incapable of falling prey to nature's terrain. Navigating modern society while living in Las Vegas had been a walk in the park compared to years of being tested by his father in the great outdoors.

After confirming he was on track, he pulled out a canister of water from his backpack and chugged some of it down. He wiped his mouth with his forearm, and screwed the top on. This better be worth it, he thought as he rose to his feet. Only the gentle babble of a creek, birds chirping in the canopy above and insects could be heard. It was peaceful. He closed his eyes for a few seconds and rested against the tree to catch his breath. He'd been up early that morning in preparation for his long trek. Jude was under the impression he was heading back to Whitefish for a couple of days to touch base with Corey but that was just a ruse. As instructed by Allie, he'd left his horse tied off to a tree several miles back. He was a little hesitant to do so with so many stealing whatever they could get their hands on but Allie had reassured him that the horse would be fine. She'd done it many a time. Her familiarity with the area seemed almost akin to his own, and yet he still knew very little about her.

Since his arrival in Camp Olney three weeks ago he hadn't returned to the town. The need to know his biological father had consumed him. Fortunately, Jude had been more than willing to share his reason for not telling him, and it was the same as Andy's. They'd both made a promise to his mother. Somewhere in the back of her mind she thought if he knew the truth, he would think less of her, but after spending the majority of his childhood around Andy, he began to see why his mother might have sought comfort in the arms of someone else. Andy was a cold-hearted bastard even before his mother died. What she had seen in him was a mystery, then again love could make a person blind to another's faults. When asked, Jude spoke of Andy in a very different light. Childhood friends, they'd grown up together, spent most of their waking hours in each other's company. Jude spoke of a funny, caring and adventurous individual. A man that inspired and made him believe the world could be a different place, that their lives didn't have to follow the same mundane route their parents had. That all changed when Dianna entered the picture.

She was the straw that broke the camel's back.

Continuing on, Tyler scanned the trees, gazed up into the blue sky and glanced at the mountain range that soared above the treetops. It would soon be fall, and the colder weather would sweep through the county bringing with it even greater challenges.

Tyler had a taken a few more steps when he noticed the sound of the forest had gone very quiet. There were only a couple reasons for that, one was there was an apex predator nearby prowling for food, and the other was humans, lots of them. He brought around his AR-15 and panned the muzzle. He cast a glance over his shoulder and took a few steps back, leaving the well-worn trail and entering thick brush. He waded through lush, leafy greenery like water with only the sound of his clothes brushing against it all. He turned 360 degrees and got this sinking feeling in his gut. It was the same kind he'd get when he felt as if someone was watching him. His eyes lifted scanning the treetops and branches. That was when he spotted the figure. The lone person was well camouflaged and had it not been for experience he may have overlooked the bulky darkness between the branches, but the sun's rays made metal glint, giving them away.

He backed up, making sure he was out of the person's line of sight and attempting to not make it obvious that he'd seen them, when instantly he heard something snap, and then his legs went out from underneath him and he soared into the air hanging upside down. It happened so fast. His rifle clattered on the ground.

Laughter followed, female, he knew who it was.

Without wasting a second, he reached for the knife in his sheath, used the muscles in his abdomen to pull himself up and cut the rope around his ankles. His body dropped, he scooped up his rifle and rolled disappearing into brush. By the time Allie made her way down from the tree and came over to the spot, he could see the look of confusion on her face. She turned her head and scanned. A smile flickered as he watched her from behind boulders nearby. He activated the red dot scope on his rifle and a tiny red dot danced on the front of her jacket. She glanced down and her eyes closed as she lifted her open hands and smiled.

"I'll give you props for the spring noose snare but it only works if you move your ass," Tyler yelled coming out from behind the boulder with a grin on his face. "Now why on earth would you go to all the trouble of rigging that up?"

"Would you believe me if I said it wasn't for you?"

He chuckled, trudging over. Tyler lowered the muzzle of his rifle. "Am I to believe you hang out here on a regular basis?" he said looking around. There was no cabin in the woods and unless she had built a treehouse, there were no signs that anyone but wildlife lived out here.

"I frequent this place often. By the way, you're fast," she said thumbing over her shoulder. "I expected to find you flailing around."

He scoffed. "If you knew my father you would understand. Let's just say it wasn't the first time I've been caught in one of those. If we didn't cut ourselves free in time, he would treat us like a piñata."

She shifted her weight from one foot to the next, and an eyebrow shot up. "Is that your excuse?"

"Can you think of a better one?"

She flashed her pearly whites and as he got closer, she pulled back her hood and dark hair flowed down past her shoulders. The surrounding forest brought out the green in her eyes. The chemistry between them was palpable. Although they had only spoken briefly a few times since his arrival at the camp, they'd exchanged glances and unless he was reading the signals wrong, she'd been throwing some serious heat his way. He felt like he was being teased every time he was around her.

"Why have you waited this long to meet?" Tyler asked.

"Because I wanted to see if he opened up to you. Did he?"

"Jude?"

She nodded, as she turned and beckoned him to follow her.

"He told me a thing or two."

"Obviously not everything, otherwise you wouldn't be

here."

"What's that supposed to mean?" he asked, glancing at her.

Instead of answering him she shifted the conversation.

"No problem finding this place, I hope?"

He smiled at the way she dodged the question. "Am I late?" he asked in answer to her question, knowing full well he was on time. She didn't respond so he continued. "What is this place? And why here?"

"You're telling me you've never been here?"

"It's a big place," Tyler replied walking beside her. "Why here? Why not back at camp?" When she looked at him with a raised eyebrow, he continued, "Too many prying eyes. Right. I get it. You know, you could be mistaken as being overly paranoid. Anyone told you that?"

Her lip curled. "Plenty."

"Maybe you should listen to them."

"That would be kind of hard. They're all dead now," she said without looking at him. Allie led him on through the knee-high brush. He glanced at the bow on her back. "You any good with that?" he said, tapping it.

"You any good at eating with your hands?" she replied in a sarcastic manner.

"Point taken. Who taught you?"

"Our mother."

"Our? You have siblings?"

"One. An older sister."

He frowned. "Have I met her?" he asked.

"No, she's not at the camp."

He let out a sigh. "I'm sorry."

She smiled. "She's not dead." Then her smile faded as quickly as it appeared. "But she might as well be."

Her brow furrowed as she forged ahead not wanting to discuss the matter any further. He did his best to keep up as she broke into a jog and led him deeper into the forest, over a rise, across a stream and towards O'Brien Mountain.

"Allie, where are you taking me?"

"You'll see," she said. "It's easier for me to show you."

By the time they made it to the location the sun was beginning to wane. He wasn't sure how long it had taken to reach the area but as they came up over a rise, she jogged up to the bottom of a tall pine tree and began to climb. It was only when he followed and they made it past some of the lower branches could he see what appeared to be a camouflaged hunters' tree stand, but instead of it being metal it was made out of planks of wood. It was like someone had begun to build a treehouse and only managed to get the floor and wraparound railing finished on it. There was a large camo netting that went over the top, and more covering the bottom so that it blended in with the foliage.

"You know, I'm really beginning to wonder about you. I feel like I'm being led around like a pup on a leash."

"Patience," she muttered. "You'll see."

She offered her hand as he climbed over the lip. As soon as he was up and brushed off pieces of tree bark, he looked around. The spot gave them a breathtaking view of the forest from above, and a clearing in the distance.

"Here, look through these. This is as close as we can get without drawing attention."

"Them?" He frowned as he brought up the binos. "What am I looking at here?"

He felt her guide them in the direction she wanted him to look. Tyler strained to see and then with a slight adjustment of the focus he saw it — a camp. Unlike Camp Olney this one looked like a summer camp site with RVs, small and large tents and cedarwood cabins. Smoke rose up from different fire pits, and he saw numerous armed men patrolling, chatting with one another or guiding in working trucks.

"What is this place?"

"That's been the great mystery, and for a while I didn't know until my sister was asked several times by Jude to go with him to bring wild game to a trading post."

"Trading post?"

"Yeah."

"How do you know?"

"Because that's what the meat is exchanged for —

ammo and medical supplies. They have a reloading machine for bullets. At least that's what my sister told me before she vanished after her last trip."

Tyler frowned. "Vanished?"

Allie pointed. "Here. Jude said that raiders attacked them on the way back and she was dead but I didn't believe that. Not for one minute. My sister is strong. Besides, no body was returned," Allie said. "Anyway, a few months later—"

Tyler cut her off. "Hold on a second. A few months later? The power has only been down for a month. Are you telling me you've been at that camp longer than that?"

Her eyebrows shot up. "He didn't tell you?"

"No. I mean Jude said Camp Olney had been in existence for over twenty years but he told me it was used as a prepper retreat, a place where they could train people and so forth. Essentially that's where Andy began teaching."

She swallowed hard and shook her head. "I've been

there for over a year, Tyler."

Her response made him stare. At a loss for words, she continued. "Anyway, as I was saying. A few months later, after my sister's disappearance, he arranged another trip with a different group."

"And you were part of it?" Tyler assumed.

"No," she said shaking her head. "I followed. They didn't know I was tracking them. That's when I saw this place, and most importantly, I saw my sister — alive."

"What? He lied to you?"

"He's been lying to many of us."

"Didn't you say something? Confront him and ask him why he lied?"

"You'll learn fast, Tyler, that confrontations only end badly. People go missing. There's always an explanation, like that person didn't like the rules of the camp and took off, or they were attacked by raiders. But there's only so many times you can hear that before you start to question it."

Tyler nodded slowly and peered through the binos

again.

"What about the others? The ones that originally went with your sister?"

"I don't know. They might be down there too."

"But why? Why would he lie? And what purpose would it serve by having her here instead of the other camp?"

"You've met Sara, Jude's wife."

He nodded.

"A little young, don't you think?"

"Yeah but…"

"I know. He has an answer for it. He always has answers. The man is a modern-day Warren Jeffs, except Jude isn't pushing religion, no, he prefers his own agenda where he presides over the people like God. But one thing he does have in common is a taste for younger women, and lots of them. I told you, he's dangerous."

Tyler stared back at her. Had that been what Andy meant? Did he know about this? No. It seemed too out there to think that someone could have that much control over others. He couldn't wrap his mind around it. Sure, Sara was younger than Jude but in the three weeks he'd been at the camp he hadn't seen any women around him. Neither had he witnessed women being treated badly or enslaved in any subservient manner.

"No. It doesn't make sense, Allie."

"Why, because he's your father? Because he seems normal around you?"

"Perhaps he figured your sister and their group were attacked on the road."

"Then how does that explain him sending more people back to this camp a few months later? This needs to stop right now. He's lying to you, Tyler. He's lying to all of us. I just don't know exactly why. But I plan on finding out and getting my sister out. But I can't do it alone."

Chapter 4

Town politics. Corey hated it. The military wasn't that much different but at least the higher-ups who barked out orders had at one time been in the thick of it. They knew what it meant to bleed in the killing fields, they'd experienced the dusty back roads and ever-present sense of danger looming over their shoulder. Hudgens and the city council on the other hand were clueless — nothing more than scared suits hanging on to titles that at one time afforded them respect, admiration and power.

All of that meant very little now that civil society had gone by the wayside.

Ferris jabbed his finger at the ground. "If these men were telling the truth, perhaps we can put a dent in their operation. But we need a skilled team."

"And what of these men? Where are they?" Hudgens asked.

"I told you, dead."

"Right." Hudgens was perched on the lip of a table. He pushed off the table and paced the cramped room where Corey, Hudgens, Ferris, Chief Bruce and Andy were gathered. "And again, how did that happen?"

Ferris glanced at Corey before rehashing the lie. He'd told them that the raid had been a success. They'd managed to drag out six and interrogate them for details only to lose control of the situation, and have one of the men kill some of their own before they took him and the others out. It explained away his mistake of sending those officers in too soon, and it covered his ass for executing in cold blood. Corey could have outed him but it wasn't worth it. It wasn't like those he'd killed were innocent.

Hudgens went behind the table and tapped a pack of cigarettes in his hand. After lighting, he sat looking up as if seeking guidance from a higher power. "Take Andy's team."

"What?" Andy looked disturbed by the suggestion.

"You have a new batch of volunteers. Now is the time to prove their worth."

"These are untrained individuals. The plan was to train them before…"

"Don't speak to me about plans. I was the one that had the idea, rallied them together. They were brought in to replace those who have already died. If you think these men were speaking the truth, then this might be our one shot at putting an end to these raiders. So far they have eaten into our supplies, crippled the town's security and made residents even more fearful. I won't stand by and see more die. Arm your group and take them with you."

"You don't get it," Andy said leaning forward and eyeing Hudgens. "It takes more than arming people to go up against trained militants."

"Trained militants? These raiders are nothing more than opportunists who have made a mockery of us." He got up from his seat and came around and got really close to Andy as if challenging him. "Unless of course you know something we don't?"

There was a pause as all eyes fell on Corey's father.

Andy's brow furrowed. "Have it your way. But their

blood will be on your hands."

"How dare you. How dare you!" Hudgens bellowed in his face. "You think you can run this town any better than me? I have been at the helm of this ship for over six years."

"And yet you have never dealt with this," Andy shot back.

"Nor have you." He looked at him smugly. "None of us have. You might have taught workshops on prepping but what you know in here," he said reaching up and tapping the side of Andy's head, "it's of no value if it's never been tested. That kid you went at yesterday. He was right. Knowledge means very little if you haven't had the experience. If anyone is capable of leading this shit show, it would be your son," he said glancing at Corey. Andy's eyebrows shot up as did Corey's along with his hands.

"Hey, woah, I served time overseas, that's a hell of a lot different than this."

"I think you underestimate yourself," Hudgens said walking away from Andy and approaching Corey. "You are your father except unlike your father you have known the heat of battle, fought in the hardest of places and gone up against armed militants. It's for these reasons I want to know what you think?"

"Hold on a goddamn minute," Andy said. "You put me in charge of…"

Hudgens brought up a hand. "*Training*. That's right. I put you in charge of training, not leading men." He turned back to Corey. "So? What are your thoughts?"

"You've got to be kidding me," Andy said casting a glance at the chief who simply shrugged. Ferris lowered his chin. "Really? Do I have to remind you that my son nearly died at the hospital? But who bailed him out? That's right, I did."

"That's not what I heard," Hudgens said keeping his eyes fixed on Corey. "You put an end to the previous threat. So, what do you make of this one?"

"Look, man, the chief wanted me to help. I'm here to do that but I'm not stepping on anyone's shoes." He cast a glance at his father. He knew he wanted this. He wanted to show them what he was worth. Prove himself and come out the other side with the respect of the town.

"I determine that. My shoes are clean. Chief?"

"No problem here."

"Ferris?"

"I'm just along for the ride," he said in a glum way, as if secretly he expected to be asked to lead after obtaining the intel.

To avoid an argument, Corey spoke up in his father's defense. "My dad is right. These people aren't ready for this. You would be sending them to their slaughter. Putting a gun in untrained hands only makes the situation more dangerous. I need to time to gather a group together."

"As much as I respect your input," Hudgens said, "time is something we are short on around here. Isn't there anything you can use this group for?"

"Target practice," Andy piped up sarcastically.

Hudgens glared at him and returned to looking at Corey. However, that gave Corey an idea. "They could be a distraction."

"A distraction?"

"In Fallujah we received intel on a gathering of insurgents on the outskirts. Time was of the essence. If we didn't move in right then we'd lose a high-value target. The problem was, there were only four of us in the area at the time. A fire team." He breathed in deeply, reliving it in his mind. "Iraqi civilians were fleeing the city at the time. Large groups were moving out to camps set up by the government and the UN because many were targeted by ISIL gunmen."

"Your point?"

He dipped his head, not proud of what they'd done. "We redirected a group, covered ourselves in Iraqi clothing and joined them." He paused and closed his eyes for a second. "We sent them through the area where the insurgents were located. It was the only way we could get close. As soon as we were within distance, we broke away and took up position in this building that overlooked the store they were meeting in. The group drew attention, allowing the four of us to take them out."

Hudgens got this broad smile. "So it worked. I told you this kid knew what he was doing."

"It worked but they all died. Caught up in the crossfire."

"But you achieved your mission, yes?"

"Of course, but at what cost?"

His father looked at him. He hadn't told him that story, nor many of the others. He couldn't. These weren't the kind of war stories that won medals. They were the incidents that caused shame, night terrors, and PTSD.

"The needs of the many outweigh the needs of the few," Hudgens said coming around and placing his hand on Corey's shoulder. "I understand."

"You don't understand shit," Corey said. "How could you?"

Hudgens cocked his head. He could see him thinking over his response. His shoulders dropped. "If you can give me a better idea, I am all ears. I'm not for putting anyone in harm's way, and... If I knew how to fire a gun, you can be damn sure I would be out there with you, side by side."

"Bullshit," Andy said, disguising his response as a cough. Obviously, it wasn't masked enough as Hudgens gave him another glare. If his glares could kill, half the town would be dead by now.

"Look, there is no way to cherry coat it. It's dangerous either way. Whether they move in with us or act as a distraction. However, under the conditions and time frame, that's probably the only option you have unless you're willing to wait for me to gather those I know."

"We don't have time," Hudgens said before continuing as if the whole idea was his to begin with. "We'll have them look as if they are leaving town. Ferris, you and Andy can blend in among them for their protection. Of course, they'll have weapons but that will be up to them to…" he mumbled unsure of it all. It was a ridiculous idea. Fallujah was one thing, this was another. Corey was beginning to regret telling him what happened. "Oversee it. Put it in action. I want it done today. If they're expecting a delivery, let's give them one." He blew out his red cheeks. "Dismissed."

Ferris was the first out the door into the hallway.

"Dad," Corey said catching up with him as he darted out and went in a different direction. "I need you for this."

"Do you? As you seem to have it all in hand."

"Put your ego aside. You think I wanted him to put this on me?"

"And yet you allowed him."

"He has a point."

"Ah, there we go. I knew it would come out eventually." Andy threw his hands in the air and walked off down the hall. Corey wasn't about to let it go. They were short on good marksmen and his father was one of the best. "Would you just listen? God, man. Why is everything a competition with you?"

Andy turned on a dime. "These people you are going up against aren't regular civilians. They have trained every waking hour for this."

"You don't know that."

Andy pursed his lips, opened them as if he was about to say something.

"Look, we have lost a lot of people. You and I know this situation isn't getting better. This isn't just about Whitefish. They are attacking surrounding towns. If we don't put a stop to this now..." he trailed off, lost in the thought of Ella. "Please."

He gripped his father's arm. There was a pause.

"Okay. But I call some of the shots and I'm not going with numbnuts over there," he said giving a nod towards Ferris who was waiting by the door to head out.

"I wouldn't expect you to."

"How do you want to do this?" His father asked.

He couldn't believe it. In all the years he'd been alive his father had never once asked for his input. "We hang the carrot out in front of them. Supplies are what they're taking, so let's give them some. We'll gather the group together and load up a trailer full of supplies, mostly the ones we collected from the cache today. And then we'll do this…" He began to share the plan with his father. At this stage they had no idea how many they would encounter but that was where Nate and Erika would come into it.

When he finished explaining, his father nodded. "It could work."

"Do you know if they've returned from scavenging?"

"Haven't been home. I'll swing by and see. What about your brother? Have you seen him?"

Corey shook his head. "Not since he left. What did you tell him?"

Andy shrugged. "Nothing. Just to avoid Jude. He wouldn't listen."

Corey squinted. "Are you sure about that? As he left in quite a hurry."

"I'm telling you the truth."

Corey leaned against the wall. "Jude. Right. I didn't think about them. Now there is a group who are already trained. Maybe if—"

"No," Andy barked.

"What?"

"Just no. I don't want us in any way to be involved with that group."

"But they could be of use to us. If it wasn't for his men coming to my aid that night, I could be dead."

"It was a power move."

"A what?"

Andy shook his head and turned away. "You don't get it, do you? Just like your brother."

"Dad, what are you not telling me?"

"Let's just stick to the plan. Forget your brother."

"But he's been gone for three weeks." Corey stared at Andy. "Even if this goes smoothly, I need to check in on him."

Andy pointed a finger at him. "Don't go up there. I'm warning you now."

"Whatever problem you have with Jude, that's between you two. But I intend to thank him. And find out what's happened to Tyler."

He scoffed. "Three weeks, Corey. Three weeks have passed and only now you are wondering what happened to him? You're in no state to be leading this group. Leave it with me. Go home. Get some rest. It was a mistake encouraging you to help the town."

Corey's eyebrow rose. "A mistake?"

"You're in grief, son. It can cloud your judgment."

"Right. You would know all about that."

Andy scowled. "Listen to me. Losing your mother was the catalyst for my downward spiral but ultimately it was my choice to ignore the pain. That is what took me over the edge. I don't want to see the same happen to you."

"You don't have to worry about me," Corey said turning to walk away. His father clasped his shoulder.

"War changes a man. Grief can destroy him. Don't mistake the two."

Corey didn't respond. He walked off heading towards Ferris. His mind was a storm of thoughts. As soon as Ferris saw that he was alone, he opened his mouth to speak but Corey nipped that in the bud right away. "Keep it to yourself. I'm in no mood."

As he walked out into the calm evening air he turned

to his left and saw Nate crouched down smoking a cigarette and looking at the ground. "Nate?"

Nate looked up at him and thumbed towards the door. "They wouldn't let me inside. Um. It's Erika. The doctors have put her in an induced coma."

"What?"

Shock took hold.

Nate brought him up to speed on what had happened. "Apparently, these things can show up weeks later. Something to do with the blood vessels in the brain. She was complaining about frequent headaches. I just assumed…" he trailed off as tears began to well up in his eyes.

Chapter 5

It felt rushed. The whole damn thing did. Hudgens was pushing for results. He wanted the raiders gone but didn't understand that operations of this magnitude and danger required more than half-assed intel. Especially when it came from those they didn't trust in the first place. It was pure madness. That's why Corey took it upon himself to go ahead as a scout and scope out the site. He didn't tell anyone except his father and he'd given him strict instructions to keep it to himself. The fewer that knew, the better. Regardless of what happened in Fallujah, there was no way in hell he was sending untrained civilians ahead without at least knowing what they were up against. His father had tried to reassure him by telling him they knew how to shoot a gun but he could tell even his father didn't like the idea. While Andy gathered the group and gave them a briefing, which amounted to nothing more than minimal information and withholding the true extent of risk, Corey lay prone on a rise looking through a high-powered night vision scope on his .338 Lapua Magnum rifle. They were at least a thousand yards out on the northeast side of the lake, facing the southwest side. Nate had joined him. He was unable to do anything about Erika's situation, and Corey encouraged him to come along as it didn't make sense to spend all his waking hours sitting in the hospital.

"It sucks, man. There is no other way to put it but she's in good hands and now is not the time to buckle."

"I know," Nate said. "I just..." he trailed off, then pulled another cigarette from his pocket. His hands were trembling ever so slightly. Since Corey had met him outside city hall he'd been smoking cigarettes back to back. "You should ease up on those things."

"Only thing that's keeping me on an even keel."

"By the way, where's Bailey?" Corey asked.

"With Erika. She wouldn't leave her side. A nurse said she would give her some scraps and water. I'll swing by there tomorrow and check in. Hope to God Erika is awake."

Corey adjusted the focus on the scope and took in the sight of the small group gathered beside Skyles Lake. "That can't be all of them."

"How many are there?" Nate asked.

"Seven," Corey said pulling away from the scope. He drummed his fingers on the ground. They'd set up a small campsite, nothing more than a few tents, one battered Jeep, and a collection of horses, but it looked temporary, certainly not ground zero for operating a large-scale group of raiders. Where was the housing? The trucks? The storehouses for supplies? The rest of them? He knew some of the insurgents operated in small cell groups. Was that what this was? Nothing more than one of many cells?

"How many were you expecting?"

"A lot more than this."

He unclipped his radio and was about to update his father when Nate nudged him. "Isn't that Andy's truck?"

"What?"

He pointed towards the road, across the tops of

towering pine trees, and handed him NV binoculars. Corey took a look and his eyes widened. He couldn't make out who the driver was but that was definitely his rusty truck. It rumbled down 93 and veered into a driveway that came out on Skyles Lake Lane. Unsure if it was his father taking matters into his own hands, he got on the radio. "Dad, it's Corey, come in, over."

There was no response.

"Dad. Come in. It's Corey."

Still nothing.

He peered through his scope to get a better look. The vehicle swung around a cluster of evergreens just out of view. Headlight beams painted the tents. A few of the men broke away to meet the stranger. All he could see was the rear end. "Damn it!" Corey said. He moved the rifle.

"You think it's your father?" Nate asked.

"No. What the hell would he be doing there?" Corey handed him the radio. "Keep trying to get hold of him. I'm going down."

"What? No. How am I supposed to get in contact with

you if… Hold on, Corey."

Corey rose to his feet, leaving the long-range rifle there. "I can't see shit from up here. I need to go in."

"That wasn't the plan."

"Neither was seeing my old man's truck roll in. I need to know who's in it."

Nate got up and lifted a hand. "Look, just wait. Maybe we can get hold of Ferris, or Hudgens. Maybe someone else can check and see where your old man is."

"There's no time."

He plucked his carbine off the ground beside him and shouldered it. He burned some energy in the jog down the slope and through the thicket. Even though his shoulder was healed, it still ached from time to time.

* * *

Nate felt uncomfortable letting him go but Corey had a mind of his own. He tried the radio a few times but got no response. He pushed the binoculars against his eyes. A lone figure stepped out of the pine trees and appeared near the edge of the water, talking with the seven men.

He was pointing to the road, and then as if he knew where they were, he directed his attention to the forest where Corey was heading. "Oh shit."

How did they know?

Corey said he'd only told his father.

He watched as some of the group began breaking down the tents in a hurry, another reversed their battered vehicle to help them load it while the other four grabbed up rifles from the back and fanned out heading for the forest. Panic gripped Nate knowing that Corey was about to walk right into the midst of them. "Damn it," he said as he scooped up his rifle and sprinted after Corey. He only had a five-minute head start.

* * *

It was one of those nights when the stars were barely visible making it seem darker than usual. Corey jogged at a steady pace, zigzagging his way down a steep rocky incline, around trees, over boulders and across creeks until he could see the lake glistening in the distance. He heard someone approaching before he saw anything. Footsteps bounding, and heavy breathing caught his attention. He took up position behind a thick bush and waited. As soon as the figure ran into view, he exploded out, grabbing them around the face to prevent them screaming and lowered them to the ground in a matter of seconds.

"Nate. What the hell are you doing?"

A few seconds to catch his breath and he spat the words out, "Four of them. Coming this way."

"What?"

"Whoever was driving that vehicle knew where we were. They pointed in our direction. Who did you tell?"

"My old man, that's it. But he wouldn't…"

"Perhaps he told someone else. Did you give him our coordinates?"

Corey was about to respond when he saw movement. He brought a finger up to his lips and both of them melted back into thick underbrush and bushes. Through the branches he could only make out one. "Listen to me. Don't squeeze the trigger. Wait here," he said to Nate, pulling off his bag and taking out some rope.

"What are you…?"

Before he could finish, Corey stepped away, knife in hand.

Shooting the guy would have been easy but without a silencer on the end of the rifle, he'd only draw attention to their location and right now that was all they had going for them. In the darkness he saw the silhouette of the man with his rifle raised. He took up position behind a thick oak tree and crouched down waiting for his moment. Sure enough, the guy stepped into view and Corey exploded upwards jamming the knife up under his chin while simultaneously clasping a hand over his mouth. The sudden attack was so swift and clean that the muffled cry wasn't heard. He didn't bother dragging the dead man out of view as it would have created noise, however, he did pull back his shirt and look at his shoulder. Sure enough there was the symbol. Like a cult, all of them were branded with that star.

Moving quickly, he carefully navigated his way into a new position after spotting another one. Using the rope he was carrying, he swung it over a thick branch and let it hang down just slightly, then waited. The unsuspecting man raked his muzzle nervously from side to side and took small steps. Using a stone from the ground, Corey tossed it just a few feet away. The man froze, inches away from the noose above. His rifle was fixed on the area where the stone dropped. Had Corey waited a few more seconds he would have missed the opportunity but instead he took it and dropped the noose. It looped over his head. Instinctively he reached for it but it was too late. Corey pulled it tight and yanked it upwards holding him there. His legs flailed around as he breathed his last. Once he stopped moving, he lowered him and was about to move on when he heard a voice over the radio. "Come in, Pete. It's Davidson. You got eyes on them?"

Two remained.

* * *

Nate wasn't going to sit by idly. He'd already moved from the spot he was nestled in to a large cluster of boulders that gave him a bird's-eye view of the forest floor below. He spotted one of the men on a radio and had him in his scope for a second before he moved out of his crosshair. Damn it.

He shifted out from behind cover and worked his way through the trees, quietly and fast, pitching sideways down the incline. He'd only taken a few steps when his ankle twisted and he lost his footing and stumbled into a roll. The rifle flew out of his hand and he felt the full force of the earth as his shoulder crashed into it and he went head over heels until he slammed into a tree trunk. It was the only thing that stopped him from going over a rocky overhang. He reached up and touched his head. Pulling his hand away he noticed he was bleeding. Damn it. Before he was able to get to his feet the same guy with the radio was upon him. There were no words exchanged between them as he came into view and raised his rifle. Nate squeezed his eyes shut expecting the end.

Crack.

Thump.

A gust of wind full of leaves blew in his face and he

opened his eyes to see the same man inches away from him, a bullet hole in his forehead.

"Get up, you idiot. What did I tell you?" Corey said dragging him out of the clearing into thick brush. A few feet away they could hear a voice over the radio. That was when Nate caught sight of the fourth man, however instead of pressing forward, he turned and made a run for it.

"Shit!" Corey yelled. "Wait here."

He burst away, chasing after the lone survivor.

* * *

Corey was pissed. He could already hear the man raising the alarm over the radio as he ran for his life. Whatever element of surprise they had was gone. Whatever hope they had of finding the rest of the raiders was vanishing by the second. He stayed low raking his barrel over the terrain as the man disappeared out of view and the sound of running stopped. Corey took cover behind a tree and scanned for the camo-style military fatigues the man was wearing.

Branches snapped and crunched and he shot out into view. Corey took the shot but it missed. Gunfire was returned a second later, tearing up tree bark and the earth around. He pressed his back against the tree and looked up to where Nate was. More branches crunched, this time getting closer. He wasn't trying to escape; he was buying himself time to raise the alarm. "Eleven o'clock," Nate yelled.

Corey turned out and using only what Nate said as guidance unleashed a three-round burst. He heard the familiar sound of bullets hitting the mark, and he pulled back.

"You got him."

Nate went to get up and a flurry of rounds made him drop.

"Stay where you are!" Corey bellowed. He might have got lucky with one shot but the guy wasn't dead, and he sure as hell was still dangerous. Corey moved around the tree and darted over to a boulder covered in green moss. There, he heard the guy move and saw his fatigues. He sprinted for another tree. Corey cast a glance over his shoulder to check on Nate and grimaced when he saw he was gone. "Damn it, Nate," he muttered before breaking off towards the man. The oversized guy had taken up position behind two trees that were close together. Every few seconds a muzzle would appear and unleash bullets his way. Due to how steep the landscape was, and the lack of cover ahead of him, he was going to have to go up and around. Corey darted out, ducking bullets that were taking chunks out of the trees. A piece struck him in the face and he cursed.

"Nate?" he said in a low voice as he came back to the spot he'd left him in. "Where the hell are you?" No sooner had he said that than he spotted him between the trees. His eyes darted over to where the man had been. "Nate. Get out of there."

Corey's voice was lost.

Nate vanished behind bushes and when he came back into view, the injured man had his arm around his neck. Corey's stomach dropped as he saw a Glock held to

Nate's head. At the bottom of the incline they stopped and looked up at him.

"Come on down," the man said. "Or I will do it. And drop the gun."

Corey hesitated for a second, keeping his rifle on them. He peered through the scope but couldn't get a clean shot. Underbrush covered their lower half and the rest of him was hidden behind Nate.

"Drop it!" the guy bellowed again.

This time Corey complied.

"And the handgun."

He paused for a second before taking it out and tossing it.

"And the knife."

Reluctantly Corey did as he said and removed it and dropped it near his foot.

"Now come on down here."

The two of them shuffled back. Nate wasn't going anywhere as he had a firm grip on his neck and the barrel of his handgun under his chin. Getting closer, Corey noticed the guy was wearing a beanie hat, had a thick dark beard and was well-built. The kind of man who looked as if he pumped iron regularly.

"That's it. Come closer."

Corey held both hands out and tried to get the man to calm down. He was red in the face and from what he could tell, sporting a gnarly wound to his thigh. He stumbled back a little, dragging Nate with him.

"Look, just let him go."

"Move your ass, that way!" he said gesturing down the slope towards the lake. The man could only control Nate using the arm around his neck and the muzzle under his jaw, all of which left Nate's arms hanging loose. Stripped of weapons, they had no other option than to follow his lead. Corey was doing his best to keep the guy calm as he obeyed his orders. All the while his mind was searching for a way out. He didn't have to think too hard; Nate took the risky leap.

One hand shot up pushing the armed man's hand away from his jaw, while he simultaneously dug the thumb of his other hand into the man's bullet wound on the thigh. He let out a bloodcurdling scream, the gun went off and the fight was on.

Corey raced forward and lunged off a boulder. His body collided like a football player gunning for an opponent, knocking them off balance. All three of them went into a dizzying roll. As soon as Corey stopped tumbling, he scrambled to his feet and was on the man. Fortunately, he'd dropped the handgun and now it was just the two of them against an injured man. Corey swung his leg but the guy caught it and brought an elbow down. He let out a cry as pain shot up his leg. Nate dived on his back and the two of them spun around as the hulking guy tried to shake him.

Then he saw the rock.

Corey grabbed up the hand-sized stone, barreled towards the man and cracked him in the face with it. Down he went, landing hard with Nate still attached to him. Not wasting a second, Nate pulled a knife from the man's sheath and plunged it into his chest, once, twice, three times, then again, and again until he was no longer moving and both of them were soaked in blood.

Not waiting for Nate, Corey hurried towards the edge of the tree line and burst out into the clearing that went around the lake. His heart sank at the sight. They were gone.

"Damn it. Damn it!" he bellowed gritting his teeth.

A few seconds behind him was Nate.

Corey turned and ripped into him, stabbing his finger into his chest and pushing him back. "You ever. Ever! Disobey what I tell you, I will kill you myself. Do I make myself clear?"

Nate threw up his hands. "Okay, okay. Holy shit, dude. Ease up."

He held him there, gripping his shirt tightly and glaring at him.

Chapter 6

They'd been watching the camp from the observation tree stand for the better part of three hours. He saw nothing that looked unusual. Sure, it was an odd place to have a campground but hey, he hadn't been in the area for over nine years. Allie scribbled inside a notebook and closed it before looking again through the binoculars. Tyler perched on the edge, studying her.

"What's in the notebook?"

She glanced back. "Dates, times, schedules. Every place including Camp Olney operates on a schedule. Guard shifts rotate at a certain time, meetings occur on certain days, people come and go every week. I've been coming here for over two months watching, taking meticulous notes."

"So you can find a chink in their armor," Tyler added.

"You've got it," she replied with a smile. "You hungry?" Allie pulled a small stove from a burlap bag that was attached to the corner of the stand by a nail.

"Sure." He watched as she took out a can of soup, used a can opener and poured soup into a small metal pot. She lit a Coleman stove and placed the pot on top. "How many times a week are you out here?"

"Multiple times. Sometimes for an hour or two, sometimes overnight."

"Two months. And they don't notice you're gone?"

"No. Like I said, everything works on a schedule."

He nodded. A strand of dark hair draped down over her face and she swept it back behind her ear. For someone that didn't wear makeup she was exceptional looking. The kind of woman that could make his heart speed up a little. Few did that. He'd dated a number of attractive women, Erika included, but there were only a small number that put his nerves on edge. "Your parents. Where are they?"

She hesitated before replying. "A plane crash. They were celebrating their twelfth anniversary. After, we stayed with our grandparents for a time but they were getting too old to take care of us and thought it was best if we went to stay with a family they knew up here, that's how we ended up in Olney."

"Before that?"

"Texas."

He nodded slowly. "I'm sorry."

She shrugged. "It is what it is, right. You?"

Tyler shook his head and blew out his cheeks. "You don't even want to know. I feel like people have lied to me my entire life." Allie sat there stirring the pot, glancing at him as he filled her in on his background.

"That's pretty messed up. So, until three weeks ago you thought Andy was your father and you had no idea about Jude."

"Crazy, huh?"

She stopped stirring and her brow furrowed. "Look, I didn't know. When I came to you in the woods that night, I figured you were an outsider. I was trying to save you…"

"From getting involved. Maybe getting a little help. I

get it," he replied.

"Had I known I probably wouldn't have said anything."

She continued stirring. After a few minutes Allie handed him a cup of chicken soup. She took a seat beside him. Their vision of the landscape before them was distorted by the camouflage netting. "So, you have an older brother. You get along with him?"

"You could say our relationship is strained. It's been that way since I left home. It's not his fault. Andy pushed us to become something he wanted. There was never any room for our thoughts or opinions." Tyler tapped on the side of the steel cup and got lost in the past for a few seconds. "Nothing mattered except for his way." He took a few sips of his soup and then took a gulp as it was lukewarm.

"So, these friends of yours…"

"Nate and Erika."

"Yeah."

"I imagine they're wondering where you are."

He scratched his forehead. "I had to know about him."

"And?"

Tyler put his cup down. "He doesn't strike me as a man given to causing harm. He's a little eccentric but so is Andy. I'm used to that. So forgive me if I find it hard to wrap my head around this."

"That's why I brought you out here," she said. He furrowed his brow and she clarified. "You asked me how I can visit here without them knowing. Look, Jude visits every week on the same day. When he's not around, the rules of the camp kind of fall by the wayside."

"He's coming here?"

"Yes." She glanced at her watch. "Soon. Not yet. He never used to but after the incident with Madison, I noticed a change in the pattern. He still sends out groups at least twice a month to do an exchange of food supplies for bullets but this is new."

"How new?"

"As in, this is a change in schedule."

Tyler nodded, rising and resting his elbows on the

edge of the railing and looking out at the camp in the distance. Without binoculars it was nothing more than specks of light in the darkness. "What if you manage to get your sister out? What then?" He turned his head toward her.

"We would leave."

"And go where?" She didn't reply to that. Tyler put a finger and thumb up to the bridge of his nose as he tried to make sense of it all. "So you think he's made some kind of arrangement with this group?"

"As far as I know."

"What if the reason your sister is down there is because she met someone? Have you considered that?"

She shook her head as she got up. "No. She wouldn't do that. Since our parents' death she's always been there for me."

"People change, Allie. My brother isn't the same as he was when we were kids. Neither am I."

She stabbed the air with her finger. "I know Madison. She wouldn't have done that without telling me first."

Allie turned, bent over and dug into the burlap bag and took out a metal canister. She twisted off the top, chugged the contents, winced and then offered him some.

"What is it?"

"Bourbon."

He took it and knocked it back. It burned like fire going down his throat but damn it was good. Far better than the shitty moonshine they served up back at camp. Tyler tapped the bottom of the canister against the wooden railing ever so slightly. "Why then? Why is she there?"

"It's obvious, isn't it?"

He shrugged. Given some time he might have a few ideas but he wanted to hear it from her.

"Slavery."

"Come on, Allie."

She stared at him. "Unrealistic? Between 2014 and 2016, ISIS drew in extremists from all around the globe. A large majority were women who went out on missions as suicide bombers, others operated as families in terror cells and others were taken in as brides, used for nothing more than sex and to serve those fighting. You think this is any different? Think again."

"That was war. Extremism."

"What the hell do you think this is, Tyler?"

He studied her. A sliver of light filtered through the netting and shadows bounced off her face. "Living like this is extreme. Trying to survive is extreme. Let me guess, you think Russia, China or Iran was responsible for the power grid going down? I'm guessing you haven't had that talk with Jude yet, right?"

He didn't reply. Up to now it hadn't really mattered who was responsible as everyone had their own theories and without government in place to substantiate them, it did little to help their daily lives. The focus was on survival, not defending their nation against a foreign threat. At least not that he knew.

"Here, I want you to listen to something."

She went over to a hook that she'd hung her backpack on and dug into it. She pulled out a recording device.

When he saw it, she smiled. "Powered by batteries."

"Ah."

She fiddled with it for a minute or two, and then pressed play.

"This was taken from a meeting."

Over the course of the next twenty minutes Tyler listened to audio of a recording that Allie had taken a few weeks back. One man spoke to those attending and told them that in signing up they would agree to go through all forms of training — marksmanship, hand to hand combat, land navigation, patrolling, rappelling, communication and code language, holding defensive positions and setting up bases. It was the kind usually given to militia.

Tyler looked back out towards the flickering lights. Entertaining the thought that her sister and others were being used as slaves, in whatever way that might be, meant accepting that Jude was something far worse than Andy. Even if he wasn't behind the group, not doing anything about it and giving to the raiders' cause made him a supporter of it. He couldn't be behind that.

Tyler's chin dipped. So many lies. He didn't know who to believe anymore but he knew that he needed to talk to Corey. "You asked for my help but you and I can't do this alone. There's too many of them out there. It would be madness."

"At this moment. Yes. But not all the time. Listen, I know you might not see the value in the risk but surely you can see the value of getting your hands on that cartridge reloading machine."

"My father probably already has one."

"And the material?"

"Possibly."

"But what about medical supplies?"

"A large number," Tyler replied.

"Not like what is down there. There is a mountain of supplies. I'm not talking about just cartridges and powder. Medication. Dry food. Cans. Enough to cover the town of Whitefish for several years. Before they hit towns, they emptied abandoned semi-trucks on the highways, then homes, then major emergency supply centers."

"And you know this because of observing them here for two months?"

"I didn't just say in this location. I've been keeping tabs on them for some time."

Tyler rested his chin on his hand and leaned against the railing. "We would need to do more surveillance."

"Everything you need to know is in here," she said, handing it over.

"I need to talk with my brother."

"By all means."

"There's a good chance he'll turn it down."

Allie shrugged. "With or without your help, I'm going in."

"You'll need to come with me."

"To Whitefish? No."

"They need to hear this from you. It can't just be from me."

She took the notebook back out of his hand and

tucked it back into her bag. "Forget it. It was a bad idea."

"Allie."

"I can't leave the camp and go with you. It would raise too many suspicions."

"Okay. Then let's hope they hear what I have to say."

She took the notebook back out and gave it to him. He took another swig of the bourbon and handed it back to her and sat down and flipped through the notebook. She squeezed in beside him and leaned over and pointed out a few sections in the book that were useful to know. As she did, her hand brushed his. Their eyes locked for a second and she cleared her throat and pulled back. "Anyway, it's all in there. If you have any questions just let me know."

"I'll do that." Thumbing through he got to the back and saw a few sketches. "What are these?" She turned and reacted as if he wasn't meant to see them. She tried reaching for the notebook but he pulled it back with a grin on his face. "Hold on a second. What's the hurry?"

"Just give it here. I was meant to…"

He flipped two more pages. A couple were of the camp, then he landed on a portrait that looked similar to him. Her cheeks flushed. "Is this me?" He asked.

"I…" She sounded at a loss for words. In the pencil sketch, she'd captured him reading. He came across another one, and another. "Look, um," she was about to explain it away when they saw a red flare soar up into the sky.

"What's that?" Tyler asked.

"Shit. We need to go. Now!"

Chapter 7

There was a traitor among them, of that he was sure. Upon return from the lake he was surprised to find the same truck outside. Corey ran his hand over the hood of the green utility vehicle. It was still warm. He pulled the handle and opened the driver's side. There were no keys in the ignition nor anything on the leather seat or in the glove compartment that could link it to the group they'd seen. "Anything?" Nate asked.

He slammed the door shut and led the way, shouldering his rifle. "Nothing."

They garnered shocked looks as they traipsed into the lobby with blood on their faces. Corey's right hand was still gloved in dry blood from stabbing one of the men.

"Where's my father?" he asked one of two officers posted by the door.

"In the back, room 201. You guys okay?"

"You wouldn't by any chance know if he left this

building over the past hour?"

They both shrugged. "Not that I recall. Then again we've been posted at the front all night."

"And the utility truck around back. Anyone used it?"

"No idea."

He continued on down the hallway and eyed the rear exit. It was possible that someone could have snuck out and driven away without anyone noticing, especially if they were familiar with the door guards' schedule. Once he found the room, he barged in. Entering, he caught the tail end of his father addressing a room full of civilians. Behind him was a whiteboard with a map of the lake and an overview of what they had talked about. Andy snapped a cap on his Sharpie. "Any questions?"

"Yeah, I have one," Corey said closing the door behind him.

Heads turned; jaws widened as they soaked in the sight of their clothes streaked with blood.

"Corey?"

"The question is for anyone in this room. Has he been

here all night?"

"What?" Andy asked, his face screwing up.

"Have you been here all night?" Corey said in a more demanding tone, now directing the question at him.

"Of course I have." Andy weaved his way around tables over to him. He placed a hand on his shoulder. "Let's do this outside." Corey shrugged it off.

"So you didn't take the utility vehicle to the lake and warn them?"

"Warn? What are you talking about? Let's head outside and discuss this."

"No. I think everyone here should know as it does apply to them." Corey walked to the front of the room and took the whiteboard cleaner and rubbed out the map. "We won't be needing this. They're gone. And someone here warned them."

Andy looked at Nate and he nodded. Ferris stood by the door, one foot against the wall, the other out straight. His arms were folded and a concerned look was on his face. "What about you?" Corey asked looking his way.

"Me? You think it was me?" Ferris pushed away from the wall. "I think you are stepping over the line."

"You want to see stepping over the line?" Corey said moving forward and flipping a small table in front of him. "Someone here took the utility vehicle and warned them. Now who was it?"

Andy crossed the room fast and gripped Corey by the back of the collar and pulled him towards the door. "Now. Outside."

"Get the hell off."

But he wouldn't let go. No amount of resisting could prevent him from shoving Corey out the door. As soon as they were outside and the door was slammed, Andy tore into him. "What the hell are you playing at? You want to undo everything we have done so far? Those people in there are under enough stress as it is. We are a hairline crack away from losing them. We already had six walk since telling them what they were going into tonight. Now you want to go nuclear, you do it elsewhere. You want to ask a question, ask me in private. But I will not have you—"

"Were you behind it?" Corey asked in a calm voice, cutting him off.

He shook his head before replying slowly. "I didn't leave this building tonight."

"And you?"

"Fuck you, Corey," Ferris said. "You want to pin this on me because of what happened with your wife?" He flipped him the bird. "Asshole."

Corey saw red as Ferris went to walk away and he lunged at him, unleashing a power punch to the back of his head. He fell forward and Andy and Nate moved in quickly to break it up. Ferris cursed at him and told him he would press charges as Andy struggled to hold him back. "Attacking a police officer. I'll have you put behind bars."

"That would require you doing your job," Corey shot back.

"Go cool off!" Andy said to Ferris. He glared at Corey before strolling away.

Before Andy could tear into Corey for a second time, Hudgens appeared with Chief Bruce. "You want to tell me what's going on?"

"The raid is a bust. They're gone. Our one chance of finding them is gone. And someone from here is responsible," Corey said leaning back against a wall and wiping his face.

Hudgens eyed Andy. "Is this true?"

"Seems so, but I wasn't there so I don't know," Andy replied making it clear to his son he was referring to him.

"He's telling the truth," Nate piped up. "We went ahead to scout out the area. Andy's truck rolled up while we were doing some surveillance. We couldn't see who the driver was as they wore a hood but it was definitely the truck."

Hudgens glanced at Andy and he shrugged. "I've been in with them for the past two hours trying to convince them not to walk after six left."

"There's only one person who knew about the scout and that was you," Corey said to his father.

"He wasn't the only one," Chief Bruce said. "Ferris overhead and told me and I informed the mayor."

Corey looked at his father and he could tell he was pissed to have his own flesh and blood accuse him.

"Is that all?"

"Well I informed the group," Hudgens said.

"Great. So it could be anyone."

"What did they look like?" Hudgens asked.

"If I knew that, do you think we would be having this conversation?" Corey rolled his eyes as he brushed past them making his way over to a five-gallon water dispenser. He snatched a paper cup off the table and filled it up, chugging it back before getting some more. Meanwhile Hudgens talked with Andy and the chief about what they should do next in light of the circumstances. His father was the only one suggesting they back off, while Hudgens and the chief were advocating beefing up support at the roadblocks and the school where they were guarding what remained of the town supplies like gold.

Corey turned to leave but was called over by Hudgens.

"Tomorrow we'll convene here and discuss the road forward. I think it would be best if we have you stay in town. The back and forth to your cabin isn't working. There is plenty of room at my home." He took out some keys from his pocket and tossed them to Corey. "Get cleaned up. Rest."

Corey clutched the keys and considered tossing them back but one glance at his old man and he figured maybe it was for the best. He didn't want to get into an argument and he could already tell by the look on his face that he was just biting at the bit to grill him over embarrassing him in front of the civilians. The truth was, it was hard to know who to trust. Anyone could have been responsible, even one of the officers. Not that he thought Whitefish had dirty cops but with the recent addition of help from Kalispell, there was no telling who might be on the raiders' payroll.

"I don't know. I don't want to put you out."

"You wouldn't put me out. It's the least I can do after

what you went through tonight."

Nate nudged him and his eyes widened.

"Okay."

Hudgens gave him the directions. "It's on Missy Lane."

"I know which one it is."

"Right."

* * *

Around the same time, many miles away inside the Kootenai National Forest, Tyler was trying to keep up with Allie as she barreled forward through the thick underbrush heading for the camp they'd been observing. "Hold up. What's going on?"

"Someone has attempted to escape. It could be my sister, I need to get a closer look," she said. Tyler managed to catch up. He grabbed her by the bicep and swung her around. "Are you out of your mind?"

"Get off me."

She tugged and tried to push him away but he wouldn't let go. "You get any closer and you risk getting caught. You think your sister would want that?"

"She'll need my help."

"If it is her, I think she's doing fine as it is."

"I need to know. You want to stay here. Fine."

He released her and she took a few steps backwards before turning and sprinting. Tyler stood there for a few seconds looking over his shoulder, contemplating heading back to Whitefish. Putting himself at risk for the sake of one person went against everything his father taught him. He looked back at Allie and shook his head. Ah man, you are going to regret this, he thought as he took off after her, swinging his rifle up and scanning the terrain ahead.

Tyler found Allie lying down in the tall grass. She was peering through binoculars when he dropped down beside her. "What we got?" he asked.

She lowered her binoculars and handed them to him. "It's not her. But I know the guy. His name is Jeremy. He used to work in the medical clinic."

Tyler took a look through. A tide of people gathered around as a man with blond hair was dragged through the midst of them. He was wearing a tan coat, leather gloves, boots and a baseball cap. He looked as if he was unconscious. A large knot of people parted as the man was thrown on the ground and turned over. The crowd pulled back to let through a guy who had a shaved head and an eye that looked white. Tyler couldn't hear what they were saying but he could tell things were about to turn nasty.

He pulled the binoculars away and looked at Allie. She sat there with a deadpan expression on her face. "You want to see what's going on?"

"No." Her chin dropped. "I've already seen it. Multiple times."

She sighed and he brought the binoculars back up.

They attached chains to the man's wrists and ankles. Tyler figured they were planning on stringing him up as an example to the rest. But that wasn't it. No, it was far worse. Four horses were brought in. They had some kind of wooden rigging system strapped over them. Tyler watched in horror as they hooked up the chains to each horse until he was splayed apart. The bald man stepped forward with a bucket of water and tossed the contents over the unconscious man's face. It splashed against his face and he spluttered and gasped for air. Within seconds he realized what they were doing and he cried out, pleading for his life. His voice was so loud it carried on the wind, turning Tyler's stomach.

The bald man took a handkerchief from his pocket and raised it into the air, he shouted something and then dropped it. As soon as he did, they let the horses loose and the man was torn apart.

"Oh my God," Tyler said, pulling the binoculars away.

"Now you understand why I want to get my sister out."

"We need to get out of here. Let the others know."

As they got up to leave, Allie took one last look before sighing and trudging on behind him. They didn't speak that much on the way back. The few times Tyler tried to engage with her she had nothing but bad things to say about Jude. In her mind, he was responsible, and yet at no point did Tyler see him down there. He understood her desire to get her sister out but he was still trying to come terms with the accusations against Jude.

* * *

Nate was like a kid in a candy shop moving from room to room, calling out what he found. "1962 Cabernet. Damn, you should see all these vintage wines. I swear I went into the wrong business. I'm getting drunk tonight." Hudgens wasn't married, and he only had few friends, so his six-bedroom, five-bath, roughly 7,000 square foot home seemed a little ostentatious, however, it wasn't his career that had given him the financial means to acquire such a property. No, this was inherited, passed down through the family. The fact was until the power went out, Ted Hudgens was considered one of the wealthiest men in Whitefish. Taking the position as mayor wasn't a necessity but a means of lording his power over others. Some admired him, others despised the ground he walked on, Corey didn't care either way, unlike his father.

Nate came up from the cellar taking a large swig from

a bottle of wine. "Okay, I was wrong about this guy. I figured he'd taken a large chunk of the supplies and was making up all this shit about raiders but barring the oversized house and the exquisite vintage wine collection, this man hasn't got shit!" Nate said, breaking into laughter. "He's just the same as us. All that money and nothing to show for it. The sweet irony," he said holding out the bottle for Corey. Corey shook his head. Nate shrugged and returned to chugging it down and running his grubby fingers across the spotless furniture. "Man, I can't wait to show this place to Erika."

He wanted to stay clear-headed. Ever since the incident at the lake, Corey couldn't push the image of the stranger from his mind. "I think it's Ferris."

"What?" Nate asked turning.

"The stranger. Think about it. What was he doing listening in on the conversation? Unless of course he wanted to give them the heads-up. And why tell the chief and Hudgens? Simple. He wanted to cover his ass. Make it look like any one of them could have done it. Probably knew Hudgens would tell the group."

"You know, Corey. I'll be the first to admit that what he did was underhanded. But, helping raiders? I just don't get that vibe from him. I think he did what any of us would have done. I mean, put yourself in his position for just a minute. All your team is wiped out and you're told if you don't tell them where one person is, they will kill your family. What would you do?"

"I wouldn't know because my family is dead."

"Corey. You know what I mean."

Corey stared at him. He'd given it a lot of thought. He knew the answer but wasn't ready to let Ferris off the hook.

Chapter 8

Ferris lied. According to him, the meeting was set for nine that morning, at least that was what he'd told Nate before he retired for the evening. The next morning, Nate and Corey arrived on time but it was already in session. Hudgens hadn't stayed at his house, otherwise they might have been able to confirm the time. They soon realized they weren't the only ones who knew that. As soon they entered the room inside city hall, a hush fell over the small group made up of Andy, Hudgens, Ferris and the chief.

"Started without us?"

"Finished," Ferris said, offering a smug grin. Corey glanced at his watch and then the clock on the wall.

"You said nine."

"Did I?"

Corey turned to Nate and he nodded.

"You must have heard me wrong, I said eight."

"No, you didn't," Nate shot back.

Hudgens rose from his chair, sensing another argument boiling. "It doesn't matter. I can bring you up to speed, but help yourself to coffee over there." Corey glared at Ferris as he and Nate went over to a table at the back of the small room. As he poured out his drink, he asked Nate again if he'd heard him wrong, being as he had drunk a lot of wine.

Nate shook a small bag of sugar and emptied it into his drink. "Trust me. He said nine."

"Yeah, I figured."

Corey scooped up an apple and took a bite out of it as he made his way down the center aisle. Either side were a dozen chairs, and at the front was a table, and a clean whiteboard. "So, we've given a lot of thought to the situation yesterday and we're in agreement. Andy will continue to offer training to volunteers, those that already have experience with guns will join the others in shift rotation at the roadblocks and critical facilities in town. Without further intel on the whereabouts of raiders all we can do is focus on ensuring the safety of residents and remaining supplies in town. Do you have any objections?"

"Whose idea was that?"

"Mine," Ferris said. "And your father's."

Corey glanced at his dad. "No point wasting valuable resources," Andy said.

"I figured it's better this way," Ferris said.

"Yeah, I bet you did," Corey replied, then took another bite from his apple.

"Well, unless of course you have a lead we don't know about? I mean I don't want to step on your toes. You know, being as the mayor put you in charge of heading up yesterday's endeavor, I just figured that since that was a bust, we should focus on the town."

It was a total power move. An attempt to swing things back his way. Corey didn't give two shits about being in charge of heading up anything. In many ways he was pleased the plan hadn't worked. He didn't want anyone else's blood on his conscience and especially not the blood of those who were unprepared for war.

The awkward silence could have been cut with a knife.

"Do you have a lead?" Hudgens asked.

Corey chewed and swallowed a mouthful of food before replying. "No."

"Then it's agreed," Hudgens said.

"Meeting adjourned," Ferris said in a sarcastic tone, pushing away from a desk with his arms crossed. Corey wanted to knock that smug grin off his face. Ever since he'd met him, he'd come across as someone on a power trip, thinking more of public admiration than getting the job done. In his mind he was a disgrace to the shield. If he could have only seen how things played out when Ella died, he was pretty certain Ferris would have been found cowering. He wasn't like some of his brothers in arms who he had fought shoulder to shoulder in combat with. Those were men that would have rather died in their boots than give up one of their own. The mentality was different. That wasn't to say there weren't good cops, brave ones, those who saw the position as more than a job but those were far and few between. Too many were vying for paychecks and an easy life. The same ones were there with their hands out hoping for some award that was gained off the bravery of others.

Nate leaned forward and put his hand on Corey's shoulder. "I'm thinking of heading to the hospital this morning to see how she's doing. You want to come with me?"

"I would like to but..."

"Ah, it's okay. I get it."

"Nate. I'm sorry if I was a little hard on you back in the forest."

"Ah it's water off a duck's back. I probably deserved it. This is all new to me. I'm still trying to figure out my way." Nate patted his shoulder and broke off heading for the door. As he sat there drinking his coffee, his father went to walk straight by him without even a glance.

"You heading to one of the roadblocks?" Corey asked over his shoulder.

His father returned. "I'm heading to the lake to see what I can find."

"You mean, anything you might have left behind?" Corey said without looking at him.

Andy scoffed. "All right, I'll bite. Why do you think it was me?"

"I didn't say it was you. I asked if it was you."

"But you're still insinuating."

"That I am. But don't worry, you're not the only one," he said glancing at Ferris who was talking with Hudgens.

"It doesn't make any sense, Corey."

"It makes perfect sense. I mean when have you ever given a shit about this town? Sure, you worked out a few deals with the city and helped a couple of neighbors with generators but beyond that, it's always been a one-man show. Hell, if it hadn't been for me coming into town and taking the position the chief offered, you'd still be back there at the cabin."

His father scoffed. "All right. I get it now. You blame me for Ella's death. Because if I hadn't come into town, she would have been there with me."

"I didn't say that."

"You didn't need to. You're doing the same with Ferris. This is how it starts, Corey."

He took a sip of his coffee. "How what starts?"

"The downward spiral." His father shifted his weight from one foot to the next. "First it's the blame, then you start drinking to deal with what's going on in your head, and then you push people away."

"Well I'm glad to see you admit your own shortcomings, Dad. That's refreshing. A little late, but refreshing."

His father jabbed his finger at him. "Don't be sarcastic with me. You want to go down this path, by all means, but you are not dragging others down with you. Or placing their lives in jeopardy. I might have made some mistakes raising you two but I'll be damned if I'm gonna let you do the same." He paused for a second. "Do you even know what Ferris did to try and save Ella? Or are you so intent on finding fault that you can't see the forest for the trees?"

Corey gritted his teeth; he could feel anger rising.

"He risked his life, and his men's lives to get Ella out of there. What happened to her was terrible, but it had nothing to do with Ferris."

"And you know this because you were there, right?" Corey turned to him and stood up, squaring off. At one time his father's size made him tremble but that was before signing up for the military. Now he paled in comparison. "That's right. You don't know shit. All you know is what he's told you."

Ferris looked over. He must have overheard. He was still talking with Hudgens but he kept glancing their way.

"The fact is you didn't care for Ella the way I did. How many times did you say she made me weak? That she was a crutch?"

"I cared for her as if she was my own daughter."

"Then why did you leave her there?"

Corey brushed past him. His father didn't say anything as he exited the room. He was done talking with them, done helping, nothing came from it. No one in the town really knew what was going on. It was a farce. They were living on borrowed time. Raiders would return. Whether it was the same group or another it didn't matter. He thought he could push her from his mind, focus on work and coast through his grief but his father was right, and he hated to admit it. All he felt was anger every day. He wanted someone to blame. Anyone but himself or Ella. For all the training he'd received from his father, none of it had prepared him for losing the one he most cared about.

Leaving the building through a side exit he made his way over to the green utility truck and hopped inside. He fired it up using a spare key and reversed out. As he drove out of the lot, one of the officers tried to stop him by getting in the way of the truck. Corey swerved around him and continued on. Would they follow? He didn't care. He drove up through the town, heading for his home. He hadn't returned there since Ella's death. As much as he wanted to, seeing it would have crushed him, but that was three weeks ago and he refused to let grief hold him captive.

He gave the gas pedal some more pressure as he passed through the town and took in the sight of burned homes and what remained of a once thriving town. Everyone had been affected by the blackout in one way or another. How many others had lost loved ones? How many others were in a worse state than him?

His mind drifted to the many days he'd shared with Ella.

Tears welled in his eyes and trickled down. He wiped them fast, a habit ingrained from being a kid who didn't want to show weakness in front of his father. His mind circled to those final moments in the hospital. He thought he'd feel satisfaction, relief from the pain when he killed Gabriel, but it had done nothing. Vengeance didn't change anything. He was still without her.

Corey eased off the gas as he came onto Woodland Star Circle.

He veered into the driveway and took in the sight of his once-beautiful home now lying in ruins. The grass was overgrown, weeds were out of control and someone had graffitied profanity directed at the government on the front of the house. His home wasn't singled out, he'd seen many like that along the way. Abandoned houses torn apart as the desperate went house to house searching for anything of value.

After killing the engine, he sat there hesitant to get out.

His mind created imaginary pictures in his head. He heard the sound of Ella's voice, bullets striking windows, and saw drywall dust explode. How scared was she? He would never know. Corey took a deep breath and pushed out of the vehicle. He made his way into the house, glass crunching under his boots. The walls were peppered with bullet rounds. It was like someone had taken a machine gun and let loose. Daylight filtered in from a hundred different places like precision lasers cutting through metal. His father's words played back in his head. Did he even know what Ferris had done to try and save her? He didn't, even though Ferris had offered to tell him. He'd refused to listen. Now as he walked through the hallway he yearned to know. Where was she? Which way out did she go? It was as if he was hoping to find a flaw in the advice given to her. Something more he could hold over Ferris' head.

Corey stopped in the doorway of the living room and spotted an overturned photo frame. He could tell from the frame alone which photo was inside. Crossing the room, he soaked in the devastation. He scooped up the photo and turned it over. The glass was cracked and covered in dirt. He pulled away some of the glass and retrieved the photo from inside. Friends of theirs had taken the photo. Ella was ten weeks pregnant. Corey was behind her, his arms wrapped around her, holding her belly. Both of them smiling, full of life, full of hope. He tucked the photo into his pocket and continued on. No one had been in to clean up the dry blood but he could see where bodies had been dragged out.

The only information he'd got was the location of where they found Ella.

He swallowed hard as he exited the rear of the home

and made his way across the yard. Chief Bruce had told him that they'd tied a purple ribbon to the tree close to where she'd fallen. It didn't take him long to spot it through the overgrown brush. He stopped walking and stared from a distance, apologizing under his breath to Ella for not being there to help her. *I'm sorry. I'm so sorry.* Tears streaked his cheeks as he waded through the high grass and brush until he made it to the spot. Corey scanned the ground for blood, anything that would indicate the exact spot. But there was nothing. Heavy rains would have washed blood away. Corey dropped to his knees, overwhelmed by loss.

The pain was so sharp he could barely catch his breath.

In three weeks he'd gone through every emotion possible, and he knew that it was only the beginning. It would take months, maybe even years before time took away the pain. The only comfort he found came from the knowledge that one day he would wake up and it wouldn't sting as much. He'd learned this from losing his mother.

He wasn't sure how long he knelt there in the grass sobbing before he heard a familiar and comforting voice. "Corey. Brother."

Still kneeling he cast a glance over his shoulder just as Tyler came up behind him and placed a hand on his shoulder. "Tyler?"

He'd never felt as happy to see him as he did in that moment. Tyler had grown a thick beard since he'd last seen him. As he hugged him, he spotted over his shoulder a woman with dark hair and green eyes with a bow over her back, and a gun in a holster at her hip. She smiled but said nothing.

"Who's this?" he asked.

"Oh. Um. This is Allie. She's from Jude's camp."

He gave a nod to her and she said hello before stepping away and looking off towards the house. Tyler patted Corey on the back. "It's good to see you. We need to talk," Tyler said. "It's about the raiders. I know where they are."

Chapter 9

"No one is to know. You understand?" Corey said. Tyler offered back a confused expression as his brother came out of the shed with a shovel and proceeded to walk to the end of the property and begin to dig. He looked back at Allie, and she shrugged, also trying to make sense of it. It was like everything he told him went over his head.

Tyler pulled out a toothpick that was wedged in the corner of his mouth and tapped the air. "First, care to tell me what the hell you are doing? Second, did you not hear a word of what I said?"

Corey sunk the shovel into the earth, and jammed it farther in with his boot before pulling out a large chunk of dirt and tossing it to one side. "I heard. But we'll be needing this." He continued digging without explaining. Allie walked over to Tyler and tapped him on the shoulder and jerked her head towards the house. He followed her so they were out of earshot.

"Look, no offense but when you said we needed help I thought it would amount to more than your brother. Additionally, he seems as if he's a little unstable."

"He just lost his wife."

"Okay, well that explains things but on the other hand it raises some serious concerns. Is he up for this? I mean you saw the way we found him — mumbling, sobbing."

Tyler looked over his shoulder. Corey was now down on his knees scooping out handfuls of dirt. That was his only regret. Spending the past three weeks at Camp Olney had meant not being there for his brother, but he assumed he wouldn't have been in a receptive frame of mind anyway. "Leave it with me. Give me a moment." He went over and noticed his brother had unearthed a green container. "Is that an ammo can?"

Corey nodded, sweeping away dirt around the edges until he was able to find the handle. Burying essentials was survival 101. Anyone with a lick of sense buried a survival cache, specifically guns and ammo just in case martial law came into effect and guns were confiscated. Goods were often enclosed in heavy-duty containers that were air-tight and used for guns, emergency gear, documents and valuables. They came in varying sizes. Most were six-inch wide PVC pipe that ranged from four to six feet in length and had a cap on either end, others were nothing more than military surplus ammo cans. "Here, give me a hand," he said. Tyler dropped to a knee and grasped a handle while Corey continued scooping out dirt to free the container. Seconds later it came free and he pulled it out. Corey cracked it open and emptied it out. Inside were a mid-length AR with collapsible stock, a Ruger 10/22, a Remington 870 shotgun, a Glock with spare magazines, plenty of ammo for all the weapons, a crank-powered radio, a two-way radio, a large survival knife, a pair of night vision binoculars, a bag of survival tools, small solar panels for charging batteries and some freeze-dried food. "That should come in handy."

Tyler's brow furrowed. "Um. Not to point out the obvious but why did you dig this up when we could just go to the cabin?"

"He can't know about this trip."

"Which brings me full circle to what I said earlier. We need everyone we can get. This is a large group and believe me, they are not playing around. I'm talking fully armed and dangerous," Tyler said.

Corey lifted his eyes as he sifted through the contents. "Someone in town is working with them." He brought him up to speed on what had occurred the day before. "It's the only way they could have known about the supplies delivery from the school. Someone had to tell them."

"And you think it's Andy?"

"Andy? Is that what you're calling him now?" He cocked his head to one side. "And, why have you been gone so long?"

"He didn't tell you?"

"Tell me what?"

Tyler rolled his bottom lip under his top teeth and then wiped a hand across his lips.

"Andy isn't my father. Jude is."

Corey stared back for a second before he responded. "He told you this?"

Tyler nodded.

"And that's why you took off?"

"Wouldn't you?"

Corey squeezed his eyes shut. "No. No, that's bullshit."

"Think about it, Corey. It makes perfect sense. All the times he would go off on me. He always treated me different from you. If anyone was getting that belt of his, it was me." Tyler stared at him. "What? You think you had some ability to talk him down from a ledge when others couldn't? He listened to you because you are his son. I'm not."

Tyler could see he was trying to process it. Hell, he'd spent the last three weeks trying to come to terms with it only to have his mind blown again by Allie. Corey blew out his cheeks and exhaled hard. "What a shit storm. Look, just grab what we have here. I have a few more of these to dig out and then we need to head to Evergreen."

Tyler frowned. "Why?"

"I just told you. We can't trust those in town. But there are some I trust."

Tyler nodded as Corey went a few feet away and began digging again. He gathered up the contents and looked over at Corey. "We can trust Nate and Erika. We'll swing by and pick them up."

"That's gonna be a little difficult." Corey stopped digging. "Erika is in the hospital."

"What?"

"In a coma."

His jaw went slack.

"Nate is with her. She's stable but…" he trailed off for a second. "She's suffering from some kind of head trauma." Tyler nodded slowly as Corey continued digging. A wave of guilt washed over him. A sense of responsibility. They were his friends, his guests. He'd just taken off without telling them where he was going. Tyler carried the can over to the truck and loaded it into the back. Once Corey had unearthed three more containers they headed for Evergreen.

The journey south would usually take around thirty minutes if they'd gone direct but as Corey had pissed off the police department by taking one of the only operational vehicles and was adamant about avoiding roadblocks, they had to add an extra twenty minutes onto that by going through Halfmoon, and past Glacier Park International Airport.

Evergreen was a small community of almost eight thousand located in Flathead County just northeast of Kalispell. Tyler hadn't spent any time there but had passed through multiple times. Most locals stayed in their own towns and occasionally ventured into larger cities like Kalispell to shop. Policed by the Flathead County Sheriff's Department they didn't expect to encounter too much trouble in Evergreen as they had their hands full in Kalispell, but to be on the safe side, Corey wanted to temporarily ditch the truck in the woods a couple of miles outside of town and hike in to be on the safe side.

"Remind me again why we're going here?"

"To meet an old Marine buddy of mine."

"Okay," Tyler said casting a sideways glance at Allie who also looked perplexed. Corey had said very little about what he had in mind.

"Look, Corey, I'm all for catching up with friends and shooting the breeze but shouldn't we be gathering together a group?"

"We are," he said looking at him for a second before gunning the engine.

The truck roared as they sped down Highway 2. Once they made it to Rose Crossing, Corey veered left and went on for another fifty yards before pulling into a heavily wooded area. He drove that truck as deep as he could inside, and then killed the engine. Once out they covered the top, back and sides with branches and brush and then stepped back and made sure it wasn't visible from any angle. "That should do the trick," Corey said.

"I don't feel good about leaving it here and especially not with that cache in the back," Tyler responded.

"Did you see anyone on the road?"

"No but…"

"It's fine," Corey said slapping him on the shoulder as they walked back out to the main road and trudged on south. "Besides, there are countless abandoned vehicles." All the while Tyler couldn't help but wonder if the whole trip was a complete waste of time. He'd wanted to bring it up earlier but Corey seemed convinced.

"What if he isn't there?"

"He will be."

"Does this friend of yours have a name?" Tyler asked.

Corey looked at him as he adjusted the carbine slung over his shoulder. "Do you believe Andy?"

Tyler frowned. His question caught him off guard. "Okay. What are we talking about? How did we go from your friend to him?"

"Forget my friend. This is bigger."

He could see it was bothering Corey. Who wouldn't be pissed to find out that they'd been lied to? It wasn't just Tyler, it was his brother.

Tyler scratched the back of his head and looked on up the road. Either side of them was a flat landscape of farms. They walked past a company that had at one time sold modular homes. The ones they had on display had been broken into, windows smashed and one even had siding ripped off it. Nothing was off limits now.

"Yes. I believe both of them. They told me they didn't say anything because of mother," Tyler replied.

Corey shook his head as they ambled along the edge of the dusty road. Allie listened in but kept her mouth closed.

"Are you saying you didn't know about this?"

His eyes widened and he shot Tyler a look of surprise. "Of course not. Don't you think I would have had something to say about it?"

"I figured you didn't but he gave me the impression that you might have known."

"No, I didn't."

The last stretch of the way was spent in silence.

It took around twenty minutes to breach the town

limits. Instead of heading straight down the main street they veered off to the right and walked down a line of railway tracks and then crossed over to Shadow Lane. "By the way. You two hang back. No matter what he does, I don't want you stepping in, you understand?"

Tyler frowned but gave a nod.

"He can be a little high strung, and we haven't exactly seen eye to eye for some time."

"I thought you said he was your buddy."

"He was. Emphasis on *was*."

Tyler threw a hand up. "Oh, great."

Once they reached a wide gravel driveway that led up to a one-story clapboard home with a blue truck outside, Corey told them to wait by the entrance. "Again, don't do anything. I don't want to have to pull a bullet out of you."

"Ah, pleasant."

They stood by as Corey walked up to a gate that had rolls of barbed wire curled around the top. The property itself had all the signs of someone who had taken great measures to secure it. The front door had steel paneling, the windows were covered in bars and the roof had wood with nails punctured through. They weren't taking any chances. Tyler noticed a curtain pull back slightly before a slat on the door slid open and a gun muzzle poked out. Corey froze. The gun went off, a round lanced into the ground near Corey's feet and Tyler and Allie reacted defensively. Tyler raised his rifle and took cover behind a tree.

"That's as far as you come, Ford," a gravely voice said.

Corey lifted a hand. "Dirk Bennington. Buddy. My old pal."

"Don't you old pal me. Where's that money you owe me?"

"I got it right here," he said, his hand sliding down.

"Careful!"

"Look, it's fine," Corey said slowly pulling out a wad of green notes. "Not that I can see this being of much use to you now. But it's all here. Twenty-two hundred."

"Place it on the truck and get the fuck out of here."

"Can't do that, bud. I need some help."

Bennington laughed. "Shit. Doesn't everyone. Cry me a river and get the fuck out."

Corey remained. "I didn't sleep with her."

"Bullshit."

"I'm telling the truth, man. It was just a prank. Wayland set it up. And your missus was pissed at you so she went along with it."

"You're still sticking to that story?"

"It's not a story. It's a fact."

"Yeah and it's a fact that I found you in the sack with her, butt naked."

"I wasn't naked. And why would I do that? I was engaged."

"Because you enjoy fucking people over."

"I brought your money, didn't I?"

"Yeah, and you waited until it was of no value."

"And yet you took it."

Corey looked over his shoulder at Tyler. Tyler raised his eyebrows and jerked his head to get him to leave. This guy was clearly off his head. Absolutely cuckoo.

"Who's that with you?"

"My brother and his friend."

"Oh, and let me guess, they're just tagging along. Please. I know you, Ford. You want me to come and collect the money and then you're going to steal what I have, aren't you?"

"Believe it or not, I don't need what you have. I need what you can do."

"Always the smooth talker. I bet you smooth talked Angela right into those sheets, didn't you?"

"Oh my God. Are we back to that?"

"We never left," Bennington said.

There was a long pause.

"Ella's dead," Corey said. "She was pregnant too."

He waited for a response but got nothing.

"Look. Maybe I got this wrong. Sorry to take up your time."

He began backing out with his hands up then turned and started heading towards Tyler.

"Ford. FORD!"

Corey stopped but didn't turn around.

The door cracked open and out came a guy who was half the size of Corey. He had to have been the smallest Marine in history. No bigger than four foot eight, the minimum standard for the Marines. If that wasn't enough, below his right knee was a prosthetic leg. He wearing a white muscle shirt, a pair of black shorts and sneakers. He had a long mullet that came down to his shoulders. Corey turned around. Dirk came out and took the money off the truck and pocketed it.

"What does it involve?"

"Killing people," Corey replied.

He stared back then broke into a laugh. "Then why the hell didn't you say so? C'mon in, and you two," he said turning and striding back in with all the confidence and swagger of someone who wasn't missing any limbs.

Tyler's eyebrows shot up and they followed.

Corey turned to Tyler and Allie as they got closer to the door. "Don't speak out of turn. He's been known to change his mind on a dime."

"I heard that," Bennington said. "Don't believe him. I haven't changed my mind about you and Angela."

Chapter 10

Andy didn't expect anything less. The irate manner in which Ferris delivered the news would have made anyone think it was his truck that was stolen. Andy quickly reminded him that it was Ford property and while he didn't agree with his son taking it, he figured he must have had a good reason.

"I don't give a damn!" Ferris replied. "Until the power grid comes back on, it was one of several vehicles that belong to Whitefish and the county. Now where has he gone?" he demanded to know. A previous conversation with Corey had hinted that he was going to head to Camp Olney to thank Jude but he didn't tell Ferris that.

"Do I look like I know?"

"Useless. All you Fords are useless."

It was only the two of them in the corridor when he said it. Under any other conditions he might have thought twice about what he did next. Andy slammed

Ferris up against the wall, pushing his forearm into his neck until his face went a beet red. "Now you listen up. I came to your defense over what happened with Ella but I will not have you drag our name through the mud. If it wasn't for me, or Corey, you assholes would be standing around with your thumb up your ass. So show some damn respect!"

He held him there for a few seconds more.

Ferris gritted his teeth and was seething as Andy released him and turned to walk away.

"You know he'll bring charges against you if the lights come back on." Andy looked over his shoulder and saw Hudgens standing in a doorway.

"Which requires witnesses, proof, and from what I can tell, he has neither." He knew Hudgens had watched it play out but the guy didn't have the balls to go head to head with him. He was too valuable to the community, especially at a time like this.

"He might speak out of line, Andy, but he has a point. Your boy can't just go charging off with property that we need. And right now, we need that truck. So, can you get it back?"

"That would require me knowing where he is."

Hudgens strolled out with a mug in his hands. Steam spiraled above it. He gazed out the window and walked over to him. "Look, I know you and I haven't seen eye to eye. It's no mystery that you don't like me but no matter how you look at this, we are in this together. I just got word that another two of our officers were shot at the northwest roadblock. If we don't get on top of these raiders fast, Whitefish will go under. Now I know you well enough, Andy, to say that you don't want that any more than I do. I thought we could take a defensive approach to this problem but it's clear we have to be proactive and that means going after these thugs. You and your son are the only ones barring Ferris that I can trust to handle that task but that means wrangling in your son and putting to rest your differences with Officer Ferris. Can you do that?"

"Of course I can. But whether I want to, that's another

question entirely."

Hudgens sucked in his lips and walked over to the window. He nursed his coffee with both hands as he looked out. "People often ask me why I ran for mayor. It's not like I need the money. I could quite easily step aside and let someone else deal with the shit that comes my way but that's not why I wanted to be mayor." He cast Andy a glance. "You and I are a lot alike. Before you say we're not, let me explain." He took a sip of his drink. "We both want to be remembered. You by your sons, me by the community. It's what drives us on, it's what gets us out of bed. You see money, yeah, it sure can make your life comfortable and even open a few doors that would usually be closed but what it can't do is give you real gratification. I'm talking about the kind you get when you lay your head down on the pillow at night — I mean, when you really know you've made a difference in someone's life. Hell, I can hand someone a thousand dollars and it might help pay for food, pay a few bills but all that stuff is surface-level shit. It's a means to an end.

Folks soon forget what someone gave them. But this," he pointed out at the devastation. "Inspiring people. Championing a cause. Turning this around even if it's only in this town, that is the stuff of legends. It's what will ingrain our names in the minds of this city long after we are gone. It's why Winston Churchill is remembered." He breathed in deeply. "You ever see those names on plaques? The ones found in parks on benches. You ever wonder what they did to deserve that? No. No one cares and yet generation after generation will sit there and look at that name and know they were a somebody among an ocean of people. They did something of significance to warrant having their names engraved into metal and put up for everyone to see and admire."

"Is that what you want, Hudgens? To be seen, admired?"

"Don't we all?"

Andy snorted. "No. I don't give a shit about that. The ones who have stood out in history weren't the ones that were necessarily liked, they were often the ones that were hated the most but stood their ground. They went against the grain, the status quo and popular opinions of their time. They were real history makers. Caring more about the moment than their legacy."

"You don't think people want to be remembered?" Hudgens asked.

Andy nodded. "Oh I believe most do, but at what cost? Becoming someone you're not? It's not for me. Too many are bent on aesthetic appearances. Smiley faces, squeaky clean images, untainted reputations and cozying up for the approval of others. No, it's bullshit. Like I used to tell my boys, give me scarred souls, those who dance with tears, wrestle with heartache and make love to struggle. Give me rejects, renegades and rebels. Give me soiled hands from clawing out of life's trenches. Give me feet marred by tough roads, and I'll show you passion and resilience that can set a world on fire."

Hudgens' lip curled. "That's why we need you. So? Do we have your support?"

"Why not just wait for him to show up?"

"Because with every hour that passes, it's getting darker out there, and I'm not talking about the lights. We need to give this town some hope, inspire them in their darkest hour before we lose everything we have worked so hard to build."

Andy frowned studying his face, trying to determine if he was being genuine or if this was another attempt at getting what he wanted without giving anything in return. "I will find my son but I can't guarantee he will help or that he'll hand that truck back."

"I understand."

Something in his response gave Andy a sense that he was grateful. As Andy turned to leave, that was when he dropped the ball. "Though one thing, Ford. I need you to take Ferris with you."

Andy frowned. "You what?"

Hudgens cleared his throat. "He's not doing us any good around here. Take him with you. He can help."

"He also pisses me off."

"Andy."

"No, I work alone."

He lifted his hand. "Fine."

"You're good with that?" Andy asked.

Hudgens smiled and narrowed his eyes. "Of course."

Andy turned and walked off down the corridor.

* * *

After visiting Corey's home, the cabin and Ella's grave, he concluded that he'd gone to see Jude. That was next on his list. He could have waited. Sat back, had a few beers at the cabin and let Hudgens sweat it out, but he was right. If the town fell, eventually so would his cabin. Even though he lived a good distance outside of the main town, looters had already begun a series of home invasions and it wouldn't be long before his place was targeted. Knowing that Jude would be anything but friendly, he opted to spy on the camp from a distance. It would also give him a chance to see what he'd done with the place. Andy had put his heart and soul into that project when he was younger, back when he considered Jude his closest friend. So much had changed. While he couldn't blame Jude alone for Dianna's infidelity, he expected better of him.

Andy saddled up a horse, bringing along one of his high-powered rifles, plenty of ammo, enough food to last him the next forty-eight hours and a backpack full of survival gear. On the journey north he thought back to those earlier days. Finding friends was hard, finding one that had as much in common with him as Jude seemed too good to be true. It turned out it was. He recalled laying out the plans for Camp Olney in front of Jude and enthusiastically sharing his vision for the future. It would be used year-round as a preppers retreat. Back then they only had five bunkers and had taken out a large loan with the bank to fund it. Any money earned from those who attended went right back into developing bunkers or paying off their debt. It didn't take long before people came from miles around and different states, and they began leading workshops on survival, bringing in speakers like military snipers, special ops and those with in-depth knowledge in living off the grid. Their every waking hour was spent working on the camp, learning new skills or developing the curriculum. It was at one of the many events they held that he first met Dianna. He saw from the start she was a troublemaker. She stood out from among the crowd with her fiery red hair and sense of humor. She was absolutely captivating in every way. It wasn't long before they were introduced and he discovered she wasn't seeing anyone. He knew right then if he didn't jump at the chance someone else would. To his surprise she said yes. It was as if he'd caught lightning in a bottle. She could have been with anyone but she accepted his request to take her out for a meal. One thing led to another and they were soon married. She moved from Idaho to Montana and joined him in the work. A companion, a friend and a lover, she was the anchor in his life. Two years later Corey was born. Things couldn't have been better. But like anything, the honeymoon period wore off, and as calls came in from all over the country to have him teach in different states, Andy jumped at the chance. It was more money but that wasn't the reason he took the offers. It was ego. He was young, foolish and trying to make his mark on the world. Trying to prove to his father that he could make it. And make it he did, garnering the attention of preppers across the nation but in the process losing those closest to him. At some point he just lost his way, too caught up, too busy and Dianna just didn't understand.

The horse trotted slowly as Andy sighed.

If he'd only turned back after that big fight, maybe it wouldn't have happened.

But it did. While he was away on trips, Jude was at the helm overseeing retreats and workshops with the aid of Dianna. Until that point their relationship had been nothing more than close friends but with Andy out of the picture, it didn't take long for a bond to form.

Andy could still see them in his mind, that night he returned home a day early to surprise her.

He recalled being dropped off by the taxi driver, inserting the key into the lock of their home and making his way up the stairs. Halfway up he heard moaning and grunting. The sound of sex was unmistakable. Pushing open the door and seeing her on top of him. A look of horror on her face, and guilt on Jude's. It wasn't rage, he felt just extreme sadness and shock as he walked away. Dianna hurried after him, pleading with him, wearing nothing but a nightgown wrapped loosely around her. He could still recall the smell of Jude's cologne on her. For years after he couldn't bear to be around anyone who wore the same scent. Andy left that night, moved out of the house and for several months he spoke to neither one of them until Dianna lifted him out of the gutter one night.

After sobering him up, she begged for his forgiveness and reassured him that there was nothing between them. It wasn't love, she said, just a need to be wanted. Although he had his doubts, he loved her too much to let her go. He said he would take her back on one condition; they would have nothing more to do with Jude. They would turn their backs on the camp, move to Whitefish and live out the remainder of their days together. She agreed. Nine months later Tyler was born. As much as he wanted to love and raise him as his own, every time he looked at that kid, he saw Jude — the one person he hated the most in the world. He might have tried to convince Dianna to let Jude take him, except that would have been a gift and in his mind, Jude deserved nothing but sorrow, pain and anguish. He wanted him to suffer. And he did. Only on three occasions did he see how much Tyler had grown.

Out of respect for Dianna's wishes, Jude never stepped in or told Tyler who he was, although Andy knew one day he would. And sure enough that day had come. For so many years he didn't think it would bother him. Why would it? Tyler had been a thorn in his side. A constant reminder of his best friend's betrayal. Was it any wonder why he didn't feel the same way for him as he did for Corey? And yet for all his pushing and keeping Tyler at arm's length, he had come to care for the boy. Maybe not in the way he would for his own flesh and blood, or even in a way that made sense to anyone looking in, but nonetheless, he cared. Andy let out a heavy sigh as he came over a rise to the last stretch of the journey.

Chapter 11

"You'll do it?" Corey asked, a look of surprise on his face. Even though he'd traveled to see him with the hope that he would assist, in the back of his mind he had his doubts. Dirk Bennington could be up one minute and down the next. A man given to liquor, it served him well. He was the only functional drunk Corey knew from the military. He was known to drink even the best under the table. Bennington gave a nod before knocking back his glass of whiskey. He'd spent the past ten minutes bringing him up to speed on the situation in Whitefish, and raiders hitting towns across the county. He figured he'd need time to digest, maybe even consider it, but he shot back a reply instantly. Bennington got up and crossed the room, closing the door to a bedroom where his sick mother was sleeping. "You're damn right I will. I have been biting at the bit to get back at these assholes since I caught wind of their escapades. Bastards robbed a truck that was bringing in supplies from Kalispell. Besides, being cooped up in here is driving me crazy."

"We could be gone for several days. What about your mother?" Corey asked, leaning forward in his seat.

"My sister will take care of her."

"Yeah? And who will look after her?"

He snorted. "Trust me. That gal could shoot the wings off a fly."

"Had the best teacher."

"Damn right." Bennington winked as he refilled his glass. He'd been a sniper with Corey's platoon. One of the best he knew. He had over sixty confirmed kills and had made a name for himself as the white devil among insurgents. That was until an IED blew his leg off. "You know a few days before the blackout I got together with Holden and Markowitz? Best damn night of my life since I got discharged."

"I bet. They still around Kalispell?" Corey asked. He hadn't seen them since leaving the military. He didn't even know that Markowitz had left but Holden had left a year before him.

He nodded, taking a seat in a recliner chair and reaching for a pack of smokes. "Holden was doing private security for some firm, and Markowitz was offering helicopter tours with Glacier Heli Tours. They're just the same as they were."

"And Perry?"

"You didn't hear?" Bennington exhaled. "Got into a collision. Died on impact."

"Poor bastard."

"Yeah, isn't that just irony for you? Bullets flying at him in the Middle East and then he returns home and gets T-boned by some drunk driver."

Corey finished his drink. "What about Gibby?"

Bennington tapped the side of his head. "Last I heard he was getting treatment for PTSD. He's been going through some heavy shit. He certainly wouldn't be up for this. Hell, I wouldn't be surprised if he decided to chew a bullet."

"Come on, man."

"It's true. Look, I liked Gibby just as much as you but damn, the last time I saw him, he looked like a bum panhandling on the street. I don't even want to imagine what he smells like now. Anyway, you want to swing by and pay our friends a little visit?"

"Yeah, but my truck is about two miles back."

"You should have brought it."

"Can't take the risk."

"And leaving it out in the open isn't taking a risk?" He laughed. "I'm pulling your chain. That's fine. I got a Jeep in the garage. Damn thing is falling to bits but the engine purrs like a kitten." He looked over at Tyler. "So, this is your little brother?"

"Not exactly little anymore, are you?" Corey said, both of them staring.

"Did he ever serve?" Bennington asked.

Corey chuckled. "Tyler? He did his time with my father. That was enough, wasn't it, brother?"

Tyler smiled and gave a nod.

"That's right. Papa Ford. Does he still have a few

screws loose?"

"Oh, they're rattling up there, all right. But he's in his element right now so everything is firing."

"I bet, well let's get a move on." Bennington got up and yelled, "Susan, get your butt out here."

A door cracked open and a kid no older than seventeen stepped out. Corey had forgotten how young she was. Now he felt bad about pulling him away. "Hey, you sure about this?" Corey asked.

"She'll be fine." He turned toward her. "We're heading out. Back in a couple of days. Keep an eye on mom, and make sure she gets her meds. The generator is out back to get some rays. Make sure you bring it in this evening. Any trouble shows up, you know what to do."

"Where you going?"

"What did I tell you before?"

She shook her head and went back into her room. Bennington tutted. "Kids these days."

* * *

Tyler couldn't help but look at Bennington's leg. They

would have to trek through some pretty intense woodland to reach the camp, would he be able to handle it? It didn't take long for him to gather a few items together in a backpack and they headed through a side exit and loaded into a dusty 1979 Jeep CJ5. Tyler ran his hand over the hood and flashed Corey a smile.

"When did you last have this out?" Tyler asked.

"Before I lost my leg."

"Are you serious? Does it start?"

"About to find out," he said tossing the keys to Corey and hopping in. Tyler had to unload a crapload of garbage out of the back to make room for him and Allie.

As soon as Corey went around to the driver's side, he glanced down. "We'll not go far on that," he said. "It's flat."

"Well change it. Damn man, you love to complain."

Corey looked at Tyler but didn't say anything. The next twenty minutes was spent changing a tire and that was all before attempting to start the damn thing. "Let's hope another one doesn't go on us," Corey said turning over the key. The engine coughed a few times and died.

"Give it some gas, she's thirsty," Bennington said, reaching into the glove compartment and pulling out a pair of aviator shades. With them on he looked like Danny DeVito in the movie *Twins*. He ran a hand over what remained of his hair which was thin and short in the front and long at the back. It looked greasy. Corey gave it a few more tries and it spluttered to life.

"There's my girl." He patted the dashboard.

Once out of the garage they got on the road hoping to arrive in Kalispell in just over ten minutes. Immediately Bennington gave directions, telling them which roads to avoid and when to hang a left or a right. It seemed Ferris was telling the truth. Kalispell had taken one hell of a hit. The city of twenty-three thousand made Whitefish look like a playground. Intense fires had swept through buildings taking them down like dominoes. Tyler's concern for their safety grew with every mile. Would they even find Corey's two friends alive? Were they barricaded inside one of these homes or had they fled the town?

While the vast majority of people didn't just up and leave Whitefish, those with a lick of sense got out before it got worse. Could the same be said for here? The Jeep rumbled down the road and bounced a little.

"We getting close?" Tyler asked leaning forward.

"He's not far from here. Just in the downtown."

"So, in the heart of hell? Great, sounds magical," Tyler added, gazing at the charred ruins, and buildings that had recently been set ablaze. Black smoke drifted through the streets.

Bennington cast a glance back at Tyler and his eyes scanned Allie. "So, you two done the double-back beast yet?"

"We're not together."

"Could have fooled me," he said looking ahead. Tyler glanced at Allie and she rolled her eyes and turned her head to look at a group running down a back alley.

"I'm sorry to hear about Ella," Bennington said to Corey who was paying more attention to swerving around stalled vehicles than listening to him. He grunted a response then changed the topic. They were a few minutes shy of Holden's home when Bennington leaned forward and tapped the dashboard. "Stop. Stop."

"Why?"

"Stop."

Corey eased off the gas and swerved slightly.

"Kid, hand me that rifle."

All of them looked ahead but couldn't see anything that would have been cause for concern. "Today!" he yelled acting more agitated by the second. Tyler handed him the rifle and he peered through the scope. "Sonofabitch." He exhaled. "Back up."

"But you said—"

"Unless you want to be ambushed, I would reverse now."

Corey didn't hesitate, he spun the Jeep around and they drove back up the road a little and then hung a left and went down another road before coming out and heading south down 2nd Avenue. "Slow down and pull over into the parking lot of Market Diner. Keep the engine running. If I'm not back in five minutes, head out without me."

"Are you serious?" Corey asked.

He gave a look that answered that. "Kid, let's go."

"Who, me?" Tyler asked.

"No, your girlfriend. Yes. You."

"Bennington," Corey said.

"He'll be fine. I just need an extra set of eyes." He tapped the side of the Jeep and they took off. For someone with a prosthetic leg he could damn well move fast. He used one of these high-tech running prosthetics that curled at the bottom. Tyler had to admit it was pretty cool shit.

"Where we heading?"

"Off to take out an asshole who killed a good friend of mine, two weeks ago."

"Okay," Tyler said in a slow manner. "And he's preventing us from reaching Holden's home?"

"No, but I've been itching to settle a score."

"Great." Tyler looked back towards the Jeep and

shook his head. They took off east down 3rd Street until they reached the back of a health and fitness center.

Bennington clambered up onto a large green dumpster and lifted his prosthetic limb. "Right. Give me a boost up."

"I thought you needed an extra set of eyes."

"Would you hurry up?"

Tyler groaned, slung his rifle over his shoulder and interlocked his fingers. Bennington climbed up and hollered for him to push. "Come on, you pussy. Higher."

"I'm pushing you up as far as I can go, I can't help it that you're a short ass."

He glared at him from above. "Higher!"

Tyler gritted his teeth and practically launched him into the air. He caught hold of the roof's lip and scrambled over the edge, then reached down to give Tyler a hand up. Once on the roof they crossed to the corner of 3rd and 1st Avenue. There Bennington took up position and shouldered his rifle. "Okay. Time to balance the scales of justice. Heads up, asshole." Tyler watched him in action. He knew his father was a good marksman but as he looked out, he could barely see where the target was. *Crack.* One single shot and he was up and running for the back. "That's a wrap. Let's move it."

"Already? You got him?"

"I never miss."

"Never? But I couldn't see him."

"Of course you couldn't."

"You got eyes like Superman?"

"No, kid, just one hell of a scope." He chuckled and threw himself over the edge and down onto the dumpster. He was as agile as a professional gymnast. He now understood why his brother wanted him. They double-timed it back to the Jeep where Allie was out of the vehicle keeping watch. Just before they reached it, Bennington said, "Keep what just happened between you and me."

"You done?" Corey asked.

Bennington nodded as he hopped in and they took off at a high rate of speed. Fortunately, Corey never asked but it did make Tyler wonder why he wanted to keep it a secret. It wasn't like his brother was averse to taking out threats.

A few more turns and they arrived at a four-story apartment block. Bennington guided them around the back and told Tyler to stay with the vehicle while he and Corey headed up the fire escape. He slipped through the gap and got into the driver's seat. Corey jumped up and pulled down a black ladder and they made their way up.

"What happened back there?" Allie asked.

"I would tell you but I get a sense he would kill me." He chuckled and they waited nervously scanning the area for trouble. They wanted to keep the vehicle idling just in case but the noise of it rumbling was enough to draw people out. They hadn't yet seen an operating vehicle on the road which meant they might as well have painted a bullseye on their backs.

* * *

Bennington banged on a window with the back of his hand and Corey looked down to make sure Tyler was okay. Five seconds passed and there was no response from inside.

"Perhaps he left town."

"No. He's in there." Bennington tried prying the window open but it was locked. "Stand back."

"You gonna break his window?"

"I gave him the chance to open."

Glass echoed loudly as it shattered with the butt of his rifle. "Holden, it's me. Bennington. I know you're in there. I got Corey Ford with me. I'm coming in. Keep your finger off the trigger." Bennington motioned for Corey to go in first.

"Ladies before gents."

"I feel like a sheep being led to the slaughter," Corey muttered as he precariously eased his body into the apartment. Inside it smelled like cigars. Holden was always chewing on a half-smoked cigar, or a mouthful of tobacco. He'd carry this small plastic container and spit into it. A few times he'd tossed it at civilians while driving through Fallujah and cracked some joke about spit.

"Holden. It's Corey."

Behind him Bennington made a hell of a noise ducking under the frame and working his way in. "How about you make some more noise?" Corey said sarcastically, so he did, tipping over a vase on a shelf. It smashed on the ground and he grinned. Crazy asshole. Some things hadn't changed.

The studio apartment wasn't large. There was a photo on the mantelpiece of his family. Like many in the military he'd been through a divorce, an ugly one. His first wife had left him for another guy while he was away on tour. Holden went ballistic when he got the news. Killed probably more insurgents that day than he had in all the months he'd been away. Instead of searching the rooms, Bennington made a beeline for the liquor cabinet. He pulled out a bottle of bourbon. "Guess I'll have to drink this by myself," he said loudly flipping the bottle.

Corey stepped into the bedroom. He wasn't in there. He checked the bathroom. No one. "Are you sure this is even the place?"

"Of course," Bennington said banging his foot three times against the floor. It sounded hollow. A second later a part of the floor opened up.

"I figured it was you," Holden said, shaking his head as he emerged.

Chapter 12

Amateurs, Andy thought as he peered through the binoculars at Jude men's patrolling the camp. He thought at the bare minimum if someone took over another person's house, they would at least change the locks. Not this guy. Nothing had changed. He had guards in the same towers, and others further afield decked out in ghillie suits. He was following the plan to a tee. To the untrained eye it might have done the job but he could spot them from a mile away. It probably helped that he'd been the one to create the blueprint. Andy turned his attention to the camp and squinted, observing the coming and going of those inside. The group had grown. He didn't recognize many of the faces. But the rest, yeah. He missed some of those friendships. All his ideas were there before him. At one time it would have pissed him off but now he didn't care. All he cared about was his sons, and finding that truck and both weren't visible. Were they inside? Was he showing them the lay of the land? Was he sharing his ideas for the future? Honestly, it didn't matter. He was more concerned with what lies Jude had told them.

Andy was about to get up from the prone position when he heard a twig snap behind him. It was at a distance but loud enough. There was a chance it was Jude's men. Had he given away his position? Did they see a glint of light come from his rifle? No, he'd been careful. Crawling up into a crouch he cast a slow glance over his shoulder. Nothing but a dark forest stared back. Moving quickly, he darted forward over a rise and swung around to see if it was an animal. He didn't think so but there was a possibility it could be a bear.

Moving through the brush like a stealthy cougar he soon spotted the individual.

He shook his head and looked at the ground.

"Are you kidding me?" Andy said stepping out of the brush, lowering his rifle.

"How did you know?" Ferris said.

"Because you have a heavy foot like an elephant."

"Damn it."

"Let me guess. Hudgens sent you?"

He nodded.

Andy grimaced and shook his head. "Sonofabitch." That man wouldn't listen to anyone. Ferris ambled over. He'd changed out of his police uniform and was now clothed from head to toe in hunter's gear. His face was smeared up with camo paint and even the rifle was camouflaged.

Ferris ambled up to the crest. "Why? What's the big deal? Why are you all the way out here?"

Not wishing to give away their location, Andy yanked him down to a crouch and in a low voice said, "Not much use wearing all that camo gear if your mouth is gonna announce us."

"To who?" he asked pulling away.

Andy pointed down through the lush landscape of greenery. Ferris strained his eyes to see without binoculars. "What is that?" Andy tutted and handed him some binos. He pulled them up to his eyes. "Well I'll be damned. An entire community operating self-sufficiently. What a place. Hell, they look like they're living better than we are."

"They are," Andy said.

"How do you know?"

"Because I designed and developed the site."

Ferris handed back his equipment with a surprised look. It changed quickly into a frown. "Then why are you up here, viewing it from a distance? Shouldn't you be down there? Is that where you think Corey's gone?"

"How about you tell me why you came all this way?"

"You already know."

"C'mon, Ferris. Hudgens isn't out patrolling the streets. You could have walked a block down from city hall, sat on a bench for a few hours and returned and he would have believed you'd followed me. Why go to all this trouble? It's not like Corey or I have given you reason. And don't say the truck."

He snorted and adjusted his position to get

comfortable. "All right. Yeah. I could have stayed in Whitefish but you could say I'm curious to know what you Fords are up to. Since this shitfest has kicked off I've barely had a chance to breathe. Hudgens has had me running errands, manning roadblocks and overseeing other officers. I figured it would give me a break."

Andy chuckled. "A break. Please. You want to tell me the truth now?"

Ferris opened his mouth but before he could say another word, they heard the sound of multiple guns cocking. Andy turned to see six of Jude's men in ghillie suits.

"Shit."

All the noise from Ferris had distracted him from those who were patrolling further afield. Several rifles were raised at them and Andy raised his hands.

* * *

Shoved like a common piece of trash, they were thrust through the open gates into the midst of curious onlookers. Eyes widened as familiar faces of old friends saw him and gasped. These were people he hadn't spoken to in years, folks who at one time had looked up to him, sought his advice, admired him even. His exit from Camp Olney many moons ago had been sudden. No word was given to the core group, at least he never heard what Jude told them. It was better that way. Turning his back on it all. Starting afresh. Had he returned sooner, he might have buckled under the request to reconsider. Leaving them all behind had been easier. A clean break.

It wasn't Jude who squeezed through the crowd to meet him but his son Maddox, who was similar in age to Tyler. He'd seen him a few times in his young years when Jude tried to wiggle his way back into Dianna's life. Looking at him now, he was the spitting image of his father when he was a youngster.

Maddox cocked his head. "What is it with you Fords? You just keep showing up without an invitation." He smirked then said, "My father's not here if that's who you were spying on."

"Actually, I was looking for my kids."

"Kids? That's new. I was under the impression Tyler wasn't one of yours?"

"Where are they?"

He shrugged looking over the faces of those gathered. "Your guess is as good as mine. Tyler left here yesterday, hasn't returned." He walked over to him, looking Andy up and down and then diverting his attention to Ferris. "Strange thing though. Around the same time a friend of ours, someone close to me, went missing. Allie. You seen her?"

"Can't say I have. Well we'll leave you to it then," Andy said turning to leave. They took two steps and were pushed back.

"Look, we don't want any trouble," Andy said lifting his hands. "We were just leaving."

"Leaving?" Maddox asked with a smug grin. "Without seeing my father?" He pulled a face. "That's kind of rude, don't you think?"

"We'll be back."

Maddox waved his finger and tutted. "No, it's

probably best you stay. It will be getting dark soon. You never know what kind of trouble you might encounter out on those back roads." There was a menacing manner to him. Like father like son, Andy thought. He glanced at Ferris.

"Fine. When will he be back?"

"Oh, I'm sure he won't be long. I imagine he will be pleased to see you." Maddox pointed a few fingers at some of the men blocking their way and gestured where he wanted them taken. As he walked away, he said, "Maybe you can explain why you were taking such a keen interest in our operations here."

"I already explained that."

"Yeah, right. Your kids."

They were quickly strong-armed away into one of the earth-covered domes. There they were led into a barred room that had nothing more than two benches. Andy looked around. "I take back what I said. I never added a jail cell to the blueprint."

He tried shaking the bars but they were solid. Built

right into the reinforced concrete above and below. He looked across the way at someone curled up in a ball. "Hey. Buddy."

The guy didn't move.

"Great. I knew I should have stayed in Whitefish," Ferris said sinking down onto a bench and putting his hands over his head. There were no windows to let light in and the one door they entered through was made of iron. No getting out that way, he thought.

"Hey. You want to let us out of here!" Andy bellowed but got no response.

"You're wasting your breath. Who is this Jude, anyway?"

"An old friend."

"Good, maybe when he shows up, we can leave."

"I'm not sure it will go that way."

"Why?"

Andy sucked air between his teeth and took a seat across from him. "Let's just say we haven't seen eye to eye in a long time. And I kept his son from him."

"His son? Corey?"

"No, Tyler."

"Perfect. Well then, that makes this really easy. I'll just tell him I had nothing to do with this and got lost along the way. I'll be out of here in no time." Ferris popped up and strolled over to the bars and turned his head to see if he could see one of the guards. He glanced over at their silent neighbor.

"Nah. You've seen the place," Andy said before chewing on the corner of his lip.

"Excuse me?"

"Prior to the collapse. Yeah. You could have come and gone from this place but now… I'm not sure he's the kind of man that hands out get out of jail free cards without something in return."

Ferris studied him without saying anything. He paced while Andy peered around at the setup. It was primitive but effective. He'd give him that. He and Jude had chewed over ideas of laws and punishment but hadn't really fleshed it out. They were so focused on training, building and teaching that they never really got around to laying down the ground rules. But by the looks of it, he had now. The question was how did it work? Did the people determine the fate of the accused? Did punishment amount to time inside or did they have more severe punishments?

It didn't take long to get his answers.

Forty minutes passed before they had company.

They heard a door clank open and Jude's voice telling the guards to wait outside. Andy sat with his back to the bars as he listened to him approach.

"Why does it not surprise me to find you here?"

Andy got up from the hard bench and stretched out his limbs. "Wow, you really need to throw a few pillows in here. Maybe provide some hand sanitizer and a toilet."

Jude smiled. "Tyler is not here. Corey hasn't visited. Now I know you, Andy, better than anyone else. You wouldn't have just let my men capture you unless of course you had some other motive. The question is, what?"

"I wanted to see the place."

"After all this time?"

"Better late than never, right?"

He grinned and then looked over his shoulder at the guy curled up. He groaned a little and looked as if he was beginning to stir.

Andy gripped the bars and got closer. "How's it work, Jude? Are you judge, jury and executioner or do you leave the dirty work for your men outside?"

He smiled. "You know me, Andy. I don't shy from guilt."

"No you don't."

Jude glanced at his watch. "I figure right about now Tyler will be speaking with Corey and we'll be seeing them very soon." He breathed in deeply. "In your wildest dreams, could you have ever imagined this situation?" Jude stared at him as if he was relishing the turn of events. He got really close to the bars and said, "Oh the things you put my boy through," before turning and walking away. "You shouldn't have come back, Andy."

"When are we getting out of here?" Ferris asked. "I'm a police officer."

"All in good time, officer. All in good time." He glanced back looking at Andy.

"Jude, just let us go."

"Like I said, Andy, you only get one free pass. And I believe you've used yours up. How sweet fate is." He turned and exited.

Ferris banged the bars and cursed. "I swear, you Fords are magnets for bad luck! First the son, now the father. Shit!"

Andy was only partially listening to his drivel. He was focusing more of his attention on their neighbor. Separating them from the cellblocks on the far side of the dome was a narrow walkway. The stranger sat upright and looked over at them. His feet were red and blistered. He swung his legs off and ran a hand around the back of his neck. He had long, dirty sun-bleached hair that came down to his shoulders, a gray beard and the clothes he was wearing were torn. "Hey buddy. Buddy."

The guy looked his way. He licked his dry cracked lips and looked around as if he'd lost his marbles.

"The name's Andy Ford."

"I know who you are," he replied in a familiar voice.

"You do?"

"How could I forget? I helped you build this place."

Andy frowned, the years clouding his memory. He squinted trying to recall where he'd seen his face. There were numerous people who had a hand in the development and engineering. "Edison?"

He raised a weary hand. "Here and counted for."

"What the hell are you doing in here?"

"Flapped my lips one too many times."

"But you were a part of the original group."

"That's right. Things have changed a lot around here since you left. Which by the way, while you're here, why did you leave?"

Andy looked off towards the main entrance. "It's a long story."

"Jude said you had a nervous breakdown."

"Is that so?"

"Guessing he was off base. Never believed it myself."

"I appreciate that."

"Though I saw your boy around here. He's grown."

Andy dipped his chin. "Yeah, yeah he has." He didn't want to say Tyler wasn't his own flesh and blood. For so long it didn't affect him. Now he felt as if he'd lost a piece of him, a piece of Dianna.

"Did you construct this addition?" Andy asked.

He chuckled. "Ah that's right, this wasn't here when you were around. No. I didn't have a hand in it. In fact, it's one of the reasons why I'm in here. Jude and I don't see eye to eye on any manner of things. This is one."

Ferris got on the ground and began doing some pushups. Both of them looked at him.

"Your friend a little high strung?" Edison asked.

Andy laughed. "You could say that."

Ferris scowled at them both.

"How long you been in here?"

"A few days."

"For what?"

He got up and walked over to the bars. He let out an exasperated breath and lifted his eyes. "Trying to kill Jude."

Chapter 13

"Corey Ford, aren't you a sight for sore eyes," Holden said, handing Corey a drink. "Last I heard, you were working for your old man. You not get down this way much?"

He shook his head. "Been busy. Sorry. How have you been?"

"You know, finding my way." He glanced at the smashed window. It didn't seem to bother him. Then again it paled in comparison to the damage throughout the city. "Now this shit storm has happened, it kind of feels like home again."

He chuckled. "Civilian life isn't all it's cracked up to be, is it?"

Holden nodded and took a sip of his drink. Holden was a bald guy with tattoos covering his arms. He had a gnarly scar across his lower lip. Close to six foot, he was pure muscle. "The upside is I don't have divorce lawyers breathing down my neck."

Corey's brow knit together. "But that was a long time ago."

Holden took another sip of his drink. "I'm referring to wife number two."

"Oh. Sorry. That sucks."

Holden shrugged. "Ah, whatever. The writing was on the wall for years. She came home one day and told me she doesn't want this anymore. I ask her why. She tells me she doesn't know. You know, the usual bull crap. A month later she's hooked up with some other guy. What a waste of time. Fourteen years of marriage down the drain. Took me a while to get the money from the house. I moved into this place and this has been home for a while." He cast his eyes over them. "But things are looking up. At least they were."

"Why did you stick around?"

"Probably the same reason as you. It isn't much better out there I hear. Besides, where would I go? Can you see me thumbing rides down Route 66?"

Corey got up and went into the kitchen and began rooting through his cupboards. "You're running low."

"Yeah, though I have a few things stashed below."

"But not enough to last you for the next year."

He took a bite of an apple. "Maybe not."

"What if there was a way to get your hands on a cache of supplies, enough to cover you for the next year or two? Ammo, and medicine as well."

"I'm listening."

Corey returned and sat in a seat across from him. He leaned forward. "The raiders. The ones that have been causing most of the damage in the towns and cities. We've come across where they're storing it all."

"You got a small army?" Holden asked. "As I heard there's a lot of them."

"No need." Corey glanced at Allie. "We have intel that they won't be around. That only a small number of them will be watching over the stash."

Holden blew out his cheeks. "I don't know."

"We could use your skills."

"It's been a while. Look, I have a kid now."

"You do?"

"Yeah, after Katy left, she informed me she was pregnant. I figured it was with the guy she was with but nope. Anyway, I got myself a healthy seven-pound boy. Katy is still in town. Lives on the west side in some upscale neighborhood. Whatever. But, I…" he trailed off looking up at a photo of him and Katy on the mantel. It was strange that he still had it there. Corey would have tossed it. Holden didn't need to explain, Corey understood. Despite the power grid being down, life continued on. Responsibilities didn't just fall by the wayside, at least those related to flesh and blood.

"She can't be taking this well."

"No, but a hell of a lot better than me," he replied taking out a cigar from his mouth and relighting it. Gray smoke spiraled up and a cloud filled the air. His face disappeared behind it. "The thing is since this shit storm has happened, she's been in touch with me more often. I think she is having second thoughts."

"That, or she just knows you have the skill set to survive this shit," Bennington said. He laughed. "Women are all the same. You are the best thing since sliced bread when you are meeting their needs. The moment you become uninteresting, exciting or unable to provide, they want to upgrade."

Holden shrugged. Corey nodded but tried harder to get him on board. "You are looking at one or two nights. That's it, man. We move in, and out. The whole thing can be wrapped up and you can return with enough to last you through to next year. Hell, it might even win her over."

"Corey," Bennington said. "Stop raising his hopes."

"I'm just saying. Allie here is confident that it can go off without a hitch. Isn't that right?" He looked at Allie for support. She nodded. "It's just a matter of deciding Holden. Are you in or out?"

He looked at Allie and shifted his cigar from one side to the other. "Look, I don't know her."

"She's a friend of my brother."

Holden looked at Tyler.

"Is this true?"

Tyler gestured to Allie and she pulled out the notebook. He handed it over and Holden thumbed through it. He was very analytical. A person who went by the book. He'd been known to pull out of a situation if he got even the slightest inkling that it could go south. Corey didn't expect him to buy it on the scribblings in a notebook.

"And how did you two meet?" He asked.

"Long story."

"High risk," Holden said as he read the notes. "Give me the abbreviated version."

Tyler looked at Corey then filled in the details. Covering how he ended up at Jude's camp, his run-in with Allie and what she'd told him about her sister.

"And you saw her sister?"

"Well, no but…"

"Then why do you believe her? For all we know this could be a trap."

"A trap?" Tyler muttered looking confused.

"You said this Jude doesn't like your old man. That he's been looking for a way to get back at him. Seems to me this would be a good way. Hurt the sons, hurt the father."

"But I'm not his son. I'm Jude's."

"And yet you haven't been in his life," Holden said rising to his feet. "Nah. This plan stinks to high heaven. You want me to risk my neck over a stranger's scribblings?" He snorted and tossed the notebook back to Allie. "And let's face it. Did you see the supplies? Did you see this bullet reloading machine? How the hell do you know these are the raiders? Everyone and his uncle have been looting stores, breaking into homes and holding people up on the streets."

Holden puttered around in the kitchen.

"Because I used to be one of them," Allie said, turning and pulling at her jacket to reveal a branding of a star. That caught all of their attention. Even Tyler looked shocked.

"Sorry. I was going to tell you, but I…" she trailed off and Tyler placed a hand on her leg.

"Get a room," Bennington said rising to his feet. "Look, Holden. It comes down to this man. Are you going to do it or not? Are you in or out?"

"I need time to think about it."

"There isn't any time. We have a small window of opportunity."

"Let me just say. I don't like this. Something about it feels off." He looked at Allie. "Working with a supposed ex-raider against raiders?"

"I'm not a raider."

"But you were," Holden said sticking his cigar back in his lips. He breathed in deeply and cast a stern glance at Allie. "Is Markowitz in?"

"We still have to see him," Corey said.

"Okay. If he is, I am."

"As simple as that?"

He nodded. Corey got up and grabbed Holden's hand and pulled him in. He patted his back and they waited for him to grab a few things together. There was a renewed sense of strength and hope among them. People could fish and hunt and that would remain one of the main sources of food but if raiders were going to sweep in and scoop it out from underneath their noses, it would jeopardize their survival.

* * *

While Holden gathered what he needed, Tyler gestured for Allie to step out onto the fire escape. He led her down to the ground because he didn't want the others hearing. He sure as hell wasn't going to lead his brother and his closest friends into a trap if that's what it was. He needed information and as this was new, he had to assume she was holding back even more.

He shifted his weight from one foot to the next, put a hand on his hip and with the other hand jabbed a finger at the ground. "You want to explain to me what is going on here?"

"Nothing."

"Bullshit! Then why didn't you tell me? I mean

because I think that would have been key to know because I just went to all the trouble of telling my brother." She dipped her head. A look of shame, perhaps guilt. Tyler continued, "Is everyone in Camp Olney a raider?"

"No."

He gave her a skeptical look.

"No. Not everyone."

He paused for a moment running a hand through his hair. "Is this another one of Jude's games?"

She stared back at him and shook her head. "No. Hell no."

"Then maybe you can help me to understand this. You told me your sister was taken by them, but yet you yourself are one of them? Which is it?"

"Both are true." She sighed and dropped her head. "The day she was taken, I was with her. That's how I know what they have down there. She was told to remain while the rest of us returned."

"So you lied to me."

"I told you the truth, I just left out some of the details."

Tyler scoffed. "I'd say you did." He shook his head. "Why should I believe a single word that has come out of your mouth? Are the women really being used as slaves? Were you really living in Texas or was that made up too?"

When she didn't answer he knew they were lies.

He threw his hands up. "God. Next you'll tell me your name is not even Allie."

"It is."

He glared at her, getting really close. One part of him wanted to kiss her, the other wanted to just leave her behind. After the death of Ella, he couldn't allow his brother to suffer any more grief. It could send him over the edge. He studied her eyes waiting for her to look away but she didn't.

"You want my help then you better start telling me the truth. What's the deal with the branding? And who is this Morning Star? Is it Jude?"

"I don't know who it is. We've never seen the person's

face. Thomas, the guy you saw with the blind eye, he's the only one that speaks with Morning Star. And he's not always at the camp. There have only been a few times Morning Star has visited the camp and only Thomas and his inner circle speak with this person inside a tent. All I know is he gets new information on places that can be raided and the group does the job."

Tyler laughed. "So Morning Star is like the fucking Wizard of Oz. Is that what you're telling me?"

"I'm telling you the truth."

"Are you?" he said taking hold of her arm and giving it a little squeeze.

She didn't reply to that so he continued to ask her to explain what the branding meant and who received it, and why there were two camps, and Jude's involvement. Allie sighed and took a seat on the edge of a curb. She straightened out her legs and picked at loose stones. "There are several groups spread out throughout the county. Branding is a way of identification. A sign of trust. I don't know who was behind it only that if you wanted to remain in the camp you had to get it. My parents didn't die in a plane crash." She squeezed her eyes closed as if she was struggling to divulge any more. "My father is alive; his name is Edison. And he was one of those involved in the development of the camp with your father. At least that's what he told me. A year ago, Jude said he'd made an alliance with a group that was about to change this country, and that everything we had been doing up until this point was going to make sense. He never said who was behind it but we soon came to learn that it was big. When the power grid went out, Jude wasn't surprised. It was as if everything was going according to plan. Anyway, several months before the blackout everyone in Camp Olney had to put their names into a bowl. Those who were selected had to leave the camp to go to the place I showed you. My mother and father were left behind. My mother tried to oppose the ruling and...was killed." Allie dipped her chin. She took a deep breath and continued. "In an attempt to keep my father quiet, Jude arranged to have me brought back to the camp. An act of generosity. Madison had to remain. My father swore to me that he would kill Jude for what was done to our mother. He also wanted to put a dent in his alliance with Morning Star. Not long after that, you arrived. That's when my father told me that he knew yours and that if anyone could help, it was him. I followed you that night in the hopes that…"

"I would get my father involved," Tyler said, saying the obvious.

She nodded. "My father told me to be careful. He wasn't sure what relationship Andy still had with Jude. I'm sorry, Tyler, for not telling you everything. I just thought it was better this way."

Tyler had been standing the whole time she'd been sharing. He plunked down beside her and picked up a loose rock and tossed it at a green dumpster below the fire escape. It pinged off the side.

"Your father. I never met him."

"That's because Jude threw him in a cell. He would let me see him but he couldn't trust him and he didn't want to kill him because they had known each other for years."

"But I saw everything in camp."

"Not everything. Jude showed you what he wanted you to see. That's why I said, he's dangerous." She sucked air in and looked up as Corey stuck his head out the window to check on them.

"You all good?"

Tyler gave him the thumbs-up.

"Are you going to tell him?" she asked Tyler.

"Not right now. It doesn't exactly change the situation. We still have to get in and out. So, you don't think this…Morning Star is Jude?"

"I don't know. Again, I never saw a face. For all I know it could be Thomas."

Tyler tapped a stone against the curb. "Morning Star," he muttered, thinking about the phrase. He'd heard it a few times.

Allie chimed in, "To the native American Indians it meant hope and guidance. It was also a name given to Christ and Satan," Allie said glancing at him.

He nodded and quoted the two familiar Bible verses. A good part of his childhood had exposed him to biblical teaching, although that influence had dissipated after his mother's death. After he said, "The yin and yang. Good and evil. Robbing Peter to pay Paul. Whoever this asshole is, maybe they justify what they do as good."

"Tyler. You ready to leave?" Corey bellowed.

Tyler glanced at Allie, unsure of what to believe. "C'mon. Time to get your sister back."

Chapter 14

What a fucking mess, Corey thought as his boots flattened ash and stepped on chunks of charred wood. Markowitz lived just off Conrad Drive in the south end of town. By the description Bennington had given, it was one hell of a private property surrounded by evergreens and thick oak trees on three sides with a spectacular view of woodland park. It was the benefits of smart investments and a thriving helicopter tour business. Now it was nothing but blackened fragments.

"You think he's dead?" Tyler asked.

Corey shrugged as he crouched and rubbed ash between his fingers. He had no idea. Had anyone told him a month ago his fiancée and unborn child would be buried in a shallow grave, he wouldn't have believed them, but there were other factors at work that they had no control over. Looting was rampant even in the smallest towns. Stores, homes, anyone was a potential target. They were living in a new world of darkness where the rules didn't exactly add up. Shards of light from the afternoon sun warmed his skin as he rose. Markowitz's two-car garage still had the burnt-out steel bones of vehicles inside it. Four of them fanned out scouring the property, hoping that he might have had a bunker or some safe house, while Bennington lay on top of the truck watching their six.

"This is a fucking joke," Holden said. "He's not here. Let's get out of here before we…"

All of them hit the ground at the sound of gunfire coming from Bennington's rifle.

"We got trouble."

Covered in ash, Corey lifted his head to see an armed group of five people fanning out in between the trees. They had obviously seen them pull in and were keen on stealing the truck or anything else they could take by force. Scrambling up and darting across the driveway to the back of the truck, he opened fire with his carbine at two individuals who were sticking their heads out. One of them he nailed in the head, while the other got off lucky. "Come on, let's go!" he bellowed at the others. Allie popped up from behind what remained of the stone fireplace and unleashed an arrow. At first Corey thought she was firing at him until it flew past his ear straight into the chest of a large fella coming up behind him wielding an ax. He gave her the thumbs-up before rejoining the fight. Two down, three to go, he thought until he saw even more. His eyes scanned the trees. Shit. Shit. There had to be another ten. What the hell? There was no way they could hold them all off, not without some cover. The advancing group had the advantage of tree cover, all they had were the few remaining stones from a house that was burned to the ground, and their own truck. Bennington was hooting and hollering as he spun around on the top of the truck like the hands on a clock, picking off one after the other. "Oh shit, I have missed this," he shouted.

"There's too many!" Corey bellowed. "Get over here. Now!"

They were turning, shooting and ducking for cover. He knew it was only a matter of minutes before one of them was fatally injured.

That was when it happened.

An explosion of epic proportion. One blast after another, like detonators going off all around them. Rock and soil rained down as the ground erupted. Several thin trees fell like they'd been chopped down. All he could do was lay on the ground as the assault on their senses played out. Smoke filled the air, and debris rattled across the asphalt before him like pebbles.

"What have we got?" Corey yelled to Bennington.

"I can't see for shit up here. Holden. You got anything?"

"Nothing, man."

There must have been at least twenty explosions.

By the time it stopped and the air cleared of smoke, many of the trees surrounding the property were on the ground as if a logging company had come through and brought it all down.

"And that, my friend, is a wrap!" a familiar voice bellowed.

Further out in the yard, a section of the earth was lifted and a person emerged. Markowitz. "Damn, you should have seen your faces," he remarked as he came up raking the muzzle of his rifle looking for further threats. There were none. Anyone who had survived had got the hell out of there.

"Please tell me that was not all the C4 that I asked you to store?" Holden said.

"Not all of it. Most though. I figured those bastards would be back." He got this wide grin on his stubble face as he came over to meet them. Markowitz was five-foot-eight and athletic. He wore a loose red shirt, beneath that was a black T-shirt, dirty jeans, combat boots, and on his skull a baseball cap turned backwards. He certainly didn't look like he'd grown up. A big kid at heart, his love of all things dangerous had taken him into flying when he was in his early teens. Unlike others who went the route of getting a license and logging flight time, he'd gone for a joyride in a helicopter at the sweet old age of fifteen. First time flying, he nearly crashed the damn thing into a resort, but some quick thinking and he brought it down in a swimming pool. Yep, insane, yet creative when it came to survival. Though that was when he was reckless and young. Now, when he wasn't flying high over Flathead County and giving his spiel on the beauty of the area, he was usually found pumping iron down at his local gym or flirting with some chick in a bar. Never married. Never had kids. He was a womanizer through and through. A pure-blooded, American-made, good old boy who was up for anything as long as it meant pussy and beer. "Hey boys," he said giving Corey a high-five. "Wondered when you would show."

"You rigged this place up?" Corey asked.

"Hell yeah. What, you think I would take them on by myself?"

"I'm not sure what disturbs me most. The fact that you rigged up your entire property with C4 or that you figured we were coming and you used us as bait?"

Markowitz laughed. "Assholes destroyed all I had. I've been watching them tearing through this town, lighting fires and killing people in the streets. If this hadn't worked, I would have taken them out one by one."

"Sounds like you," Holden said making his way over and giving him a hug.

Markowitz stepped back from the truck and looked up at Bennington. "You got any beer?"

"Are you kidding me?" he replied, peering over the roof. Then Markowitz laid eyes on Allie.

"Hello, lady love."

"Um, Markowitz. A little young for you."

"Please. Let the lady decide," he said wandering over. Allie brought up her bow and he backed up. "Whoa. Shit girl, don't you be pointing that at me."

"I would probably back off," Corey said. "She's a damn good shot."

"As am I, in the sack!" He grinned. He diverted his eyes away to Tyler. "Is this who I think it is?"

Corey wrapped an arm around Tyler's neck. "My little

brother, yep."

"Looks like you. Is he as mad as you?" He laughed before sniffing hard. "So, what brings you down this way besides the obvious need to be in my glorious presence?"

"Real glorious," Bennington said sliding off the top of the truck and making his way over to the fallen to make sure they were all dead. They heard him put a round in someone before moving on to another. Holden filled Markowitz in on the details. Told him he was in if Markowitz came.

"Well your timing couldn't have been better," he said motioning to the house. "I just put the house on the market."

They all laughed.

Corey saw Tyler wander over to the area of the yard where Markowitz had crawled out. Markowitz saw him and called out, "It's a dugout. Nothing more." Tyler lifted the cover and looked inside.

Markowitz turned back to Corey. "Sounds risky. Fun. I'm in. But we need to pick up Gibby. I told him I would be by today to check on him. He's not been in a good frame of mind since this kicked off."

"Um, maybe we should leave him," Corey said.

"I'm not leaving him. He goes or neither do I."

Holden got closer. "You think that's a good idea? Last time I saw him he was wasted on drugs with a needle in his arm."

"He's been clean since the power grid went down. A little hard to get your grubby hands on heroin when money has no value now. But food does and I'm sure he'd want in."

Corey ran a hand over his head and grimaced. "I dunno."

"You don't have long to decide," Markowitz said. "Those explosions will attract attention." Corey lifted a hand and looked at the others. They shrugged. No one was really in a position to argue. The stakes were high and the more people they had, the easier it would be. Besides, years of working side by side in Iraq had given them a trust that few would ever experience. Sure, Gibby was suffering from PTSD but how bad could it be? "All right, where is he?"

"In the dugout," Tyler said still holding the entrance covering open.

Corey frowned. "But you said we need to pick him up? I thought he was…"

"Yeah, off the ground. He's wasted."

"Shit. Man, we don't have time for getting him clean."

"He's clean. It's alcohol. He'll soon sober up. You got coffee?"

Corey raised his eyebrows and shook his head as he went over and looked into the dugout. There he was, laid out fast asleep. He'd just slept through explosions and one hell of a firefight. He mumbled under his breath. "This is a bad idea."

Holden gave him a hand lifting him out of the hole in the ground. There wasn't much to it. It was simply an area dug into the earth with a flat roof covered by strips of grass sod. Inside there was wood paneling to prevent the earth from caving in, and a couple of bunks. Essentially it looked like a sauna room in the earth. They were easy and quick to make and perfect for concealment and protection during warfare or hunting.

Keen to put Kalispell in their rearview mirror and not lose daylight, they loaded Gibby into the back of the truck and hightailed it out of there. On the way out, Markowitz brought them up to speed on what had occurred since he'd last seen Bennington.

The truck bounced as Tyler drove. Allie cast a glance over her shoulder listening in on their conversation as they caught up.

"I guess my situation is similar to you all. I had Gibby over and was trying to convince him to get off the smack. His doctor had him on all these pills. Anyway, I was helping him kick the habit. That's why he was at my place. I told him I would watch him for a week, you know, make it through the sweats, the shaking and night terrors. I had to literally cuff him to a pipe. He pleaded with me to get some heroin. Anyway, I got him over the hump and that's when those assholes showed up a few days later. At first it was only a handful. I was able to push them back with some force but they returned one night like a mob ready to hang us. I took a few of them out but then they set the house on fire. We escaped by the skin of our teeth." He leaned forward and motioned for Tyler to pull off and head down to the Flathead River.

"We should get out of the city," Corey said.

"No, he needs to sober up."

They pulled off Conrad Drive down a narrow gravel stretch of road that ended in a small parking lot near the winding river. Markowitz hopped out and instructed Holden to give him a hand by grabbing Gibby's wrists while he took hold of his ankles. Corey already knew what he was going to do. Without coffee on hand, there was only one other way to quickly sober him up, and that was the dunk. They shuffled over to the river and when they reached the edge, they swung his body a few times and then released. Gibby hit the water and as if someone had jabbed him with adrenaline, he came up gasping for breath and cursing. Markowitz cracked up laughing. "You might want to step back," he said as if knowing something they didn't. Holden frowned looking at him then back at Gibby.

Gibby waded out of the river, his legs sloshing water onto the stony shore. No sooner was he on dry land than he let out a yell and charged Holden, throwing a fist that caught him on the chin. He went down and Gibby continued on like a pinball now coming at Corey. Corey ducked his jab and shoved him. All the while Markowitz thought the whole event was hilarious. He was cracking up laughing, staying out of the way as Gibby swung and jabbed at anyone close to him.

It was Tyler that put him down in the end. He clotheslined him with his left forearm and then placed his knee against his shoulder. Gibby struggled beneath his weight but it was useless. Tyler had him in such a way that made it almost impossible for him to get out. "All right, all right," Markowitz said coming over laughing. "I'll take it from here."

Tyler released his knee and backed up.

"Hey buddy, it's Markowitz. Remember?"

Gibby squinted and then Markowitz offered a hand. Gibby grabbed it and as he came up, he swung and caught him on the jaw taking him down. "Next time. You're going in!" He then turned his attention to the rest of the group. "What the fuck are all you staring at?" He cracked his head from side to side. Gibby was blonde, and had an average build. He was the youngest in their platoon but a damn fine soldier. A good-looking kid who had witnessed some seriously fucked-up things over in the Middle East. The worst of it came at the hands of insurgents who managed to lure him away from their platoon. For six days they tortured him to give up information about his platoon but he never once buckled. Had it not been for some helpful intel from an insurgent there was no doubt in their mind he would have died at their hands. Instead, he survived. He later recounted how they had taped his eyes and mouth shut, starved and tortured him with electric wires. They also taped shit-filled diapers around his face, hung him by his neck until he lost consciousness and then woke him up only to flog his naked body with a strip of rubber. All the while keeping him in a blacked-out room where they told him he wouldn't leave until he was dead.

Corey could still see the look on his face as Marines burst in, killing his captors and finding his emaciated and battered body lying in a pool of his own urine and feces. They actually thought he was dead. Markowitz had been the one who had flown him by medical helicopter to a nearby base where he was nursed back to health.

Long after, he still showed crisscrossed scars across his back, thighs and chest from his beatings, and burn marks from being shocked. But it wasn't the physical aftermath that haunted him, it was the memories. The military soon discharged him and his journey back to feeling human again began. After Markowitz left the military, they formed a close bond and had it not been for his influence in his life, Corey was sure Gibby would have committed suicide.

Chapter 15

"Sit down, you're annoying the hell out of me," Andy said as Ferris paced. Several hours inside that cramped cell was starting to wear thin his patience. No one had given them food or water, and the accommodation was less than desirable. Every few minutes Ferris would try to shake the bars, filled with indignation.

"I'm an officer of the law. Let me out of here!"

"You can yell all you want. Your title means nothing to him."

That was when Ferris turned the tables.

"We're in this position because of you!" Ferris yelled.

"Oh yeah, I convinced you to follow me. Please, take some responsibility for your own decisions." Andy rolled his eyes as he lay back on a hard bench with his hands behind his head. He glanced over at Edison who was leaning against his bars. "I still can't believe you thought I could help."

"I figured you were friends. Perhaps you could get through to him."

"We were friends. That was a long time ago."

"Yeah, well he's gone off the deep end. He's not the man we once knew."

"Tell me about it," Andy replied.

They heard the clunk of metal and two guards walked down the narrow pathway that led up to their cells. Ferris shot over to the bars gripping them tightly. "Finally. At last. I have a good mind to take you all in."

"That's really going to help," Andy said.

They unlocked their jail cell and Ferris went to walk out when they pushed him back in. "Not you. Him," they said pointing to Andy. "Jude wants to see you."

"Are you serious?" Ferris bellowed. "Get the hell out of my way."

He tried to press forward but was met by a wooden baton to the gut. Ferris let out a groan, doubled over and dropped to his knees. Andy stood over him and shook his head before following the two guards out. He glanced at

Edison and gave a nod before heading out into the bright afternoon. They led him a good two hundred yards east, through a section of trees and back into the main living area. Andy scoffed as he saw where they were taking him. It was the original bunker they built, the one he'd created for himself. Jude was now using it.

Led into the earth-covered dome he saw Jude waiting for him in the living room area. He was standing with his hands behind his back.

"Sir," one of the guards said. Jude turned.

"Very good." He gave a nod. The guard cut Andy's binds and then stepped outside. Andy looked around.

"I should have figured you would take this as your own. You have a hard time keeping your hands off another person's property, don't you, Jude?"

"She wasn't your property."

"Maybe not, but she sure as hell wasn't yours."

Andy looked around while Jude went over to a liquor cabinet to pour a drink. He returned with two glasses and handed one to Andy. He contemplated tossing it in his face but opted against. As he took it, he said, "I'd say I like what you've done with the place…but it looks like shit," hoping to piss him off.

Instead, Jude smiled and walked over to a luxurious sofa where he took a seat, wrapping one arm around the top edge and crossing his legs. He rested the glass on his leg and turned it slightly with his hand. "Take a seat."

"I'll stand."

"Suit yourself." Jude took a large gulp of his drink.

There was a moment of silence as Andy scanned the room. On the mantelpiece he spotted something. Jude's eyes darted to it and he smiled as if enjoying his reaction. Andy walked over and squinted. It was a photo of Jude and Dianna, his arm wrapped around her, taken when she was still pregnant. Andy shook his head slowly. "All these years and you still can't let it go. I wonder, Jude, how does your new wife feel about that?"

"Dianna was my friend, as were you."

"Really? How is it then I don't see any of you and me?"

Jude didn't respond to that but shifted the conversation away. That was always his way. When things got hard, he would try to make light of the tough issues and focus on the ones that made him look like he cared. "There are bigger things afoot here, Andy. You and I knew this day would come. Hell, we were like prophets, spreading the word, trying to prepare the nation and here we are at the crossroads. The question is what choice will you make?"

"I've already made my choice. I want my sons and I'm out of here."

"Out of here? And go where, Andy? To your cabin?" He smiled. "Oh, you didn't think I knew about that addition? I think you'll find there is a lot I know about you, about your relationship with Dianna." He took another swig. "And let's not forget Tyler. Wow, now that young man is just full of stories." He looked up at Andy. "What were you hoping to achieve, huh?"

"Achieve? Okay, let's talk about that, shall we?" Andy said making his way around and standing across from him. "Edison's wife, Rosalie. Really?"

"That was an unfortunate mistake."

"A mistake? Is that how you justify killing a man's wife? Someone who stood by us when we built this place from the ground up?" Jude didn't respond so Andy continued. "I'm curious, how did you justify fucking my wife?"

"Oh, I think you and I know that she stopped being your wife long before she came to me."

"Came to you? Bullshit. You moved in on her. You knew I wasn't around and you used that to your advantage. You saw a vulnerable woman. You saw something you couldn't have and that just pissed you off, didn't it?"

Jude turned his glass on his leg and a smile appeared. "And here's you telling me I can't let go?" He stared intently at him. "Tell me, Andy, do you honestly think she wanted to be with you? Do you think she chose to stay because of her great love for you? Is that what you think? Or was it because of Corey?"

Andy pursed his lips. He could see Jude trying to push his buttons but it wasn't going to work.

"What are you playing at?"

"Playing at?"

"Is this some kind of retribution for keeping Tyler from you?"

"I think you know me better than that."

"No, no I don't think I do," Andy said. "The Jude I knew wouldn't have moved in on his best friend's wife. The Jude I knew wouldn't have killed a woman. What happened to you?"

He finished his drink and placed it on the table in front of him before reaching for a box and opening the lid. Inside were Cuban cigars. He offered one to Andy but he declined. Jude took one out and clipped off the end, placed the cigar between his lips and rolled it as he lit. A few hard pulls on it and it glowed to life. He blew gray smoke out the corner of his mouth, keeping his gaze firmly fixed on Andy as he leaned back in his seat.

"You know, I'm glad we can have this talk. I was

surprised at the way you reacted when it all went down. You simply walked away. You didn't attack me. You didn't even ask why, you just walked." Andy dropped his chin. "Even now you can't ask me, can you?"

Andy shot back a reply, "I already knew. I didn't need to ask. You were jealous."

"Jealous. Oh that's beautiful."

"Face it, Jude. I got the girl. I had the ideas. I was the one called upon to give talks throughout the country while you sat back supervising and watching Dianna, just waiting for the right time to move in."

"Man, you really are full of yourself. Just like Tyler said. If you honestly believe I gave a damn about what you had, you have deceived yourself. Man. That's some crazy, whacked-out shit." He blew out more pungent smoke. "I saw the way you treated her like she was undesirable, an annoyance, and yet you had gold in your hands but you couldn't see that. That's because all that mattered to you was that next speaking gig, that next workshop, that next great idea. Well, here's a great idea.

Don't forget the ones you leave behind because one day they'll overtake you and strip you of all you had."

Andy smiled and scanned the room before letting his eyes fall upon him. "Is that what you're doing, Jude? Stripping the towns of what they have?"

He chuckled and cocked his head to one side. "I have no idea what you mean."

"Of course you don't. Just like when I asked you if you felt anything for Dianna a month before I found you in the sack with her. What was your response?" Andy screwed his eyes shut and said, "That's right. 'Andy, why would I do that to my closest friend?'"

He stared blankly at Andy. "You're reaching."

"Am I?" he paused. "Morning Star."

Jude snorted, then laughed. "You think I'm Morning Star?" When Andy didn't respond, he broke into a full belly laugh. "Oh, that is priceless. You believe I'm behind the raids on the towns. That I would brand people in some sadistic manner to show some kind of allegiance to me? Is that right? Man, the years have been unkind to you, my friend." He tapped the side of his temple. "You know there is therapy for instability."

"Perhaps you should try it," Andy shot back.

Jude rose to his feet and Andy thought he was going to strike him as he got really close with a stern look on his face. Instead, he brushed past and refilled his drink. With his back turned to Andy he continued talking. "You are not seeing the bigger picture, Andy. You never did. I will admit you had some great ideas, you were visionary, ahead of your time some might say. I admired that in you. But your biggest mistake was thinking too small. It was always about this place, preparing, workshops and teaching but when it came down to it, you just weren't ready to pull the trigger."

"And you were?"

"Look around you, Andy. What do you see?"

"Weakness."

Jude turned, a flash of anger on his face.

"That's the Jude I remember," Andy said.

Aware that he was baiting him, Jude smiled and

walked back to his seat. "One month and already we are thriving. How long do you think you will survive out there?"

"I taught you everything."

"Not everything," Jude replied. "Only a fool walks away from what he's built and leaves it in the hands of another. What do you have to show for it? Nothing. How does that feel, Andy?"

"Is that why you brought me here, to gloat?"

"No. Strangely enough, it was to extend an invitation." He closed the distance between them until Andy could smell the alcohol on his breath. "Join us."

"Why? Huh? Why would you want me? Hell, why would you think I would want to be around you?"

"Because you want to be around Tyler. That's why you're here, right?" He turned and walked over to the photo on the mantel. "It's what she would have wanted."

"You have no idea what she wanted."

"I think you know that's not true," Jude replied looking at him. "Did you know that the reason she stayed with you was because of me?" He paused, looking at Andy and allowing his words to sink in. "That's right. She told you it was her decision. That she turned her back on me. That she somehow talked me into accepting that she loved you and if I wanted what was best for her that I would let her go, but that's what she wanted you to believe. It was easier that way. The truth was she came to me and was ready to leave you. She had her bags packed, Corey in the truck and was ready to turn her back on you, but it was me who persuaded her that it was wrong. That what had happened between me and her should have never happened. I told her I didn't want her. That's why she came back to you. That's why she stayed."

Andy clapped his hands giving him an applause. "Bravo. How self-sacrificing."

"It's true," Jude replied.

"You expect me to believe you would turn your back on your own son?"

"At that time, I didn't know she was pregnant. I found that out later. By that point her resentment for me had grown. She used Tyler like a knife, twisting into my back, using it as a way to get back at me. So call it what you will, Andy. The reason she stayed was because of me." He breathed in deeply. "But that is neither here nor there. Water under the bridge. The question is now, whose side are you on? Will you join me, join Tyler?"

"Is that why you saved Corey, to try and win him over?"

Jude smiled. "That wasn't done for him. I did that for you."

Chapter 16

It was nightfall by the time they ditched the truck many miles from the clearing near O'Brien Mountain. They would have to hike the rest of the way through the Kootenai National Forest just northwest of Libby. Holden and Tyler finished up concealing the truck with branches and camouflage netting while Corey handed out bulletproof vests, weapons, ammo and tactical comms equipment. They'd dropped off Allie back in Olney while they surveyed the camp. She knew there was supposed to be a delivery of wild game to the camp the next morning, and that most if not all of the raiders would be out looting, leaving the camp vulnerable to attack.

"No one told me we would be hauling ass through the forest," Bennington griped as he trudged on, his prosthetic leg getting tangled up in thick underbrush.

"Stop bellyaching," Holden said. "We've been in far worse. At least you can breathe here."

He was referring to the heat in the Middle East. Even though it was a dry heat, there were days it felt like the sun was burning them alive. Sometimes it got so damn hot in Baghdad with temperatures soaring up to 102 degrees, it felt like they were in a sauna. The crazy part was that wasn't officially summer. Loaded down with heavy body armor and a uniform, you could easily add another 10 degrees to the heat. Heat exhaustion was very prevalent, especially if a soldier didn't stay hydrated and drank too many caffeine drinks. Corey could remember the commanders making sure the convoy had a cooler full of ice with water and Gatorade to keep everyone's electrolytes high. They would monitor the group and anyone complaining of headaches, dizziness or nausea was quickly dealt with. The only upside was anywhere they went in Iraq there was water. He always remembered his commander telling him them that if they thought they were drinking enough, they weren't. Dehydration had a way of sneaking up on a person.

"You remember the first time they sent us to Kuwait?"

Markowitz said. "And they had us stay there for a couple of days to get used to the heat?"

"Oh yeah," Corey muttered. He smiled but it soon faded as he glanced at Gibby who had been silent for most of the trip. His PTSD worried him. There was no telling how he could react if they came under attack, but Markowitz said he was confident he'd be fine. Prior to the blackout, he said, he'd taken him down to the firing range to get used to the sound of guns going off again. But that wasn't what concerned Corey. It was the flashbacks. The torture. All he'd endured at the hands of insurgents. No amount of bombs going off over your head, or bullets snapping nearby could deal with that level of trauma. It had to be worked through with a professional, meds and therapy and by the sounds of it he was only on meds.

"You good, Gibby?" Corey asked, just checking in with him.

He eyed him but didn't reply. Meanwhile the others continued to shoot the breeze as Tyler led them through the same route Allie had taken him. Bennington pulled out a canister of water and downed it.

"Hey kid. We getting closer?" Bennington asked.

"You're kidding, right?" Tyler asked cradling his rifle and looking back at him.

"Tell me something. You trust this girl?"

"I don't trust anyone," Tyler said.

"Well that would have been good to know before we left." Bennington turned and looked at Markowitz. "You remember that pretty Iraqi informer you had eyes for? What was her name again?"

"Zina," Markowitz replied, looking around casually.

The crunch of their boots and the sound of birds was all that could be heard.

"Zina. That's right. Damn, she was a fine bit of ass, and yet one hell of a liar. With a deadpan expression she told us about that cell group. That bitch cost us the lives of Charlie and Liam. And what made it worse was she got away with it. How many other soldiers did she do that with?"

Corey recalled that day. Informers that played both

sides of the fence were as dangerous as suicide bombers. The military relied on accurate intel to remain safe. Insurgents knew this and so instead of just hiding in the shadows or sending their women out covered in C4 and a mass of 3-mm steel balls, they would send in an attractive Iraqi woman from a respectable family to gain the Americans' trust. From there it was a simple process of leading them like the Pied Piper into a building rigged to go off.

Corey caught up with Tyler. He'd noticed he'd been quiet since leaving Kalispell. Tyler shot him a sideways look as he fell in step. "Well this will either go south or turn out to be the best thing we've done since this shit storm. I've been meaning to ask you about your time with Jude. How did it go?"

"It was all right."

"That's it?"

"What do you want me to say, Corey? That he isn't anything like Andy?"

"I just figured in three weeks you might have noticed

things that weren't right. I mean, if Allie is telling the truth and this is the main camp for the raiders, he could be leading them."

"No, I don't buy it."

"Why, because he's your father?"

Tyler looked at him but didn't respond.

"You know, this doesn't change anything between us. You're still my brother. We might not have the same father in common but we are connected through our mother, and our time growing up together."

He nodded and adjusted his grip on his weapon and pressed on.

Corey fell back and made sure all their comms were operating.

"Hey Corey. You know, if the situation looks bad, I'm pulling out," Markowitz said. "No point losing our lives over food."

"This is more than food we are talking about here. It's pushing back the tide before it sweeps over our towns and drowns us."

"No. These people are opportunists. Like those assholes who showed up on my property. They look for the weak."

"Tell me, Markowitz, if you were starving and I offered you bread, what would you do for it?" Corey asked.

"Depends. Are we talking sucking dick or...?"

"Nope. Shit, man, why do you always make everything sexual?"

"You said what would I do for it. That had sexual connotations to it. Didn't it, Bennington?"

He nodded and looked back. "It kind of did."

"You two need to get your heads out of the gutter. It's a loaf of bread. Geesh."

They both roared with laughter and he joined in. He missed the old banter. Although Corey enjoyed working in search and rescue, it didn't come close to the brotherhood he had in the military. There was something to be said about being shoulder to shoulder, in the grime and heat of the Middle East.

Right then Tyler's fist shot up in the air, then he placed it to his ear to indicate for them to listen. All of them dropped to a crouch in the thick leafy brush at the sound of a dirt bike engine in the distance. They moved quickly to find cover behind some of the thick conifers and cedar trees. Another bike shot into view. They seemed to be following the same trail. Corey motioned to each of them not to do anything. The only thing they had going for them right now was the element of surprise. There was no telling who they were. Under the canopy of tree branches they watched four dirt bikes bounce down a trail. All of the riders had rifles on their backs but were wearing biking gear. All of them shot by at lightning speed but it was the fourth that slowed. Corey put his finger on the trigger and prepared to take him out. He turned his head towards them and lifted the visor on his helmet. What had he seen?

Tyler was looking directly at Corey, sweat beading down the side of his temple.

"Keep moving," Corey said under his breath. He

turned his head ever so slightly to see if the rider had spotted an animal. Perhaps they were out hunting for food? Corey brought up his eye to the scope and had the guy's face in the crosshair. Just give me a reason, he thought. He watched his eyes shift from side to side. That was when he saw another one of the bikes that had gone ahead return. It slowed and the other rider was asking him what he'd seen.

Corey's heart sped up.

This wasn't a good situation. They might be able to take out two of them but if the other two caught wind of it, they could easily escape and raise the alarm and what little window of opportunity they had would be gone.

Fortunately, the rider shook his head and flipped down the visor and both of them took off at a high rate of speed. The five of them waited in the brush for a few more minutes before continuing on, changing direction to ensure they didn't have them come up behind them on the way back from wherever they were heading.

It didn't take them long to reach the rise that

overlooked the clearing.

Corey's eyes widened as he saw the setup. They spread out to get a better view of the place. Over the comms unit he heard Holden say, "Okay, how the hell did they get all this shit in here?"

Tyler replied. "There is a road off US-93 called the 17 Mile Road. It connects with Quartz Creek Road and then forks and cuts through the forest down to NF 4681."

"NF what?"

"It's a single trail mostly used by loggers and campers. But from the trail you can't see this place. It's hidden behind that mountain."

"So how did they haul in all of these supplies?"

"ATVs and trailers."

"You have got to be kidding me," Bennington said. "Then how do you expect us to get the shit out of here?"

"Same way," Tyler said.

This new information didn't sit well with any of them including Corey. He figured as did they that if a large supply was being stored in a campsite, they had to have a means of getting it there. ATVs couldn't haul large amounts of supplies. It would require multiple trips. And there was no way in hell he could manage to get his truck through the forest, it was too dense. Out here, dirt bikes, ATVs, that was the only way to slice through God's country.

"Corey. A word with you," Markowitz said. Corey got up from the ground where he was peering through high-powered binoculars. He handed them to Tyler and at a crouch made his way over.

"You didn't say anything about kids."

"I knew less than you, buddy. Look, if you don't feel good about this, we'll pull out. I just know these people are going to keep coming. Volunteers are dropping like flies at the roadblocks in Whitefish and I expect it's the same in Kalispell and surrounding towns. They don't think twice about killing and they aren't going to stop. The only way we can put a dent in their operation is to take the war to them."

Markowitz stared back at him. He didn't need to

explain what that meant. Hell, they had for years served overseas taking the war to insurgents, chasing them out of their hideaways and putting an end to their reign of terror. But back then they had air support, large platoons of soldiers and the whole goddamn U.S. military behind them.

"This requires more people."

"We don't have them," Corey replied. "This is it."

"Why?"

"I told you why. We don't know who to trust right now. The last raid in Whitefish was compromised. Now I don't know who tipped them off but the fewer people who know about this, the better."

"I don't like it."

Tyler overheard and walked towards them. "It's a simple matter of timing," he said pulling out the notebook belonging to Allie. "She knows their schedule down to a tee. They won't bat an eye over those three ATVs leaving the camp. They'll expect it. What they won't realize is one of them will be carrying out the cartridge reloading machine. Look, I understand the hesitation, I really do, but I trust her."

"You don't know her," Markowitz said. "On the way up here you told us that you had only known her for three weeks and most of that wasn't spent with her and now you want to go out on a limb to get her sister, who you don't even know if she is down there? Am I the only one who sees how absurd this is?" He turned away from Tyler and directed his attention to Corey. "You should know better than anyone else that this is the reason why this is not a viable mission."

Corey turned to Tyler. "Give us a moment, would you?"

Tyler nodded, looking at a frustrated Markowitz. He walked back to his spot. Corey turned to Markowitz. "We get one shot at this. It's not just food that is down there, its medical supplies, generators, gasoline and most of all, a reloading press, and more ammo than we could ever find. In the wrong hands that shit is devastating. Now I don't know about Kalispell but Whitefish is running out of ammo. Food, well, we can hunt and fish. That's not a problem so if you want to leave that behind, fine. But the ammo, gas, medical supplies, that shit is golden now. And don't tell me it isn't."

Markowitz was thinking it over.

"I've already lost a lot. Ella, the baby and good friends of mine in Whitefish. Today it's a friend, tomorrow a brother. I won't lose more people."

"I get it," Markowitz said. "But you can't control the future."

"No, I can't but we can stack the odds in our favor," he said jabbing his finger towards the camp. "Right now, they hold all the cards and they won't stop until all that is left is people, and you know what happens then."

"Slavery. Executions."

"That's right and child soldiers. War crimes. It's happened before and it will happen again. Right now, we have an opportunity to turn this around, to stack the odds in our favor and hold on to a sliver of what remains but I can't do this by myself. If I have to I will but…" He trailed off and looked over at Gibby, Bennington and Holden before shaking his head. "Haven't you missed it?"

"You know I have," Markowitz said.

"Then stand with me. Because let's face it, what do we have to go back to?"

He nodded slowly. "More of the same. Perhaps worse."

"Perhaps worse," Corey repeated his words before running a hand over his sweaty face and squinting into the distance. Darkness had wrapped itself around the forest and a light rain had begun to fall.

Corey patted him on the back. Markowitz sighed. "Man, the shit I do for you all."

"So you're in?"

"Do I have a choice?"

Chapter 17

Nate ran his thumb over Erika's hand and stared at her with a heavy heart. She was still in an induced coma. The doctor had told him that it varied based on the situation but in most cases, patients could be in it for a few days up to two weeks. Anything longer than a month was rare. It was done only when patients were at a high risk of brain injury from physical trauma, a drug overdose, a disease like meningitis, rabies or a life-threatening seizure. The knock she'd had to the head had caused a fair amount of swelling. That's why she'd been suffering from headaches and acting agitated. While they were confident that it would work, he didn't mince words with Nate and was clear that it carried some risks, like risk of chest infection which was common because it affected the cough reflex. He'd also warned him to not be surprised if she awoke scared and confused. Patients emerging from sedation often experienced hallucinations.

"Can you hear me?" Nate waited as if expecting her to reply. "I don't know if you can hear me but I really need you to fight this. I know you can. You're strong." He smiled and then snorted. "I'll be honest with you, when I first met you I didn't think you were. In fact," he clenched his teeth then continued, "I kind of thought you were a whiner, a daddy's girl who didn't have backbone but you proved me wrong. You proved us all wrong, Erika. I guess that means we should probably withhold judgment about people until we know them better." Nate cast a glance out the window. "You know, I've never considered myself a wuss but when I was in that bunker, I don't know what I was more terrified of, that mad cow Denise or seeing you harmed." He sighed. "You aren't missing much here." He looked at smoke rising in the distance. "Whitefish is quickly turning into hell. They are losing people and can't replace them fast enough. Andy is still a dick, the mayor, well, bless his heart, he's trying." He paused for a second, placing a kiss on her hand. "Oh, and if by some strange twist of fate, you wake up and can't remember who I am, I want you to know that I'm going to do everything in my power to remind you. Okay." He smiled then kissed her hand again. "I miss you, Erika."

After that Nate got up and went over to Bailey who was lying at the foot of the bed. He ran his fingers through her hair, and her ears perked up. She sniffed his hand and licked it. "Hey girl. You want to come with me?"

She lifted her eyes but didn't look interested. "No. I get it. She'll pull through. You'll see." He looked back at Erika and swallowed hard. "She has to. I'm not facing this shithole alone." A tear welled up in his eye and he wiped it away. He got up, strolled down the hall and refilled her bowl with water from a holding tank they'd brought into the hospital. Most of the water in the city was being sourced from a number of places. Local homes were using manual pumps if they had well water, those who didn't, collected rainwater from rooftops or anywhere water pooled. The city took things to the next level and started bringing it in from the reservoirs, rivers, streams and lakes in the area. Of course, all of it needed to be filtered and boiled, making it a slow process, but at least no one was going without. Food, well that was another matter entirely. Fortunately, there was an abundance of fish in Whitefish Lake, and wildlife in the forest. The challenge was making sure you didn't get shot in the process. He'd been out with Andy a week ago and what should have been a peaceful and relaxing time was anything but. The sound of gunfire was crazy. Dotted throughout the forest, survivors from towns in the area wore bright orange vests to avoid getting shot by the steady influx of people seeking out food.

The challenge the city would soon face would be dealing with the greedy, those who were taking more than their fair share as a means to extend life. That could only last so long. It was inevitable that the abundance of wildlife would soon dwindle with every man and his uncle hunting. What then? Well, everyone would revert to fishing but how long would that last before they realized it was easier to let someone else do the hard work and then swoop in and take it by force? That was why Corey saw the importance of taking the fight to the raiders. Nate? He was torn. Just as the city was replacing those who died, wouldn't the raiders do the same? The offer of having your needs met was enticing in this new world.

Nate returned and plunked the bowl down. Bailey looked at it despondently as if she'd given up the will to live. It reminded Nate of what Andy had said. Only the strong would survive. He'd already come across those who had taken their lives. One month in and people had given up. He couldn't imagine it was possible but Corey told him that many in the nation had grown up with parents who had filled them with fear of the end times. Would Denise and her batshit clan have done the same thing? Swallowed the Kool-Aid and joined Jim Jones on the other side? He shook his head at the thought before leaving Erika. He tapped the door frame a few times and told her he would be back soon.

Before leaving he managed to bum a smoke off the security guard. On the long forty-minute trek back to city hall that evening, he thought about how he'd acted in the bunker and dwelled in the regret of what-ifs. What if he'd acted sooner? What if he'd been the one to escape? As he came into the residential area of the city and went to cross Riverside Avenue, he heard a woman screaming for help. Her cries cut through the darkness as he looked east. The street was empty. He waited a second thinking he might hear it again but got nothing so he continued on, making it to 9th Street before he heard the scream again, this time it was close. He looked up US-98 contemplating continuing on. Andy had told him and Erika that under no circumstances were they to engage with anyone if it meant putting their lives at risk. He was by himself but even as he ignored the scream and crossed the road, he couldn't help but wonder what was happening. Still, Andy's words echoed in his mind. *Stay on course. Don't detour. There's nothing you can do to help.*

The screams got louder. Nate glanced down 9th Street

and saw trouble. A woman was running down the road in torn clothes. Behind her, three guys on mountain bikes followed, overtook and circled her. They would do a figure eight around her, and take turns prodding her like cattle with the end of a baseball bat.

"Oh, come on, don't play hard to get."

Nate scanned the street for cops. *Typical.* When needed they weren't anywhere to be found, and when you wanted to avoid them, they were everywhere. He hesitated for a second, Andy's cautionary words echoing in his mind, then decided, screw it. He removed the AR-15 slung over his shoulder and brought it up. He moved down the street crossing over front yards, weaving around trees and bushes until he got close enough to make out their faces. They were in their late teens. Wet behind the ears. They reminded Nate of self-entitled jocks who would get drunk on weekends and then boast about getting laid the following Monday. The girl stumbled as one of them prodded her a little too hard. She landed hard on her knees and the three broke into laughter. "All this could have been avoided if…" one began.

Before he could finish, Nate emerged from a front yard and fired a warning shot near his bike. The look of fear on their faces spoke volumes. These weren't gang members, thugs or even opportunists, they were immature assholes. The one he fired near, froze, his hands shot up while his two friends whipped their bikes around and pedaled the hell out of there, only taking a moment to look back. Nate jogged over, rifle aimed at the guy. "You don't understand, man. She deserves it."

"Deserves it?" Nate shot him a disgusted look.

The girl was on her hands and knees looking up at him, surprised, maybe relieved? Although her clothes were ripped, her attire was modest. It wasn't as if she was sending out the wrong message. She had these baby blue eyes, was around five foot four and had short cropped hair that formed a perfect frame for her heart-shaped face. As he crouched to help her, the other guy swung his bike around and took off. Nate bolted upright and considered firing another round to scare him but chose not to waste it. He cast his gaze down, and then offered her a hand. She took it and he pulled her up. She was as light as a feather. "You injured?" He could see a few scratches but besides that there was no noticeable sign she was hurt. Her white shirt was ripped exposing her bra, and her pants were torn at the knees revealing a scrape. She shook her head.

"You live near here?"

She motioned with a finger to US-98.

"The cat got your tongue?" he asked when she didn't say anything. Her response was a shake of the head. He gave a thin smile. "The name's Nate." When she didn't reply with her name, he shrugged. She was still breathing heavily so he waited for her to catch her breath before he asked, "You know those guys?"

She shook her head.

"You don't say much, do you?" He looked off down the road. "Look, I'll walk you home, okay? Just in case those assholes decide to come back." He motioned her forward. "Lead the way."

She was silent for a good ten minutes, glancing at him occasionally before she uttered her first word. "Mariah," she said.

"You can speak," he replied. "You want to tell me what all that was about? Did you know them?"

Her head dipped then nodded. "Guys I went to school with. The one that froze is Jacob Rawlings. He always wanted to date me but I didn't want to know. The other two were his pals."

"Ah like that."

She nodded. As they crossed East 7th Street, two cops came into view riding bicycles. Nate snorted. "Isn't that just the way. A little too late but…" He raised his hand to get their attention but Mariah pulled it down. "What?"

"No. Please. I don't want to deal with them."

"But look at you."

"Please."

The cops had seen his hand and they yelled over to him. "You okay?"

He looked back and hesitated. "Yeah. Fine. It's

nothing."

Mariah pulled her top closed to cover up and ran a hand through her black hair. Either it was too dark for them to see or they were already on route to another call but they didn't stick around. As they pedaled away, Nate looked at Mariah. "Look, it's none of my business but if I'd gone through what you just had, I might be inclined to tell a cop. At least that way they could watch over your house, follow up with those bozos and possibly prevent it from happening again."

"I don't want to," she said.

"Suit yourself. Now where is your home?"

"Just off 6th and Columbia Avenue."

They crossed a yard and heard people yelling at each other inside a house. Nate imagined arguments between spouses would have been at an all-time high with the stress of trying to stay alive. How many couples had separated since the power went down? How many had seen the situation as their way out? Mariah was startled by a pit bull slamming into a chain-link fence and barking at them. Nate put his hand on her back and moved her over to the other side of him. Once they made it to Columbia Street and she pointed out which one was her house, he looked at it and noticed all the lights were out. It wasn't uncommon. Not everyone had flashlights, batteries or even candles. Some chose to only use them at certain times of the night. It was a simple one-story, cream-paneled house with white shutters, a green metal roof and a garage. A short paved driveway divided her home from her neighbors.

"Well here we are. You gonna be okay?"

At first she nodded, thanked him for his help and started making her way up the driveway. Nate turned to leave when he heard her say, "Do you want to come in?"

He pulled a face. "I really should be getting back. My friends. Well…"

"It's fine," she said lifting a hand and turning towards the front door.

Nate stared down the road. "Okay. Just for five minutes. Just to make sure everything is good inside," he said, trying to come up with a reason for following this girl who was at least ten years younger than him. She unlocked the front door and beckoned him inside. A part of him wondered if this was some kind of trap. Perhaps she knew those guys. Maybe they were waiting for him in the house. One look at her convinced him otherwise. There was a timidness to her, a genuine fear.

The home was even smaller on the inside than he thought. She shuffled past him and collected a flashlight left on a small table that held a telephone, a notepad and pen. She flashed it on with the beam facing up, illuminating her face. No, it wasn't creepy or anything, Nate thought. She quickly turned it and pointed it into the living room. There she retrieved some matches and lit several candles around the house. That was when he got his first look at the place. A narrow corridor ran the full length of the home from the front to the rear kitchen. There was a living room off to his right, a bedroom to his left and one more bedroom in the rear, with a washroom close to the dining area. The décor was outdated. Early

'80s if he had to guess. Flowery wallpaper, and shag carpet. However, the place was immaculate. Everything was in its place. Not a spot of dust in sight.

"Your parents not here?"

She didn't answer that but returned from the kitchen with two bottles of beer and handed one off. *Five minutes?* Maybe he could stretch it to ten.

Chapter 18

The raid on the camp was set to occur in the early hours of the morning. That night from the concealment of the forest Tyler watched a large number of raiders leave on ATVs. Emotions were running high. The air was tense with anticipation. They heard engines roar, saw clusters of men and women taking rifles with them. Whatever commands they had been given, whatever town they were going to hit next, they were planning on striking in the dead of night. At first, they'd used distractions like lighting fires, or causing trouble on the opposite end of a town, to draw away law enforcement, but that only worked for a while before towns and cities caught on. According to Bennington, word on the street was that armed groups were hitting supply houses without anyone aware they had hit until it was over. They next morning police and city officials would walk into empty storehouse and find holes in the roof where they'd lifted back shingles, broken through the wood and extracted goods.

It was fast, clever, and very effective. It was why their numbers were high and why they were probably having no problem recruiting people to help them. Who wouldn't want to be part of a group that was sitting on the lion's share? At first Corey doubted it. He thought they would have taken it by force but that meant putting their necks on the line and no one with a lick of sense was going to do that. These weren't stupid people. Even as they watched the assembly of ATVs and trailers disappear into the night, and the glow of the red taillights blink out, they hadn't left the camp unguarded. It was hard to tell how many were still there, patrolling the area or inside the camp, so the risk was high.

Tyler sat in the camouflaged treehouse preparing to get some z's while two of their group stayed vigilant for the next couple of hours. After, he would take a turn. Tyler glanced over at the bag that held a few cans of food and a Coleman stove. All he could think about was Allie and what she'd told him. Was this a trap, a means of luring out those who could be a thorn in the side of the raiders? After all the lies, it was hard to know. Women at the best of times were hard to figure out but she had one hell of a poker face. The sound of boots against wood made him glance towards the opening. Corey emerged. "You still awake?"

"Nope. I can't sleep," Tyler replied, casting a glance his way.

"Me neither." Corey pulled himself up and took a seat beside him. They gazed out over the tops of the trees towards the camp. Two fires flickered in the distance, and they saw the silhouettes of people walking from tent to tent. "Tomorrow. If all goes well, Dad was thinking about going south for a couple of days. He's been chatting with Lou on the ham radio. Things have got really bad down there. Lou and Aunt Barb left a few days ago and made their way north to Lou's old army buddy Ralph Brunson."

"Oh, that guy."

"What do you mean?"

"We were going to drop by his place but got sidetracked on a different route." He frowned. "So Andy's thinking of leaving his cabin? After all that stockpiling?"

"Not for good. We'd return in five days. He was hoping you could watch over it."

Tyler screwed up his face. "He was, was he?" He said it in a way that came across as sarcastic as he knew what Andy was like and after all the crap he'd put them through, he was always wondering what his end game was. "More like he was looking for a reason to pull me away from Jude's camp."

Corey groaned and ran a hand over his tired face. "That's not it at all."

"No?" Tyler shot back. "Then what is it? Because from my standpoint he has made it very clear that he didn't want me around. And what, now he needs someone to watch over his shit, I become valuable to him again? Please. He has another thing coming if he thinks I'm doing anything for him."

Silence stretched between them.

"I know you're angry."

"Angry. You don't know the half of it."

"Of course I do. Have you forgotten? I was there through it all. You might have got the worst of it but I didn't scrape through with a pat on the back. He was hard on me too. But you don't see me whining about it."

"Let's not go there, shall we. It never ends well, Corey."

He thought back to the last argument he had in Vegas with him. He was close to knocking him on his ass over the comments he made. "Look, just think it over, okay?"

Tyler took the binoculars and looked out. All was peaceful down in the camp.

"You know Nate was real torn up about Erika," Corey said.

"And?"

"I just figured you might be."

"She's a friend."

"That's not what I heard."

"Then you heard wrong."

Again, there was a pause. Corey took his rifle and began the process of cleaning it. Tyler rolled over and tried to get some sleep but Corey wasn't done.

"You given much thought to who this Morning Star could be?"

Tyler grunted. He heard him clearly but didn't want to get into it.

"If he's behind this, you know what we'll have to do," Corey said.

"If who's behind it?"

"You know who."

He knew he was referring to Jude.

"Who's to say that it's him? For all we know this could be the work of Andy."

"Are you kidding me?" Corey asked.

Tyler rolled, turning his way. "Think about it. He built Camp Olney with Jude and then walked away from it. All that time, all that money in preparation for what? Is it too much of a stretch to think that he might have started his own thing? His own camp?"

"I would have known."

"Really? Like you would have known he wasn't my father. Got it."

"Don't be sarcastic."

"You said yourself that there were only a few people who could have known about the plan that was in place in Whitefish. Who else had access to that truck? Why did they cover their face? Simple. They knew you were out there. After all the crap that Andy has pulled, I wouldn't be surprised if he tipped them off and then got the hell out of there."

"I don't believe it."

"You don't need to believe it, brother. You just need to read the writing on the wall. His connections with the mayor and the city allowed him to know. Sure, Ferris might have overheard and told the others but..."

"No buts!" Corey stopped cleaning and glared at him. He knew it was getting to him. Despite Andy being a royal asshole, he was still his father and blood defended blood. He would have been lying to say that he hadn't given thought to what that meant now that he knew Jude was his father. Andy and Jude were at odds, would the same happen to him and Corey?

* * *

Allie thought she would slip in unnoticed; wow, was she wrong. She was on route to her dome when Maddox blindsided her, grabbing her by the arm and pulling her into a tent that was used for medical. "You want to tell me where you've been for the past two days?"

She thought denial was her best bet.

"I don't know what you're talking about. I was here," she said before trying to brush by him. He grabbed her arm. "Get off me." He shoved her farther back into the tent.

"You know what I think. I think you've been talking."

She smelled alcohol on his breath and tried to use that to her advantage.

"Maddox, you've been drinking. Go sober up."

Again, she tried to move past him but he wouldn't let her. He shoved her forcefully back against a table, so hard that it moved and a collection of medical utensils dropped to the ground. Maddox pressed himself up against her and brought a hand up to her throat. "You know what happens to those who speak," he said squeezing her cheeks until the tip of her tongue stuck out. In an instant he brought up a knife and pressed the blade against it. "It would be a real shame to waste all of that," he said before planting his mouth on hers and French kissing her. At first, she wriggled within his grasp but he was too strong. For a brief moment Allie considered kneeing him in the nuts but then it dawned on her what to do — what better way to gain his trust than to give in to him, give him the sense that she was enjoying it. As Maddox pulled away and looked as if he was about to walk out, Allie grabbed his wrist and pulled him back in. A look of surprise filled his face, then that smug look as if he thought she really was into him. Like a hungry animal, he pushed her against the wooden table again, pressing his lips against hers. She pressed back, aggressively raking her fingers down his back. His eyelids popped open and she saw a glint of excitement in his eyes. Putting the knife back into the sheath, he hoisted her up onto the table and continued to kiss her in an aggressive manner. He tore at her top and mauled her breasts with his hands before flipping her over and yanking down her pants. There was no resistance on her part. It was all playing out as expected. Although she hated every minute of him grinding up against her, she knew that too much was riding on this and with Maddox as an ally there was a chance she might be able to convince Jude to let her take supplies in and see her sister. Hours from now, Tyler would be waiting with Madison and they would leave all this behind.

When Maddox was done, he hiked up his pants and leaned in for one more kiss. "Damn, I read you all wrong. I had a sneaky feeling you were into me but I didn't expect that."

"Who wouldn't?" Allie said in a believable way before covering herself up.

"Who wouldn't what?"

God, this guy was dumb. She traced a finger down his chest. "Who wouldn't be into you?"

He gave her another one of those smug looks. "Yeah, you're right."

The guy was full of himself. A total loser. Had there not been so much riding on this she would have cut him from balls to sternum.

As he turned to leave her alone, he said, "Meet me here tomorrow morning."

"That's actually going to be a problem."

He scowled looking back. "Why?"

"Because I was hoping to do a run to the camp. You know, I haven't seen my sister in a long time."

"And?"

"Well I…" She sidled up to him and ran her fingers down his arms. "I thought you might be able to put in a word with your father."

He scoffed, bringing up a finger and wagging it in her face before looking around. "And why would I do that?" he asked. His reply caught her off guard.

"I..."

"You thought this would change anything?" he said twirling his finger around to indicate what had just happened. When her chin dropped, he burst out laughing. "I'm fucking with you. Of course I can put in a word. Though I don't know why you'd want to go there. The place is a shithole compared to here. But you know my old man. Always thinking ahead." He nodded, eyeing her carefully. "I'll speak to him tomorrow," he said.

"No, it has to be tonight."

He gave her a strained look.

"Because. Well. I won't get another chance for a while and..."

"And you want to see Madison."

She pursed her lips and nodded.

"I'd like to help. Really, I would but there is a little matter of where you've been. You see, that's out of my hands. I'm not the only one that noticed you weren't around. Since your old man pulled that stunt and tried to slice my father from ear to ear, let's say that we've been keeping a close eye on you. My father knows you left the camp."

"Does it matter?" she asked.

"With all that's happening right now, damn right it matters." Maddox began walking around keeping a close eye on her. "Now again, it can all go away if you have a good reason."

She knew he was toying with her. Allie was aware she was under the watchful eye of Jude's men and that was why she'd gone to great lengths to avoid being detected when she left, however, leaving was one thing, returning another.

"I needed to get out. I wanted space. You don't get that though, do you? You get to go anywhere you please." She was laying it on thick, hoping he would see her frustration and put two and two together. "This place has been suffocating me. All the rules. Do this. Do that. Go here. You can't go there. Don't you ever just want to blow off some steam? Escape it all? Live by your own rules?"

"All the time," Maddox replied. "So where did you go?"

"Whitefish. I just told you."

He walked over to her and got really close. "It wouldn't have anything to do with that asshole Tyler Ford, would it?"

That was why she hadn't approached Tyler in the three weeks he was in the camp. She knew Maddox and others would be watching. If she'd been seen talking to him, they would have concluded she was in league with him.

"I don't even like the guy."

Maddox's lip curled. "Now that's my girl." He ran the back of his knuckles over her right cheek. "That's going to come in real handy."

"With?"

"I have to go out on a limb here for you. You know that, right?"

"And?"

"Well my father isn't stupid. He'll want real answers.

Not the kind you've given me. Now me, I don't give two shits where you've been as long as it doesn't come back to bite me in the ass. Now I can help you but I'm going to need you to do a little something for me in exchange."

"I just thought I did," she muttered.

He ran his hand around the back of her neck. "Oh let's be honest, Allie. You wanted that as much as I did." She nearly vomited in her mouth. His breath stank like cigarettes and hid body odor was even worse. "Didn't you?"

Now he wanted confirmation? Something to stroke his ego?

"Yeah."

"So…it's simple. When Tyler returns, I'll make a few arrangements for him to go hunting with us. When he does, that's where you come in. You're pretty handy with that bow, aren't you?"

"Not bad."

"I want him dead."

"Dead?"

"Gone. Out of here. My father won't do it. No. He's got his son back. He thinks the sun shines out of that kid's ass but I know better. A Ford is a Ford. Like father like son. There is a reason he's back here and I don't trust him one bit. I'm taking him out before shit goes south. You hear me?"

She didn't reply.

Maddox put his hand around the back of her neck. "I'm going out on a limb for you. All I ask is for something in return."

She stared at him in disbelief. Although she wanted to tell him he was out of his mind, she realized Tyler wasn't coming back to the camp, so it wasn't like she was ever going to be put in that position. Still, she had to give him a sense that she was shocked by the request.

"Not liking someone and killing them is quite a leap. I'm not sure I can do that."

"You take the shot. If it doesn't kill him, I'll finish the job myself."

"But Jude will know," she said.

"No he won't. Leave that part to me."

She scowled. "Why not just do it yourself?"

"Because I'm not the one that has a sister I want to see. Now am I?"

She stared back at him. Man, he was a piece of work.

"Do we have a deal?" he asked.

Allie took a second to reply before she nodded and said, "Yes."

"Good. Stay here while I go have a word with my father."

Chapter 19

Andy rolled his eyes, and rocked his head back. "You're preaching to the choir," he said in a loud voice, trying to make it obvious that he wasn't interested. He'd had enough of listening to Jude's drivel. Not for one minute did he believe he wanted to bury the hatchet. There was always an agenda at work running subtly in the background. It might not have been obvious in that moment but it was there.

"You're not helping your situation," Jude said.

Andy rose. "Are we done here?"

Jude was about to say something when Maddox walked in.

"I'm busy," Jude snapped.

"This can't wait."

Maddox glanced at Andy as he crossed the room and made his way around his father's table. He leaned in and whispered in his ear. Andy couldn't make out what he said and he couldn't care less. Jude scowled. "Why didn't someone tell me sooner?" Maddox shrugged. Jude looked over at Andy and then smiled. "Bring her in."

"Look, Jude. The past is the past. I'm heading back to Whitefish," Andy said turning to leave.

"You're not going anywhere. Sit down."

Andy ignored him and made it to the entrance before he was stopped by two of his men who shoved him back in. "What do you want of me?" he asked Jude directly.

"I just told you."

"I've got nothing to give you that you don't already have," Andy said.

"That's where you're wrong. I saw the way the people looked at you when you walked into the camp. They remember you. Respect you. Admire you. It's taken me years to earn that kind of trust. With the new ones it's not a problem but the original core group, I've never really won their hearts or minds."

"What are you talking about Jude?"

"We are in a war, my friend. Whether you agree or

not. The only way forward is with people. It's about winning hearts and minds."

Andy couldn't believe what he was saying. "You really have lost it."

"Quite the contrary. I've never been clearer. You see, that's what I learned from you." Jude got up and talked as he walked with his hands behind his back. "Food, medication, ammo, these can persuade a lot of people. It can even give the illusion that people are with you, that you've captured their hearts, their allegiance, but what happens when you have nothing left to give? What happens when I have to go out there and tell them that supplies are low, that the forest that once held an abundance of wild game is barren?" He turned towards him. "That's when we'll see who is behind you and who was with you for what you could provide." He breathed in deeply. "You always had a way of rallying people behind you long before you gave them anything. Together," he said placing a hand on Andy's shoulder, "we can secure our future."

Andy broke into laughter. At first it was light, then he roared.

"Then we can secure our future? Oh that is beautiful," Andy said clapping his hands and giving him a round of applause. "Bravo."

The smile on Jude's face vanished. Andy saw him clench his fist but before he could act, Maddox returned with a woman no older than Tyler. Jude cast a glance her way. "Andy, you remember Edison and Rosalie, meet Allie, their youngest daughter." Jude walked over and placed a hand around her shoulder and brought her in. "We were just talking about your father," he said. "You had us worried, Allie. We had a lot of people out there looking for you."

Allie looked concerned. She flashed Andy a look.

"Yeah, I just needed to get out. Clear my head," she replied.

"I understand. It can become quite claustrophobic in this camp at times. I was just telling my old friend Andy here about some of the visions I have for expansion. He's not as convinced as I am but I think he'll come around, what do you think, Allie?" he said, holding her tightly beside him like a child.

"I guess."

"I guess." He chuckled. "Well I'm glad to see no harm came to you. But then I imagine that's because you had Andy's boy with you. Oh, that's right, I meant, my boy with you."

Maddox frowned and shifted uncomfortably.

When Allie didn't reply but looked confused another girl came into the room and put her arm around Maddox's waist. She had fiery red hair and pale skin, and had an AR-15 slung over her shoulder. "That's right, isn't it, Ann?"

Allie swallowed hard. "I have—"

"No idea. Right," Jude said, cutting her off. "I thought you might say that." Jude held out his hand but kept looking at Allie. Ann crossed the room and placed in his palm a cell phone. He powered it on and made a remark about there still being ways to generate power using solar and wind. He slid his finger across the phone a few times and then turned it around. Andy caught a glimpse of the image. Tyler was untying a horse and standing beside him was Allie.

"You see, as much as I love my son, I'm afraid it takes time to earn trust. I had to have him followed."

"You bastard!" Allie yelled at Maddox. She made a dash for him but was stopped with a clean punch to the face by Ann. On the floor, nursing a bloody nose, she glared at Maddox as he strolled over and bent slightly at the waist to address her.

"Why would I help someone who agreed to kill my brother?"

Her eyes widened, and he pulled out a phone and turned up the volume so they could hear a recording of her agreeing to the deal where she would get to see her sister in exchange for killing Tyler. Maddox stepped back as Jude bellowed for two of his guards to take her away. "Throw her in with her old man. I'm sure they're just aching for a reunion."

"No. No!" Allie bellowed as they dragged her away kicking and screaming.

As quick as a flash, Jude turned to Andy with narrowed eyes. "And you? Have you made a decision?"

"Jude."

"Maybe you need more time to think about it." He made a gesture with his head and Andy was led away, back to his cell.

"JUDE! Don't do this!" But his words fell on deaf ears.

Chapter 20

Mariah was dodging questions. Something didn't add up. Nate should have stopped drinking after the first beer but he made the fatal mistake of accepting another. He gazed through bleary eyes at the label on the bottle, trying to see the alcohol content. It felt much higher than five percent. Usually he could hold his liquor but this was kicking his ass. "Help me out here. You were out looking for your father, is that right?"

She nodded, dipping her hand into an oversized bag of chips and stuffing her face.

"And he went missing a week ago, you say?"

"That's right."

"And you ran into Jacob and they wanted some action."

"Wanted. Yes."

"Why did they say you deserved it?"

She shrugged. "Can I get you another one?"

He laughed. "I should really get going."

"Just one more," she said. "Are you in a rush?"

"Well I'm not in a rush but..." He looked at her and lifted his hands. "What the heck. Go ahead."

"I'll make us something to eat as well."

"Sounds great."

She got up and headed out into the kitchen. Nate widened his eyes and ran a hand over his face. What the hell was in this stuff? He couldn't remember Budweiser being this strong. He got up from his seat and stumbled, bracing himself against the coffee table and chuckling a little. "Oh, if Erika could see me now," he muttered. Holding his bottle, he took another swig and wandered over to a table in the living room to look at one of the photos. He picked it up and squinted. It was a snapshot of a couple in their late forties with a young boy. Was it her brother? If so, why wasn't she in the family shot? He scanned the room and saw more photo frames just above the fireplace, though these were face down. Nate turned them over and noticed that the glass was cracked in two of them and again not one photo had her in it. It seemed odd but then again not everyone wanted their photo taken. He set it down as he heard Mariah return. She came in and he turned and she narrowed her eyes as if trying to determine what he was doing. "Here," she said handing him an opened bottle. He took it.

"Thanks." She clinked hers against his and he took a hard pull on it. "There a bathroom around here?"

"Just down the hallway."

"Wow, maybe going without alcohol has made me more sensitive to it. This stuff is strong," he said stumbling a little and bracing himself against the wall. He squeezed his eyes closed and staggered down the hallway, stopping only to look back. Mariah stood in the doorway watching him. He smiled and entered the bathroom, closing the door behind him. It smelled so bad inside but then again, every house he'd entered over the past few weeks smelled rotten. Stumbling over to the toilet he lifted the seat and grimaced. It was full of feces and piss and reeked to high heaven. Holding his breath, he unzipped and went about relieving himself. While he was doing that he glanced at the medicine cabinet. To the right of him was the bathtub with the shower curtain closed. He might not have given it another thought had it not been for the bloody handprint on the edge. "What the hell?" he muttered. A quick shake, and he zipped up and pulled back the curtain. Then he stumbled back, his eyes widening. "What the fuck!?" Piled up inside the bathtub were the couple and young son from the photo. They had multiple stab wounds to the neck and face and were covered in dried blood. Their faces were pale and lips blue. Flies buzzed around their heads, and maggots had eaten their way into what remained of their flesh.

He swallowed hard, bringing a hand up to his nose. He wanted to vomit but nothing came up. Suddenly there was a knock at the bathroom door, and Nate's head jerked to the side. His heart sped up. His hand went for his sidearm but it was gone. The rifle was in the living room.

"Everything okay in there?" Mariah asked.

"Yeah. Yeah, just finishing up."

Bringing a forearm up to his face to block the overwhelming stench, he closed the curtain and went over to the door and opened it. Mariah was blocking the way. She glanced past him and he swore he saw her lip curl ever so slightly. "You feeling okay?" she asked. "You look a little pale."

"I think I had too much to drink. I should go."

He brushed past her and stumbled again, this time landing on the floor. He rolled over and the ceiling was spinning. It had been a long time since he'd been this drunk. However, something about this didn't feel right. What was in that beer? Had she spiked it? And if so, why?

Nate staggered to his feet and banged into the wall. He held on to it for dear life as if he was teetering on the edge of a cliff. The world around him spun out of control, a dizzying kaleidoscope of images broken up into fragments. He looked at Mariah and could see eight versions of her. "What did you put in that?" he asked her.

"Nate, it's okay. I'll look after you," she said, trying to

guide him into the living room. He threw his arm up, shrugging her off, but it was pointless. He could see darkness creeping in at the corner of his eyes. "What did you give me!?" he yelled, cursing her as he bumped against a table.

"You just need some rest."

"Get off me," he said pushing her back before collapsing on the glass coffee table. The whole thing smashed and then he lost consciousness.

* * *

As the sun peeked over the horizon in the early hours and lit up the forest floor, Corey and the others prepared to move in. A heavy rain had turned the ground to slush and threatened to make the whole operation miserable. Tyler peered through the binoculars, then checked his watch. An hour remained and Allie was still nowhere in sight. The plan was straightforward enough but it relied heavily upon timing and Allie's knowledge of what occurred in camp when supplies arrived. As discussed, Allie and a group from Jude's camp would arrive with multiple ATVs and trailers full of wild game in the usual exchange for ammo and medication. This would create a distraction on the northern side of the camp while they entered from the south. The first order of business was taking out six guards who patrolled the perimeter. Bennington would then cover them from a sniper's position on the outskirts of camp, scanning for further threats they couldn't see from their vantage point. Once inside, all five of them would plant C4 explosives throughout the camp in preparation for the return of the rest of the raiders. Corey and Tyler would extract Allie's sister Madison as soon as Allie indicated where she was located. Bennington would give them the heads-up via radio communication and once Madison was safely out, Allie would once again serve as a distraction while they loaded into the back of a trailer the cartridge reloader and supplies. By that point the ammo and medication would already be loaded. From there they would ambush the trailers and disappear into the night, cutting through the forest. Once they were clear of the camp Corey would remain behind to remotely detonate the explosives upon return of the raiders, which was set to occur within the hour. There was so much that could go wrong and it heavily relied on Allie but there was no way around it.

"Your girl better show," Bennington said peering through his high-powered scope.

"She'll be here. Don't you worry."

"Well the clock's ticking, kid, and my patience isn't what it used to be," he replied. Tyler shot Corey a look and he raised a hand as if to say, don't worry. But he was worrying. How could you not?

* * *

A few hours earlier, Jude was sitting in his office contemplating the previous day. He hadn't slept much that night. His mind had tried to make sense of the intel Ann had provided. Though it was clear where their focus was, the intent was unknown. In the three weeks he'd spent with Tyler, he got a feeling that he was honest, smart, but more importantly a street-savvy kid who'd grown into a man anyone would be proud of, despite his upbringing at the hands of Andy. He had high hopes for him but this changed everything. His initial impression was Andy had put him up to this. That he'd sent him in like a Trojan horse to spy out Camp Olney, and make a connection with Edison's daughter, but that didn't add up. That made him conclude that the whole meet-up with Tyler was driven by Edison. He'd put his daughter up to this but why? What did they hope to achieve? Who else was involved in this? That was why he hung the carrot out in front of Andy to see if he would take it. If he'd agreed to join, it would have confirmed his suspicions but instead he outright refused. He knew him well enough to know if he was lying and he could tell by the look on Andy's face that he wasn't. He truly was put off at the thought of putting the past behind them. So where did that leave him?

Jude took another sip of his coffee.

Camp O'Brien was a valuable asset to their survival. Only a handful of his closest confidants knew its true purpose. Knowing what was on the horizon he had taken every measure to ensure there was enough dry and canned food stockpiled to last at least three years at Camp Olney. Ammo and medical supplies was another thing entirely. His continued relationship with Thomas was vital. Nothing could jeopardize that. Each camp relied on the other for what they provided. Working on a hunch, Jude asked one of his men to bring Allie in to see him.

* * *

Allie was beyond distraught. The thought of never seeing her sister again tormented her. She was angry at herself for thinking she could con Maddox into making the arrangement, and overwhelmed at the thought of Tyler placing himself in harm's way. "He'll be expecting me anytime now," she said to her father. Jude's men had placed her in the cell beside him. Though the bars kept them apart, they chatted through the night. Her father reached through and clutched her hand to reassure her that everything would be okay, but it wouldn't. How could it? If Jude knew what was planned, all he had to do was ensure she didn't show and Tyler and the others would be screwed.

Allie looked across to Andy's cell.

Hours earlier, she'd brought him up to speed on her interaction with Tyler, Corey and the others, and the original plan. He'd listened intently then retreated to the back of his cell without saying a word.

"I need to get out there," she said. "There must be a way out."

Right then one of Jude's men entered and made his way down. "Let's go," he said, unlocking her cell and making a gesture. She looked at her father and slowly rose from her hard bed and made her way out. No sooner had she stepped a foot outside than she made a break for it. She fired a foot into the guard's shin and bolted towards the exit. Bursting outside, she was stopped in her tracks by two armed men pointing rifles at her.

Her hands slowly went up as they ordered her to get on her knees.

The guard she injured came over and slapped her across the back of the head, and she found herself on the ground eating dirt as they clamped her wrists with a zip tie and strong-armed her off to Jude's.

She wriggled within their grasp as she was thrust into his office. Allie turned and spat at the guard. "Piece of shit!"

The guard looked as if he was about to strike her when Jude intervened.

"Enough. Leave us alone."

The hulking man scowled and turned away.

"You really are a firecracker," he said before chuckling.

Allie turned and glared at him.

"Fresh apple juice?" he asked pouring into a glass. She wanted to say no just out of spite but she was thirsty. Jude walked over and cut her ties before handing her the glass. She looked at him through skeptical eyes trying to determine what he was playing at.

"I wanted to speak to you about Tyler. He's my son. I care a lot for him, and I would hate to see harm come to him."

"Then you should speak with your other son, as I

don't think he shares the same sentiment," Allie replied with a disgruntled glance.

He smiled before gulping down some of his juice. "Maddox just needs time to get to know him better. Even I do. But one thing that is important is discipline. Without it we are like a rudderless ship. It's what keeps us on track, reminds us of our duties."

"What are you going to do with him?"

Jude motioned for her to take a seat. "Well that depends on you, Allie. I know you were watching the camp. Your interest is obvious. You want to see your sister again. But why Tyler? Why get him involved if your purpose was to get Maddox to convince me to send you in with supplies? Where does he come into all of this?"

She shrugged.

"Come on now. You know I will eventually find out."

She refused to say anything. It was the only hope she had of protecting him.

"Allie. One way or the other. I'm going to know. Now you got him into this, do you want him to come to harm?"

She shook her head.

"Do want him to suffer for your decisions?"

"No."

"Then do what's right. Tell me what you had planned. Where is Tyler right now?"

Her chin dipped. Once he saw that she wasn't going to speak, Allie thought he would just send her back to the cell but that wasn't what he had in mind. Jude rose from his desk and came around and perched on the edge. "Maybe I'm going about this the wrong way. You want to see your sister, yes?"

She lifted her eyes but said nothing.

He continued. "I will take that as a yes. What about if I said that Madison could return here? Live with you? What then?"

Her mouth opened ever so slightly and her heartbeat sped up.

"You know I can make that arrangement, don't you?" He paused. "But I need you to do something for me."

He was beginning to sound like Maddox, or maybe that was where Maddox learned it from. Either way she didn't trust him anymore than his son.

"What?" she asked naively. "I won't kill him."

Jude snorted. "Maddox. He's, uh…quite the wild card. No. I'm not asking for you to kill him. Don't worry. No harm will come to Tyler. He's my son after all. Misguided but that's to be expected after years under Andy's thumb. No, he's my son and in time I should be able to unravel, redirect and create new bonds of trust. But as it stands, I can't do that without knowing what you told him."

She stared back unsure.

"I need to know, and I need to know now."

Allie couldn't hold it in any longer. "I told him the truth. About this place. You. My sister. He was going to help me get her back."

"Okay. Now we're getting somewhere." He sat down on the edge of the desk and ran a hand around the back of his neck. "So, how did you intend to get Madison back?"

She took a deep breath, hesitating to say anything more than that.

"You do want to be with your sister, yes?"

Allie nodded.

"What if I said you could see your father too?"

Her father meant everything. After losing her mother she would do anything to protect him. "What do you want of me?"

He lifted two fingers. "Come closer and I'll tell you."

Chapter 21

"Where the hell is she?!" Markowitz yelled in Tyler's face as he lowered the binoculars. Tyler glanced at his watch. Cold rain splashed against it and ran off the top of his rain jacket. Everyone's nerves were on edge. It had been years since they'd worked together and even longer since they'd tackled any operation as dangerous as this. Tyler took the binos from him and scanned the terrain. She should have been there by now.

"I knew it. I knew this would happen," Markowitz said lifting a hand in the air

"Calm down," Holden said. "Not everyone operates on your schedule."

"My schedule?" he said getting up in his face. "Do I have to remind you that this entire operation relies on timing? Get that wrong and we'll find ourselves buried in a shallow grave." He shook his head. "I say we pull out. It's too risky."

"We didn't come this far to leave now," Corey said.

"You want to take the risk. Be my guest but…"

"There she is," Tyler said acting all theatrical and pointing towards the northern side. There was a line of three ATVs hauling trailers with canvas covering the meat, some of which was sticking out the back.

The rest of the group turned his way and Markowitz was the first to confirm it. He slapped Tyler on the back. "You're lucky, kid. Real lucky."

Tyler looked at Corey and gave a strained smile.

"Let's move out," Corey said grabbing up his soaked backpack and cradling his rifle. The sky above was a gunmetal gray with brooding clouds squeezing out the faintest rays of sunshine. The sound of thunder rolled in the distance making it clear the weather wouldn't get any better. Their boots sank into the wet earth as they trudged down through the forest towards the camp.

It didn't take them long to get into position.

Six armed guards shrouded by heavy hooded jackets eyed the perimeter and walked back and forth. "What we got, Bennington?" Corey asked over the comms.

"Tyler's girl has entered the camp. A group of ten have gone out to meet her. You are clear to engage. I got the first one in my sight."

Corey, Tyler and Bennington prepared to take out the guards. Only the heavy rain and noise of the ATVs on the north side masked the sound of their suppressed gunshots as three of the guards buckled and dropped out of sight. Moving fast, Corey shifted into a new position and took aim. Over the comms he heard Bennington tell him that he'd taken out the fourth. "Tango down." He breathed out slowly and squeezed the trigger, and got a clean head shot, sending the fifth on his way. The initial attack was over before the last guard who Tyler dropped had time to know his comrades were out of service. With the perimeter clear, the five of them moved in leaving Bennington to watch for threats and guide them safely through the maze of tents. Rain tapped against tents, earth and trees, beating out the rhythm of nature as it washed the world clean. The rules were clear. Engage only when necessary. This wasn't about killing everyone in sight, only covering their tracks and ensuring they got in and out with the least amount of damage. The C4 would take care of the rest. Markowitz and the other two fanned out as soon as they breached the main campground.

"Corey. Hold. Two Tango's at 3 o'clock," Bennington said as Corey was coming up between two tents. "Hold." He dropped to a knee and kept his rifle out ready to squeeze off two rounds if needed. But there was no need, the couple turned at the last second and entered a tent. "All clear, they're gone."

Corey raised two fingers and motioned to Tyler to press on.

Due to the size of the camp they anticipated that anything of value would be at the center, no doubt in the wood cabins. As they moved through the camp, they planted C4 and waited for Allie to give them a clear indication of where her sister was being held. Markowitz came over the comms.

"That's the south and east covered."

"Copy that," Corey replied before ducking inside an empty tent and looking around. It was basic. Military-style folding cots with green blankets and white pillows. These folks weren't living the high life despite all the supplies they were stealing. He peered out the tent slit at some of the silver Airstream RVs. There was hierarchy to this group. Tents on the outside, RVs inside of that and a few cabins at the core. Besides the cabins it seemed as if they had it set up ready to move out if push came to shove. How many more were set up like this throughout the county? And which one contained Morning Star? Who the hell was it? He'd entertained the thought of his father, or the mayor or even Jude, but could it be that it was just some random lunatic, much like Denise? Someone with a history of prepping? No. They had to carry some weight to convince this many people to get behind them. His father said that many Americans would flock to FEMA camps when disaster struck out of desperation even though they knew their rights would be trampled. People were finicky — driven by basic needs that had to be met even if it meant going against what they believed.

"I have eyes on her sister," Bennington said, then repeated it.

"Roger that. Markowitz, how's Gibby holding up? Over."

"No problem."

"Tyler. Where you at?"

"Look out the tent. I'm at 11 o'clock."

Corey peered out and saw him in a tent holding a knife up to a woman's throat. "What the hell?"

"She walked in on me. I had no other option."

"Take her out," Markowitz said.

"I'm not doing that."

"Then I will."

One second Tyler was standing in the entranceway holding a struggling woman, the next he had red mist all over his face and a limp body hanging on his arm. There was a bullet wound to her head.

"Damn it!" Corey said in a low voice. "You could have

injured my brother."

"You wanted her to raise the alarm?"

"Markowitz."

"It's done."

"Would you two shut the fuck up? We have a job to do here," Holden said.

Before he could get into it with him, Bennington told him to head out. "Now's the time. Go. Go." From between the tents Corey could see Allie hugging her sister and pulling away while others loaded up the trailers. Madison disappeared into the tent as Allie went to assist the others. She cast a glance over her shoulder as if looking to see where they were. She made a low gesture with two fingers towards a cabin, the signal for which one contained the ammo. Chances of her seeing them were slim to none. They moved like shadows in the early dawn, sidling up behind RVs. The plan was straightforward, Tyler would head in and collect Madison while Corey led the others to the cabin. He had no idea how large the machine was but Allie was convinced it was moveable.

Corey had seen a few while growing up. They varied in size but were constructed in a similar manner. There was an area to load brass shell casings, and a tube that could be filled with powder. Shells would drop down, get filled with powder and a bullet would be placed on top, it was standard. Some were more complex than others but that was the guts of it.

As the four of them converged on the cabin, darting in and out of the spaces between RVs, Corey caught sight of Gibby choking a man out. He lowered him to the ground and continued on using hand gestures mostly and whispers over the comms only when needed. Drenched by the rain they made it to the rear of the cabin and Corey peered through the windows. In the distance they could hear raiders yelling as Allie and crew instructed them on where to put items in a trailer. Water rolled down panes of glass as Corey tried to see if there was anyone inside. No movement. "Moving in."

He tried the handle and it opened. Pulling back the door he ducked inside. As soon as he entered, he could hear three people talking. He figured they would have someone watching over the machine, as well those working tirelessly to create more ammo. It was the lifeblood of survival for a society that was lost in anarchy. The new form of currency wasn't food or water but a projectile. Beans, bullets and bandages was what his father would say. Yet bullets took precedence over everything else. Without that an individual was working at a disadvantage. Of course it would only last so long. Eventually powder would be hard to get hold of and in time humanity would have to go back to primitive methods like bows, knives and swords.

Holden came up behind Corey and patted him on the shoulder, he made a gesture and peeled away to the left through a doorway while Gibby went to the right. Markowitz was covering the outside. Silently they crossed the breadth of the home until he heard movement from a room off to his right. Corey slid the rifle behind him and pulled his knife. The door opened and a man stumbled out doing up his zipper with his head down. He glanced up, his eyes widened and before he could open his mouth Corey grabbed him, hand over mouth, and jammed the tip of the blade up into his skull. He dragged him back into the bathroom and laid him out.

By the time he made it out, Gibby and Holden had taken care of the other two. There before them in a large living room were boxes and boxes of brass casings, primers and bags of powder. At the center, several seemingly average-size cartridge reloaders were attached to a thick table. They were a common product that nearly anyone could buy but often were forgotten by preppers. Yet it was vital if you wanted to stay ahead of the curve.

"How the hell are we gonna get all this shit out of here?"

"We'll need to pull one of those trailers around."

"It's already been taken care of. Allie said it was the last trailer to be loaded. They often fill the other trailers with dry goods and medication and leave loading the ammo until they're just about to leave."

Holden stared at Corey. "That's how we're getting out

of here, isn't it? Under the tarps covering the goods."

He nodded. "We'll be meeting up with Tyler, Madison and Bennington later. Once we are out of sight of the camp, Allie will stop the ATV, causing the others to come to a halt. That's when we'll take the rest, cut through the forest and..."

Holden swept back his rifle. "Hold on a minute. But what about the others? Jude's men. Allie isn't alone."

"Casualties of war," Corey said. "Now let's get this shit loaded into those boxes over there." In the next room boxes had been stacked up with the names of people scribbled down the side. Corey ran his hand over some of the ones that were ready to go out. Jude's name was on eight boxes. Others had different names. Well, I'll be, he thought. The raiders had been smart, they weren't hogging everything they were taking for themselves, they were trading it to others at a cost. It was like selling on the black market. Jude's camp had to deliver wild game in exchange for what they wanted, for another camp it could be something else. There was still so much about the raiders' operation that was unknown. Who was Morning Star? Did he or she even exist? Allie said they answered to the one-eyed man, Thomas. Maybe it was just him creating some mysterious persona in order to give people a symbol, a figure to rally behind. Like a guru of a religion.

"Markowitz, you see that trailer yet?"

"They're still loading up," he replied.

"Tyler. You got Madison?"

"Closing in. Had a few difficulties. Nothing I couldn't handle."

Corey returned to loading the ammo machines into the boxes along with casings and powder and burying it all below what they already had been assigned.

"You know they're going to come in here," Holden said.

"Of course. And we'll take care of it."

He didn't need to explain what that meant. There were those that had to die. They had no qualms about killing these people. Willing participants or not, they had taken out many good people in Whitefish, officers, volunteers and even a few close friends and family. In his mind they were just like Gabriel, each and every one of them.

"Corey. Here she comes," Markowitz said backing into the cabin and retreating into the darkest recess. Corey and the others moved into position taking cover behind doorways, in the bathroom and behind furniture. Sweat trickled off his brow. He knew this would be the closest they would get to the alarm being raised. All it would take was for one of them to spot them and yell, and they would have a battle on their hands.

"Listen up. Use weapons only if required. Knives only. We get this done, we are home free." The sound of an ATV rumbling in got Corey's nerves on edge.

They heard voices, several outside, Allie's was among them. "We'll give you a hand bringing it out," she said.

"No. You stay here."

A storm door creaked open and heavy footsteps walked in. Corey peered out the bathroom door as three men made a beeline for the storage area where boxes were stacked. "Grab those." One by one they lugged them out, all the while not realizing they were doing the hard work for them. As they came in to collect the last load, one of them must have spotted Markowitz, as he lunged forward driving his knife into the man's chest.

In an instant, all hell broke loose.

Chapter 22

A dull light stabbed Nate's eyes as he awoke with the worst headache ever. It came with double vision, which confused and disoriented him. As his sight cleared and he remembered where he was, a shot of cold fear went through him.

Mariah. Beer and staggering into the bathroom. The dead family in the bathtub. The world spinning. Crashing into the table. How long had he been unconscious? Where was he? He could hear music playing lightly in the background. It took a few more seconds to recognize he was in the dining room at the head of the table. It was prepared with cutlery, a plate in front of him, a teapot, cups and another setup at the far end. At the center was a flickering candle. The drapes to his right were pulled back and he could see into the backyard.

Nate tried to move but couldn't.

He looked down and saw the rope. His wrists were

tied to the chair as were his ankles. *What the fuck?* Why had she done this? He squirmed in the chair but it was useless. She'd made sure that he wasn't going anywhere. He tried to rock it back but there was little room between him and the wall. It was as if someone had shoved the table up close to prevent him from trying anything. Nate listened for signs of Mariah, expecting her to enter. Surely she wouldn't tie him up and just leave him here?

"Hello?"

No response. No one came. Well at least he was alone. Maybe there was a way he could get out of this. He squeezed his eyes shut, feeling a band of pain around his head. He'd woken up with hangovers many times but nothing like this. She'd spiked his drink with something strong. I've got to get out of here, he thought as he tried rocking to the side. Before he could build some momentum, he heard a door open, and someone entered humming.

Mariah. She was back.

She appeared in the doorway wearing a pretty dress

with her hair pulled back in a bun. Nothing about her screamed lunatic but that was who he was looking at. She had to be unstable to do this. "Oh, you're awake. I was just out picking some flowers. Aren't these beautiful?" She carried in a white vase of purple wildflowers and set them at the center of the table near the candle. She leaned forward and smelled them, beaming with delight.

"Why are you doing this?" Nate asked.

"We're going to have breakfast, silly."

He tugged at his restraints. "This," he said gritting his teeth.

She didn't give an answer but left the room, returning minutes later with a bowl that was filled with fruit. She took his plate. "I hope you like oranges. It was all I could find in a can. They taste delicious."

"Mariah!" Nate bellowed tugging again to make it clear that she still hadn't answered him. The smiled disappeared from her face and she scowled at him.

"Now don't be rude. No one likes a rude guest."

"Untie these ropes now!"

"No. No. We need to have breakfast. You know it's considered one of the most important meals of the day. My mother once said…"

"Mariah."

She snapped. One second she was rattling off something to do with her past, the next Mariah grabbed a fork and jammed it into the top of his left hand. Nate screamed in agony.

"Now look what you've made me do!" she yelled at him.

Blood streamed out and down his hand pooling between his fingers.

She left it there, sticking upwards so that every tiny movement of his hand caused him further agony.

"You batshit crazy bitch!" he bellowed back.

Not liking that reply she grabbed the knife in one hand and his throat in the other and squeezed tightly. "Don't make me pluck your eyes out," she said seething, spit forming at the corners of her lips. "Now are you going to behave?" She squeezed his throat tighter until he started choking. Nate couldn't believe this was happening to him. He never imagined that the person he came to help would turn out to be a psycho. He nodded and she released her bear grip. Instantly her scowl disappeared and she went back to scooping fruit onto his plate. "Looks like we are in for some bad weather so we won't be able to go out today." She scooped some fruit onto her plate and placed it at the other end and took a seat. Nate glared at her. She took a few bites, smiled and then frowned before placing her fork down. "Oh, I'm sorry. How rude of me." She got up and dragged a chair over and removed the bloody fork from his hand and wiped it with a napkin before stabbing some fruit and bringing it to his mouth. Nate pursed his lips and turned his head.

"Come on now. You need to eat."

When he wouldn't open, she slammed an open hand on the table causing everything to bounce and clatter. "EAT IT!" she shouted before returning to a gentle voice. "Or I'm going to…"

Nate opened his mouth and she shoveled the fruit in.

"That's it. Very good."

He chewed a few times and just when she thought he was going to swallow he spat it in her face. Her head jerked back in surprise before a scowl formed. He expected her to react violently but she didn't. She slowly lowered the fork in her hand, took a napkin and wiped her face before rising and leaving the room.

He snorted, a sense of satisfaction washing over him. It didn't last.

He listened. The sound of cutlery, then cupboards banging. "Ah, there it is," she said before returning to the room holding a crème brûlée torch. She crossed the room with a blank expression and grabbed his bloody wrist. "Can't have that wound getting an infection. Now can we?"

"Get off me. Nah, nah, come on. Don't be stupid. No. No! NO!" he yelled getting louder as she brought it up and hit the red button on the back. A tightly formed blue flame shot out, hissing. Mariah brought it down on his hand and singed his flesh until he passed out from the pain.

* * *

A detonation of pure adrenaline jolted Corey into action. Reacting fast, he burst out of the bathroom and threw the blade in his hand at the raider closest to him. It spun multiple times before plunging deep into his back. His legs buckled and he collapsed, still alive. Holden took out the third by slashing his throat from behind.

Corey pounced on his guy, pressing his face into the ground and using the knife multiple times to end him.

The young man that was part of the crew that came with Allie turned to flee but was blocked at the door by Gibby. "Don't kill him," Allie yelled. "He's with me. He's just a teen." The scared boy looked at Gibby's blade that was inches away from his neck.

"Gibby," Corey said trying to break him from the trancelike state he was in. His hand was shaking. "Gibby, put it down. It's okay." He scrambled over to the boy and got between them, pushing the teen back towards Allie and telling her to keep a hold on him. "It's all right, man." And just like that Gibby snapped out of it. It was as if he was frozen in time and was somewhere else in his mind.

Corey shot a glance at Markowitz. He was wiping his knife on the dead man at his feet. "What? He saw me."

There was no time to dispute that.

"Just get the last box and let's get out of here."

While his guys finished loading up the trailer and getting beneath the tarp in preparation to leave, Corey had a word with Allie inside the cabin. The boy she was with stared at the bodies around him, a look of shock, horror perhaps as if witnessing death for the first time. "Tyler has your sister. We are nearly home free. Can we trust him?" he asked looking at the boy.

She nodded.

"Is there anything that I need to know before we leave?"

She shook her head.

"You sure?" he asked. They were taking a big risk. There was a chance that the raiders would stop them on the way out to check the load, but he asked Allie and she told him that it was fine. The load-ups were done by raiders to avoid them taking more than they should. Still, it made him feel uneasy. Once underneath that tarp, they wouldn't be able to do shit until she stopped on the outskirts of the camp.

"How many were in the crew?"

"Four others."

"We going to have a problem?" He was referring to when she would fake a flat tire and stop. That would be their signal to emerge from under the tarp and take the three trailers. He knew they were armed, everyone from Jude's camp was.

"Where is my sister?"

"As I told you. You'll see her soon."

Corey glanced out just in time to see Bennington slip under the tarp. Unconvinced that Allie had a handle on the boy, he approached him, still holding the bloody knife he'd killed the raider with. "What's your name?"

"Sully."

"Well Sully. You see this," he said holding the knife out. "I won't hesitate to use it if you say anything, or give anyone any indication we are under that tarp. You hear me?"

He swallowed and nodded.

"Do what she says. Deviate from it and today is going to end badly for you. Do I make myself clear?" He nodded but Corey was still unconvinced. "Yes or no?"

"Yes," he said.

"You're scaring him," Allie said putting herself between them. Corey studied both of them for a few seconds more before he nudged them out. He cast a glance back at the fallen men and exited, climbing underneath the tarp, out of sight. The heavy sound of rain tapping against the tarp made it hard to hear what Allie was saying to the boy before the ATV roared to life and they felt a jolt as it took off transporting them to the north side to join the others. As daylight filtered in, Corey looked at Markowitz. He watched him adjust his grip on his rifle. Water trickled off his face. Humidity and wet clothes sticking to their skin made the short ride a misery. The ATV came to a halt and the engine turned off allowing him to eavesdrop on the conversation Allie was having.

"Thomas, do you have news?" She asked.

"We do. Tell Jude that Morning Star has approved his request. It will be set up for two days from now. As the final light of day casts a shadow over the foothills. Have him come alone. He will be taken to the cabin up on the ridge. He knows where it is. If there is anyone else who follows, it will be called off and he won't be given another opportunity." He heard the sound of boots in sludge as if Thomas had got closer to her. "And remember, we have eyes everywhere."

"Understood."

The ATV rumbled to life and Corey jerked forward as it pulled away. The short trip away from Camp O'Brien was a bumpy ride. They had to cling to the boxes to prevent themselves from bouncing out. Allie was the first in the line of three ATVs hauling trailers out. They had no idea when she would pull off, only that it when it happened, she would release the hooks on the tarp and they would burst out and take the remaining four at gunpoint. It was agreed they wouldn't be killed, only captured along with Allie to make sure suspicion didn't fall on her. She would later say that she had no idea they were there, drawing attention away and giving her a solid alibi. A day later Allie would join her sister in Whitefish and leave behind Camp Olney for good. It was straightforward. Simple even.

As they traveled along the trail back to the road, they heard the sound of an army of ATVs approaching. It was the raiders returning from the night of pillaging towns in the county. Their off-road vehicles shot by them not stopping. Minutes from now they would hear the sound of explosions as charges were detonated remotely by Bennington and Camp O'Brien and all its inhabitants would be buried under debris.

Tyler, Madison and Bennington would then head to the rendezvous point.

By evening they would be chugging back beers, and celebrating putting an end to one of the largest threats facing Flathead County.

Another twenty minutes of riding and then he felt the ATV swerve to the edge of the road. The engine shut off and Allie yelled that she had a flat. Behind them they heard her crew slow down. Out the corner of his eye, Corey saw Allie's boots beneath the tarp as she came up and unhooked the tarp on one side before going around and doing the same. In that instant all four of them burst upwards, rifles on the ready.

What occurred next was not what they planned.

Instead of finding themselves staring at four shocked and scared people, they heard the sound of guns cocking and saw rifles and handguns aimed at them. Surrounding them on all four sides were at least twenty horses, all of them ridden by Jude's men.

Corey turned slowly as they commanded them to lower their weapons.

There was hesitation but they weren't fools. They

knew when they were outnumbered. Seated high up on a dark black horse was Jude. He leaned forward staring directly at Corey. "I'm shocked. Really, I am. After what I did for you, Corey."

"This is between us and the raiders."

"Not if my informer is correct," he said glancing off to his right. Corey followed his gaze and looked upon Allie. She lowered her head, guilt overwhelming her.

"I'm sorry," she muttered. "I had no other choice."

"Don't be hard on her. She did it for her sister. I'm sure you understand the value of blood. To be honest, she really didn't have any other option. It was that or..." He stopped and raised his hand to his ear. "You hear that?" he asked looking back at Corey. "Silence. Though I'm sure you were expecting something else, am I right?"

Corey gritted his teeth. Sold out. Why would she do that? They had her sister. She was free. Something must have gone wrong, or maybe not. Perhaps Tyler didn't know her. Maybe his men were right.

"I knew it," Markowitz muttered under his breath.

"You bitch," he said aloud.

The sound of horses snorting, and their hooves adjusting in the rain-soaked mud dominated. "Your father is waiting for you," Jude said. "All I need to know is where is Tyler?"

What did that mean? Was his father in on this? Was he Morning Star? Corey's eyes shifted towards the forest and Jude noticed. He jerked his head towards the lush green trees. "In there?"

If Tyler could have heard, Corey would have shouted for him to run but he knew they were miles away inside the forest.

"Toss your rifles," Jude said. "It's over." Reluctantly, one by one they released them. Rain continued to pour, soaking through their clothes as the sound of ATVs coming from Camp O'Brien got closer.

Chapter 23

The remote detonator hadn't worked. Bennington tried multiple times until he cursed and tossed it at the ground. "Something's not right."

Tyler stood near a tree with Madison beside him. She was taller than Allie, blond hair but with the same eye color, and was wearing tight jeans, a dark tight-fitting top and a black baseball cap.

"Obviously," he replied. "Maybe one of the guys rigged it wrong."

Bennington shook his head. "Kid, in all my years in the military we never once had it not work. No. It's something else." He raised his binos and scanned the terrain of the camp. "Damn it. There is no chance of getting back in. There are far too many in the camp. We need to abort the mission."

"Abort? Not without Corey. No, we stay with the plan. We're meant to meet them at the rendezvous point twenty minutes from now."

Bennington turned and handed him the binoculars. "That was if there were no problems. Look towards the east."

Tyler brought them up to his eyes and squinted. On a trail heading out of the camp were ten of the twenty ATVs that had originally left. "And?" Tyler asked.

"Isn't it obvious? The mission had been compromised."

"They're leaving the camp. That's all."

"Shit, kid. The explosives never went off. The raiders just returned and now half the group has left. Do the math. If we leave now we stand a chance of making it back to town before we find ourselves as the hunted."

"You don't know that."

"You ever served, kid?"

Tyler shook his head.

"When you spend enough time in places where even angels fear to tread, you get a gut instinct for this." He reached down and snatched up his backpack. "I'm heading out, with or without you. And before you say anything, it's what Corey would have wanted."

Tyler stabbed a finger towards the earth. "I'm not leaving my brother behind."

"Or my sister," Madison was quick to add.

Bennington stopped walking and turned, his prosthetic running limb digging into the ground that had quickly turned to slush. Rain trickled off his forehead.

"Five minutes. That's all you get. Then I'm out."

Tyler nodded and they took off through the forest towards the rendezvous point.

* * *

Nate awoke to find he was still in the same shitty situation. The ropes cut into his skin, that's how tight they were. But Mariah wasn't going to trust him to be loose in the house. There was a reason behind all of this. Perhaps he stood a better chance of escaping by finding out why than struggling to resist. After all he was still alive. That had to count for something. Still bound to the tall chair with his forearms held firmly against the armrests and his ankles tied to the legs of the chair, he waited for her to return from the bathroom. Mariah eyed him carefully as she took her seat, smoothing out her pants before tucking into her plate of fruit.

"They're not your family, are they?" he asked.

She lifted her eyes and chewed without replying. He would need to probe deeper to get even a crumb. "I saw the photos, you're not in any of them. So, who are they? Neighbors? Someone that hurt you?" When she refused to speak, he shrugged and tried to use the us vs. them approach. It was an old-school marketing technique he'd learned when he'd taken a job in car sales. Just as people would rally behind the underdog, groups loved to stick together over the same issues. Religion, politics, the government, you name it, when you could get on the same page as someone else, they would often open up. Car sales was no different. It was — I'm not really a salesman, I'm your friend, I'll make sure you get the best deal on this car by giving you my salesman discount. When in reality it was just a farce, a means of luring people into a false sense of security. The deal was there regardless but the customer didn't know that. It was all about positioning yourself as being on the same team. Rubbing shoulders. Friends. Letting them in on a secret.

Nate shook his head. "Whatever. I actually thought you were different from those out there. The mindless sheep that wander through this town like they think the law doesn't apply to them. The ones that hurt others to get their needs met. That's why I helped you. I figured you were a victim like me."

She stared at him. "Like you?" Mariah took the bait.

"Yeah," he nodded. "Let me guess, you were taken advantage of by someone?" He snorted. "I know I was. I trusted them and they broke that trust." He lowered his chin and shook his head as if trying to give the impression he was reliving the moment. "That's why I was out there. On my way over to set things straight but I spotted you and…" he trailed off. "Look, for what it's worth. Whatever reason you have for tying me up I expect it's a good one. I can't say I understand but I want you to know that I don't hold it against you."

Her brow furrowed as if she was looking for a crack in his façade. Of course that's what it was. He had every intention of putting her two feet underground when he got out but first he needed to earn her trust. "You think I can get some of that fruit now? I'm kind of hungry."

Reluctant to repeat the same scenario she sat there staring at him until Nate tried to lean forward and reach the plate. A feat that if achieved would have been quite remarkable being as he could hardly move a muscle.

Mariah set her fork down and made her way over. She picked up his fork and without saying a word stabbed some of the fruit in front of him. A final moment of hesitation before she brought it to his lips and he opened, chewed and swallowed. "Wow. That's pretty good," he said. As if he were a child unable to feed himself, she fed him the rest of the fruit without issue. Then she gave him a sip of water and wiped his lips with a napkin. He thanked her and breathed out. The frown on her face didn't leave. She still didn't trust him but that would change given enough time. The question was, how long would it take? He wasn't sure he could handle being strapped to this chair for much longer. His hands were beginning to turn a light shade of purple.

* * *

Tyler grew anxious as twenty minutes passed without any sign of them. Bennington leaned up against a tree trying to take shelter from the steady downpour. Madison sat on a large mossy boulder, gnawing the skin on the edge of her thumb.

"Time's up, kid," Bennington said. "They're not coming."

Tyler shook his head, unable to accept that. "I need to see for myself."

"You got a death wish?"

"He's my brother."

"And he knew the risks. He can take care of himself. Now let's go." Bennington pushed away from the tree and cradled his rifle as he trudged off leaving them behind. Tyler looked at Madison and could tell from her expression she wasn't comfortable leaving without first knowing what had happened. He was done trying to convince Bennington.

"You coming?" Bennington asked.

Tyler gave one shake of his head. He extended a hand to Madison and she crossed the forest clearing and took it. "Go on without us," Tyler said before turning to head north.

Bennington sighed. "Stubborn asshole. Just like your brother."

* * *

Not far from Tyler's location, the four of them sat in waterlogged soil with their hands tied behind their back. Corey was cold, wet and miserable. He didn't need to see Thomas to know how this would end. However, his mind wasn't on whether he lived or died but only on Tyler and Bennington. All he could hope for was they were as far away from there as possible. A slew of ATVs swerved nearby filling the air with the smell of gas and kicking up dirt. "Thomas," Jude said approaching him. The one-eyed man dismounted and glanced at them. "It's all under control."

Without saying a word, Thomas motioned with a gesture of his head for his people to take Corey and the other three. Jude immediately intervened blocking their way. A few of his own backed him up.

"Step aside, Jude, this is between us and them," Thomas said in a controlled voice as though he was in the habit of being obeyed.

"You have my word it will be handled, but not here or by you."

Thomas' brow furrowed as he got closer to him. "They killed nine of ours."

"And there will be punishment for such an act but we are taking them with us. I have unfinished business that requires them alive."

Thomas smiled and stepped closer. "Do I have to remind you how this works?"

"They are coming with us," Jude said in a firm tone.

Thomas smiled, turned and walked among the twenty-odd people that had come with him. "Convenient." He breathed in deeply. "These men show up and kill our people, stow away in your trailers and you want to be the one to take them and dish out justice?"

Jude didn't respond.

"If I'm not mistaken, I almost get the impression that perhaps you were behind this attack."

"Us? You're out of your goddamn mind."

"Am I?" he sneered, snapping back. "Then tell me this. If you knew this raid on our camp was to occur, then why did you wait until our people were dead? Unless of course you hoped to benefit from this."

Jude looked back at him in disbelief. "Why would I do that when we are days away from the merger?"

"Perhaps you changed your mind and wanted to be at the helm of this ship." Thomas said, giving him a steely look before walking over to the trailers and rifling through boxes. He removed one of the cartridge reloaders.

Jude chuckled. "You have no clue. Trust me when I say that we are doing you a favor, not the other way around. You don't see the bigger picture."

"Don't I? You are doing us a favor? You are nothing but a face in an ocean of people who can deliver what you have traded." He waved him out of the way. "Now step down or we will take you with them."

"I'd like to see that," Jude said. In an instant, rifles were raised on both sides. The sound of guns cocking could be heard, and everyone yelling at each other. The tension could be cut with a knife.

"Enough!" Thomas bellowed raising a hand. Silence fell upon them, except for the pitter-patter of rain striking clothes, trailer tarps and the earth. Thomas eyed Jude with a look of disgust. Jude was unmoved by the show of force.

Corey had to admit it was a ballsy move. But it raised a question. What was the unfinished business? And what was Jude's bigger picture?

"I don't see what interest Morning Star has in you but be assured of this. What has occurred here today will be made known. How that will affect the merger will be determined. Mark my words," he said shaking his finger at Jude. "This is far from over."

Thomas raised a hand and at a simple click of his fingers his people fired up their engines. Thomas returned to his ATV, casting a stern glance back one final time before he spun his tires, leaving them in the wake of tension. Jude exhaled and lowered his head for a second before turning his attention to his men.

"Take them back."

Maddox approached his father. "And Tyler?"

"He'll return."

"You know he's out there, Father. Let me take a few men and bring him in."

He nodded and Maddox gestured with two fingers to eight guys to follow him. They quickly mounted their horses and galloped away heading for the tree line.

"Unharmed. Maddox. You hear me?" Jude shouted.

Maddox didn't reply.

Chapter 24

Minutes earlier, from the covering of the forest, Tyler zoomed in on the gathering of horses and ATVs surrounding Corey and the others. His heart stuck in his throat feeling helpless. Unable to hear the conversation, he could only imagine as he watched the confusing confrontation play out between two headstrong men. Jude's men on horses lifted their weapons at the raiders while yelling ensued. For someone that was supposed to be in league with the raiders, Jude's actions brought that into question. What the hell was going on? Was Jude coming to the defense of his brother? Or was this a battle of egos? Leadership gone awry?

The thought of killing Thomas passed through his mind as he centered the crosshair of his carbine on his head. One squeeze of the trigger could change everything. But would it? Wouldn't someone else just step up? And then of course, if he opened fire now, he would give away his position and bring the whole goddamn army down on him. Tyler removed his finger and kept it on the outside of the trigger guard. He panned the rifle across the faces of the team then slowed as he focused in on Allie. What had happened? Had she given them up? Turned coat? Was she working for Jude all this time? No. He didn't get that impression, and yet despite his reluctance to accept it, his eyes told him another story.

"Allie," Madison said in a low voice as she caught sight of her sister. She went to step out of the tree coverage when Tyler pulled her back.

"You will get us killed."

"But…"

"No."

He turned back in time to see Thomas and crew pulling away and Maddox talking with his father. A few more seconds and he and eight of Jude's men galloped away heading directly for them. A cold chill washed over him as he pulled Madison back and told her to run. They had minutes before they would be upon them. They needed to get deeper into the forest where it was so thick that horses would have a hard time getting through. There were only so many clear trails, the rest was overgrown and dense brush.

"Go. Go!"

The moment of hesitation was cut short as rounds lanced away from the riders tearing up the dirt nearby.

They'd been spotted and talking wasn't in the agenda.

Scared and confused, Madison broke into a sprint leaping over fallen trees.

Tyler knew they wouldn't make it unless he held them off. Seeing Madison disappear into the forest, he turned and aimed his weapon and unloaded a single round that struck one of the eight men in the chest, knocking him off the back of the horse. *One down, seven to go.* It wouldn't stop them but it would momentarily slow them. Sure enough he saw Maddox pull on the reins and yell at the others. Tyler rose from his knee and caught the eye of Maddox before he fled deep into the forest.

His thoughts flashed to when he was younger. Another

one of Andy's survival tests. He recalled being let loose in the forest, pursued by multiple people. Tyler swallowed hard, beads of sweat forming on his brow as he ran. He was reliving the whole damn thing again. At least back then he had darkness as cover. Now it was morning, and the sun was rising high in the sky flooding the forest floor with bands of warm light. The odds were stacked against him. It would have been easy to let panic set in. Tyler purposely slowed his breathing trying to get a grip on the fear before it got the better of him. It could be both an asset and a curse, Andy would say. It didn't take long to catch up with Madison. He found her huddled behind a mossy boulder as he leapt off the top. There was little time to come up with an effective plan and these weren't just average people he was going up against. They would have been trained by Jude, trained to be cautious and spot danger. He knew they were in deep shit. If only Bennington had stuck around.

Rounds suddenly chewed up the trees and dirt near them. Tyler lunged forward taking Madison to the earth with him as a flurry of bullets snapped at the boulder above. "Can you fire a gun?" he asked. She pulled a face. "Of course you can." He hesitated for a second but knew that he'd increase the odds of their survival if both of them were packing heat. He handed her his Glock and an additional magazine and wrapped both of his hands around hers as he said, "No heroics. Stay here behind cover. I'll try and draw them away. If you get a clear shot, take it. The quicker we lower their numbers, the better."

She nodded. He wriggled away across the ground. He couldn't believe it had come to this. Having looters, inmates, even psychotic religious freaks shooting at him was one thing, but not his half-brother.

Scrambling to his feet he darted out returning fire and drawing them to the west of Madison. They'd dismounted their horses and tied them up and had fanned out throughout the forest.

"Only one way out of here, Tyler," Maddox said.

"Jude approve this?" Tyler bellowed before changing position and dashing from one tree to the next. Each time he took the risk of being hit but he needed to put some distance between him and Madison. Right now they had no idea she was behind the boulder and he planned to keep it that way.

"You should have stayed in Whitefish," Maddox replied.

"Come now, brother, you wouldn't kill your own blood, would you?" Tyler shot back knowing it would rile him up. In the three weeks he'd spent in Camp Olney, Maddox had made it crystal-clear that he didn't accept him, not as a friend, and sure as hell not as a half-brother. Tyler tore forward across the ground and pulled himself behind another large boulder. He tried to keep Madison in his line of sight to be sure that Maddox's pals weren't coming up on her. One tried, unaware she was there, and Tyler forced him back with a round that took off his ear.

More bullets whizzed overhead. Pieces of wood from tree trunks shot out and rained down, a sliver catching him in the face and making him bleed a little. Tyler smeared the blood with the back of his hand.

"We wouldn't be in this situation if it wasn't for your girlfriend." Maddox laughed. "Oh, by the way, she was one hell of a good lay. When she returned to the camp she practically begged me to give it to her."

It was a failed attempt at getting a rise out of him.

However, it worked for Madison.

"You bastard!" Madison yelled appearing off to his right, unloading multiple rounds at them.

"Madison!" Tyler yelled. "Get down."

She ducked, escaping the return fire. He motioned to her with an angry shake of his fist. That was all he needed. Now he had her to worry about. Tyler darted out again, trying to make his way back so he could watch her six but it failed. Rounds pushed him back to cover as bullets tore up the ground in front of him and ricocheted off rock.

"Oh this just got better," Maddox yelled. Tyler pressed his back against the boulder and turned his head towards Madison. She gave him a look as if to apologize for losing it. The tables had turned. Maddox's group divided into two. Trouble was now breathing down both their necks.

* * *

Mariah was a foster kid. That was why there weren't any photos of her. Nate had finally managed to get her to open up to him. She'd bounced around the system and had arrived at this family's home five months ago. That was all she'd tell him. She was tight-lipped about how they died. Any mention of the family only enraged her. He put two and two together and figured she'd done it. The question was why? Then again, did it matter? It was clear she was mentally unstable. He'd met his fair share of foster kids on the streets of Vegas, guys and girls who'd run away before the age of eighteen. Most foster homes were good, but there were always those that did it for the paycheck. Abuse was rampant and few would believe the children, especially if they had a track record of lying, running away from home and violence. Had that been the reason?

He couldn't get a straight answer out of her and eventually he gave up and focused on trying to convince her to let him go.

"If you're worried that I'm going to tell anyone. Who would I tell? Hell, who would even care?" Nate said. "The town out there has gone to shit. Law enforcement is barely hanging on by a thread. No one gives a rat's ass about a few people who died. Like I said, you probably had a good reason for doing what you did."

"I didn't kill them," she snapped. "They did."

"They?"

She nodded. He craned his neck, anticipating clarification. Nothing.

"Look, Mariah. I can't help you if you won't tell me."

"I don't need your help," she said rising from the table and disappearing out of the room. He heard her banging shit around in the kitchen. Cupboards slamming, plates smashing, a chair overturning and multiple hard thumps as if she was taking out her pent-up frustration on the fridge.

It went quiet.

"Then maybe you can consider letting me go?" he

hollered. "You know, my fingers are tingling and going numb." He paused. Still nothing. He continued, "What I did for you, Mariah, has to count for something? I could have walked on by."

She returned holding his rifle, and for a brief second, he thought this was where it would end. Staring down the barrel of his own gun. Victim of a psychotic girl he should have never helped. The irony wasn't wasted. There was him thinking he was being lured into a trap, that somehow she was connected to the three guys that surrounded her in the street, and yet they weren't the threat — she was.

"Listen to me," he said, his eyes bouncing from her face to the barrel. "I don't care what happened here, or what you think I will say. I have seen worse. You have my word. Untie me, and you will never see me again."

She got close and pushed the barrel into his cheek causing his head to turn.

"Mariah. Please. You don't have to do this."

In all the years he'd been alive, he had brushed with

death many times but nothing felt as real as right then. He swallowed hard.

"Shut up and look away."

He forced his face back at her and stared. If she wanted to kill him, she was going to have to look him in the eyes.

"Put the gun down."

"No, you are with them."

"Them? Help me out here. Who are we talking about?"

"THEM!" she bellowed loudly, her spit reaching his face. If she was on meds...clearly, she hadn't taken them in a while. How many others had lost their minds since the power grid went down? Perhaps she was telling the truth. Maybe her foster family were the victims of a home invasion. Maybe they took her for their own desires and she'd managed to escape. Who the hell knew?

"Them? I'm gonna need a little more than that," he replied.

"It doesn't matter as I'm going to take care of them. Yeah," she said nodding, a smile forming on her anguished face. "Then I'll deal with you."

And just like that she turned and strode out of the room.

"Mariah! MARIAH!"

Locks unlatched and a door was slammed closed. Silence permeated.

Was she gone or was this a trick, some way to determine if he could be trusted? Nate cursed loudly and then waited for what felt like an eternity but was probably no more than fifteen minutes. Convinced she was gone, he began rocking the chair from side to side. If he could just build up some momentum, maybe, just maybe he could break the chair and escape.

* * *

Rounds cut into the landscape. The staccato of automatic rifles drove home their intentions. They didn't want to bring him in alive. He steadied himself and scampered over a rise. He pitched sideways and was trying to scan the trees when he lost his footing. Tumbling head over heels he rolled down and narrowly missed plowing into a boulder, instead he wound up in a stream. He slapped in another magazine as he scrambled to his feet and raced into the coverage of the dense forest. Madison was engaging with them and had managed to take one of them out, bringing the group down to six.

A chorus of yelling signaled their approach. Tyler managed to elude them with the hopes of circling around and coming up the rear, however, that was harder than he anticipated. One of them spotted him and announced his presence to the others. Bullets snapped overhead. Tyler dropped to the waterlogged ground and wiggled his way towards a tree and rested the barrel of his rifle on a root rising out of the ground. He could hear boots getting closer and knew they were nearly upon him. Hold, hold, he told himself. A bearded man emerged. His eyes locked on to Tyler and he went to react but it was too late. A single round straight through his forehead and then Tyler shifted ass. He tried to make his way over to Madison, fearing for her life, when he was cut off by the bark of carbines. He ducked and bullets speared the trees around him. Thinking fast he tore off one of the EG18 high-output smoke grenades from his pouch, pulled the pin and tossed it. It kicked out an insane amount of black smoke which drifted and blocked their view as he darted back the way he came and slipped past two of them without problem. When he reached Madison, he was relieved to see she was still alive and unharmed. He threw her another magazine before resting his rifle on the top of the boulder and panning for threats.

"Tyler!" Madison yelled but before he could react, a gun cracked.

He turned to find one of Jude's men dead only yards away. He must have spotted him and waited until his back was turned before coming up the rear. Tyler looked at Madison thinking she'd killed him but she simply shrugged. His eyes scanned the trees. Was it a case of friendly fire or... He got his answer when he saw another collapse. Neither one of them had shot him and he could clearly see the other three.

That meant only one answer — Bennington.

He couldn't see him but he knew he was out there, probably tucked among the brush with his crosshair firmly fixed on… Crack!

Another dropped.

"What was that you were saying earlier, Maddox?" Tyler hollered, turning his face towards Madison, his lip curling ever so slightly. Maddox didn't reply but he sure as hell didn't back off. A torrent of gunfire was unleashed tearing up the trees all around them as they tried to throw everything they had at the wall with the hope of getting lucky. The onslaught of rounds put every other attempt to shame.

A surge of hope filled Tyler as he darted over to a tree to get a better lay of the land. He knew how many were left, but he needed to know where. He snuck a peek nearly losing his face in the process. He felt the air change, and the snap of bullets that were too close for comfort. A risk that had afforded him the exaction location of the last two. The only one he couldn't see was Maddox. Had he turned and fled, leaving his pals behind to chew on a bullet? No, he was too egotistical to back down and accept defeat. Returning home to Jude with his tail between his legs wasn't an option. *Where are you?* Tyler moved with purpose, ducking and darting from tree to tree, getting closer by the second to the last two. Another crack of a distant rifle and he saw one of them slump. *Damn, Bennington, you are one hell of a sniper.* Barring Maddox, one remained and within seconds his number would be up. Tyler clambered up a rise that would bring him up the rear behind the final shooter. Sure enough, there he was. Tyler brought his rifle up to take the shot when he heard a rustle to his left. He turned expecting to see Maddox but there was no one because the asshole was above him. He should have figured he'd go for a distraction. So focused on readying himself for the kill, he'd dropped his guard. Tyler felt the sheer force of his weight collapse on him before they rolled down the steep incline.

When a tree trunk broke his fall, it took the wind out of him at the same time.

Gulping air, he managed to take in two lungful before Maddox kicked him in the face. There was no pain as it happened too quickly but the assault that came next was brutal. A knife came down with Maddox behind it. Tyler reacted fast, rolling to avoid the collision of steel and flesh. A hard elbow to his back wasn't enough. Maddox lunged with the knife hoping to stab him in the ribs. Had he not grabbed his wrist, it would have sliced into him, for sure. Clasping his arm, he banged it four times against the earth before he released the knife. Maddox brought a sharp knee up, striking him in the groin while they lay side by side fighting for control. Another loud crack of a gun. There was no telling if it came from Bennington, or the final shooter. So intent on trying to block his knee, he wasn't fast enough to stop the second attack. Maddox pulled Tyler in and slammed his forehead into Tyler's nose, busting it open. A direct hit to the nose brought tears to his eyes. That was followed by two hard jabs to the face before Maddox hauled him up and threw him against a boulder. Blood was gushing down Tyler's face.

The taste of iron filled his mouth as he tried to catch a breath.

Maddox came forward again, this time striking him with a side kick to the gut. Tyler buckled straight into an uppercut. "You sack of shit." On the ground Maddox rained down his foot, pounding his ribs. Tyler balled in defense taking everything he threw at him. Another flash of his childhood. The endless self-defense drills Andy put them through played out. In that moment it wasn't Maddox beating him but Andy. Calling him a pussy. Telling him to get up. Striking him as Corey looked on unable to help.

Something primal rose in him, a will to survive that no one could teach, as it was in every human being. Tyler's arm lashed out like a cobra latching onto Maddox's grounded leg as he raised the other, he yanked it hard bringing him down like a sack of potatoes. Pushing pain from his mind he scrambled over, straddling him, raining down punches, one after the other, each time not seeing his face but Andy's.

He wasn't sure how long he beat him only that when Bennington pulled him off, his knuckles were raw and Maddox was unconscious and unrecognizable. Like waking from a nightmare he snapped into the present moment. Madison stood at the top of the rise looking down, while Bennington dropped and checked Maddox's pulse.

"Still alive." Bennington pulled his weapon to finish him when Tyler put out a hand.

"No. I need him alive."

Chapter 25

"You lied to me!" Allie said loudly from inside Jude's office. After returning to Camp Olney, Corey and the group were placed in cells and told they would stand trial for their crimes once Jude had conferred with the council. Jude leaned back in his chair with a cup of coffee in hand like he was some kind of god among men.

"First, watch your tone!" he replied with a stern look. "Second, I didn't lie. You will be joined with your sister in due time once Maddox returns."

"I'm not speaking about that. My father. You said you would release my father."

"I think you misunderstood me. I said you could see your father. I didn't say he could be released. Do you honestly think I would pardon a man who attempted to kill me?"

"But..."

Jude set his cup on his desk and leaned forward. "I like

you, Allie. You're smart and resourceful, and I probably haven't given you enough credit but surely by now even you should understand how things work around here. There is a system, a flow to every community whether that be in a city, a town, a village or a settlement like ours. There must be some semblance of order otherwise people suffer. If I release your father what message does that send to the rest of this camp?"

"That you are merciful," Allie replied without missing a beat.

"No. Weak. Indecisive. Unable to protect. We are living in precarious times, my girl. Survival is at the core of all we do. Why? Because we wish to live. That means not being in fear for our lives. If I release your father, and someone else attempts to take my life or someone else's in the camp, they will also want me to extend the same mercy. Eventually someone will take it for granted and upon release they will return to finish the job and that time they might get away with it. As much as I would love to see Edison living among us as a free man, he made a decision and for that there is a consequence."

"You're going to kill him?"

He smiled. "What is it with people thinking I love to kill?"

"Because of Alexander."

Jude blew out his cheeks and shook his head. "Alexander took the lives of three innocent people in this camp and he would have taken more had I not put an end to it." Jude tapped the side of his temple. "He wasn't all there, Allie."

"And you are?"

He gave a warm smile, the kind that won over the hearts of those who had joined the community over the years. There was a charisma to him that was attractive. He had a way of making people feel welcome and yet on the other hand, he could turn on a dime. There was something very Jekyll and Hyde about him. "I never asked for this position, Allie. I never forced my way to the top of the chain. I started this camp with friends, a core group of people who I respected and admired. We had a similar vision for the future. After Andy walked away from it all, what was I meant to do? Do the same? No, I couldn't turn my back on it as easily as he had." He paused for a second. "You should walk in my shoes sometime. It's not easy."

If he was looking for sympathy, he'd come to the wrong person.

"When do I get to see my father?"

"When your sister returns."

"No. I want to see him now."

Jude stared at her intently and she got a sense she was overstepping the line.

"I could have you put in the cell with him for what you did. So if mercy is what you want, know that I have already extended it to you." She shifted her weight from one foot to the next and looked down. "Ten minutes. You'll see him longer when your sister returns and I've spoken with both of you."

"Thank you, Jude," Allie said backing away. Jude gestured to one of his guards to go with her. Escorted over to the community jail, she felt a wave of embarrassment at the thought of seeing Corey and the others again. What did they think of her now? What choice did she have? She was caught in a tight spot and it was either agree or find herself thrown into a cell. At least right now she was in a position to turn this around if the opportunity arose. The problem was she was being scrutinized by every one of Jude's men. They were fully aware of her transgression and what a liability she was. She stood behind the hulking guard as he unlocked the entranceway. She entered the humid and foul-smelling cellblock. It reeked of bad body odor.

There he was. Her father was standing near the bars talking with Andy across from him when she entered. "Allie."

"Dad," she muttered before hurrying over to him. She reached through and hugged him and he placed a hand on her head. "I tried, Dad. I really did. But…"

"Ah there she is." Markowitz rose to his feet and crossed to the bars adjacent to her father's cell. "The girl with a plan. Except she forgot to mention the part where she screwed us over."

"Settle down," Corey said.

Allie cast a glance over her shoulder but didn't reply. Her father spoke on her behalf. "Whatever she did, she probably had a good reason."

"Oh, I'm sure she did. Like saving her own ass!" Markowitz slammed a hand on the bar and it echoed. The guard at the far end of the corridor shouted a warning. Allie dipped her chin, looking despondent.

Her father lifted her chin with two fingers. "Tell me what happened." She sighed and brought him up to speed.

Edison exhaled hard and stepped back and paced. He looked over to Andy and then got close to the bars to tell her his idea. As soon as he was finished, she frowned. "That won't work. All it takes is one of them to say something and I'll be thrown back in here."

"Trust me, Allie," Edison said with a strained smiled. He glanced at Andy again and this time Allie looked behind. Could it work? It was possible but so much time had passed. Would they even care now?

No sooner had the thought passed through her mind than the door at the far end of the corridor opened and another guard stepped in and spoke with the other. A glance towards her and she was beckoned out. "I was told ten minutes," Allie said when she reached him.

"There's been a change."

As soon as she stepped outside, she knew why. Multiple armed guards were ascending the steps to the top of the gates. That meant only one thing — a threat.

Chapter 26

What on earth was I thinking? Nate squirmed in the chair that was now sideways. He'd rocked it from side to side until it finally gave way and landed hard knocking the wind out of him. For the first few minutes he did nothing except try to catch his breath, then he struggled for what seemed like forever to turn the chair so he could use his feet to knock the table and get one of the knives to land on the ground. He worked every muscle in his body. Every creak of the floorboard had his senses on high alert. Had she returned? It had been at least an hour since she'd left. If she caught him like this he wouldn't fare well. Nate jammed his feet between the table leg and the chair, and with the back of the chair pressed against the wall he pushed the table in a jerking manner. He could hear the plates and cutlery shifting. "Come on!" he yelled. As hard as he tried the table wouldn't budge. As he grunted and pushed, sweat trickled down his brow and dropped onto the wood floor. For the first time, he considered the possibility that he might not be able to pull it off. That desperate thought amped his strength into high gear, and he gave the table one giant heave. With a thud the table tipped but then rocked back into place. *Damn it!* Enraged, he tried again. To his surprise it gave way. The table shifted and his plate and the cutlery clattered onto the floor nearby. Now he'd given himself another challenge.

If he could just shift himself over to the knife, he could possibly… He groaned, realizing it wasn't the sharp knife that had fallen, just a butter knife. He sighed, realizing he wasn't getting out. She'd find him on the ground and he'd have to come up with some lame story about losing his balance. Of course she wouldn't believe him and would probably take that damn crème brûlée torch to his hand again. He felt a growing dread. Perhaps she wouldn't bother and would just put a bullet in him, and Tyler and Erika would find him weeks from now piled up in the bathtub — or worse, no one would find him and he would rot away. His entire being was awash with horror. Had he come all this way, escaped from the dangers of the city only to die at the hands of some lunatic girl? Another swell of anger and he tried to claw his way over to the cutlery, figuring he could at least try to use the fork and pick away at the rope. The most insane and desperate thoughts went through his mind as panic gripped him.

The sound of a window opening, and then footsteps caught his attention. Had she forgotten her key? His mind shifted to how he was going to explain this. Any second now and... A face appeared in the doorway, but it wasn't Mariah.

It was a kid, no older than sixteen. He was wearing a Nike baseball cap, dark sunglasses and a bandanna around his face. As soon as he removed it, Nate's eyes widened. It was one of the three teens he'd driven away. The same one that had frozen and warned him before hightailing it out of there.

"You should have listened," he said. He stood there

looking around. "What a fucking mess this place is."

"You want to get me out of here."

"Oh, yeah, sure thing. I'm Danny by the way."

"She said your name was Jacob."

Danny hauled him up so that the chair was straight again.

"That girl is two sandwiches short of a picnic. I don't even know anyone by that name." He dropped to a knee, withdrew a sharp knife from a sheath and began cutting through the rope. "We first encountered her a few days back. That bitch attempted to kill one of us after we got out of a home over on Sun Crest Drive. Don't even ask me why. She kept talking about some Jacob kid, and a group of his friends. I told her we didn't know who the hell she was talking about. Anyway, we gave her a free pass the first time. Figured she was off her meds, you know. A day later we came across her using a baseball bat on some poor kid. There was no hope for him but that's when we figured we'd intervene."

"Tease, you mean?" Nate asked. "Hasn't anyone told

you about poking a wasp's nest?"

"We didn't tease her. We came over to check that the kid was okay and she turned on us. I swear that bitch was high or something because her strength was inhuman. Anyways, you caught up with us minutes after that. We were on our way to the cop shop."

"I bet you were," Nate said in a disbelieving tone.

Danny stopped cutting. "Look man, I don't need to help you."

"Ah forget it. Im sorry. I'm just exhausted and want to get out of here."

"I hear yah." He glanced at the table. "Having a tea party, were you?" He snorted and continued cutting. "After you took off with her, I followed. I figured shit would go south and I was right."

Nate frowned. "So why did you wait until today?"

"Ah, I got a little sidetracked with the cops. Sorry about that."

"What?" he said just as his wrists were freed. The comfort of not having rope cutting into his wrists was exhilarating. Danny moved on to his ankles.

"Looting. They've had me on their radar for some time since I hit up one of the stores with a group of my pals." He stopped cutting. "I know what you're thinking. Look, I'm not proud of it but we have to survive and the city isn't exactly helping. Though I would have gladly served up that loony bin of a girl to them on a silver platter. Can't have someone out there putting mine or my pals' necks at risk. There's enough danger as it is."

Danny continued to rattle on about how he'd managed to survive so far. He had just got done cutting the rope around his left ankle when Nate saw movement in the corridor.

"Danny!"

He turned just as Mariah shot into the room and brought a large ornament down on his head. Nate lunged forward with his wrists and one leg free and plowed into her, driving Mariah across the room into the wall. His right leg was still attached to the chair so that came with him, clattering behind and causing him to stumble and land on top of her.

The fight was on.

Her face was enraged as he pressed her wrists to the floor and tried to hold her there. It was like trying to wrestle a wild animal. She tried to buck him off her using her hips but he had her pinned. He turned his head to shout for Danny only to have her latch on to his ear with her teeth. Nate let out a scream as she sank her teeth into the lower part of his earlobe. He'd never felt so much pain. It was pure agony. Nate saw red at that point. As blood streamed down the side of his neck, he switched gears and wrapped his hands around her throat and began to squeeze. Her eyes bulged and went bloodshot. Mariah clawed at his chest but he wouldn't let up for even a second. It seemed to take forever for her to die. Minutes passed but slowly and surely Nate watched the life in her eyes disappear. Convinced she was gone, he rolled off her, exhausted, and lay there, staring up at the ceiling. Danny moved and clambered to his feet sporting a gnarly gash on his forehead. He looked down at them. "She dead?"

Too tired to respond he answered with a simple nod.

Danny cut away at the rope around his ankle and Nate breathed a sigh of relief.

As they came out of the house a neighbor across the street looked at them in horror. They were a mess with blood coating Nate's neck and Danny's forehead.

"I told you she deserved it."

Nate looked at him and shook his head. "Let's get to the hospital."

"Hospital? But it was just a knock to the head."

"Trust me on this." His thoughts turned to Erika as they staggered south.

Chapter 27

The shotgun angled at Maddox was rigged with a tightly wound pantyhose around his neck so that if he attempted to run or swipe at it, it would only quicken his death. In addition, Tyler had secured his wrist to the gun to ensure that if anyone shot him, unless they got lucky with a head shot, he wouldn't be dropping the gun. It was just one of several tactics he'd set into motion, including having Bennington watching his six. It would have been a lie to say he felt no fear as they strode up to the settlement, but he figured that it would give Jude one hell of a dilemma. Which son was he willing to risk losing? As far as Tyler saw it, he had one hell of a bargaining chip.

He stopped fifty yards from the gate and waited.

"You got eyes on them?" he muttered into the comms.

Bennington replied. "Of course. They're agitated, that's for sure."

The gate pulled back and a number of Jude's men

fanned out, rifles aimed at him. No one said anything until Jude appeared, squeezing his way through the curious onlookers. "Tyler. Glad to see you're safe," he said walking towards them.

"That's far enough," Tyler said when he was roughly twenty-five feet away. He scanned the men to his left and right that were arching around him. "That goes for your men. They get any closer and you'll be picking up brain matter, and I'm not talking about Maddox here." That got Jude's attention. His eyes bounced from Tyler to the hilly forested landscape. He could only imagine what was going through his mind.

"Where is he?"

"He? You think I'd be brazen enough to walk up here with only one sniper?"

Jude surveyed the hillside. "Don't play games, Tyler. Allie told me how many there were." He turned his attention back to him and lifted a hand. "What are we doing here? Huh? Let him go and let's talk about this."

"We are done talking. I was wrong about you. I

wanted to believe you were different. That you weren't playing both sides of the fence but I know now you are."

"It's called survival, Tyler. I think you know a thing or two about that."

"Is that how you justify supporting raiders who pillage and have killed good people in Whitefish?"

Over the comms he heard Bennington say that he'd spotted two guys circling around from the west. Tyler looked but couldn't see them. He figured they must be coming through the forest area. "I'll take care of it."

"Hold," Tyler said.

"What?" Jude replied thinking he was talking to him.

"Unless your two men want to die today, I would advise them now to back off."

Jude glanced at Warren, a close friend and confidant of his. He'd obviously made the arrangement. "It's your call. But my sniper never misses."

Jude turned and leaned into Warren. He got on a radio and mumbled something before looking back at Tyler with a disgusted look on his face.

"You do that again, and Maddox here is going to sing with the stars."

"Maddox. You okay?" Jude asked. His face was busted up beyond comprehension, a swelling mass of bloody flesh. Both eyes were almost sealed closed, his nose was off to one side and his lips were split revealing two teeth he'd knocked out.

"Oh, he's just dandy," Tyler said. "Now I want you to go and get my brother, Andy, Allie and the rest of the group and we're going to leave here and you can go about your business."

Jude smirked. "Son, you know I can't do that."

"Don't call me your son. Andy might have stepped over the line more times than I can recall, he may not be winning the father of the year award anytime soon, but he sure as hell knows where his loyalties lie. Unlike you."

The tension could have been cut with a knife.

* * *

Inside the camp, Allie knew this was her window of opportunity. Those that scrutinized her were distracted. If her father was right, they would only get one shot at this. She sought out Caroline in the nursery. There she was watching over the youngest along with several other women. There wasn't a sense of danger because not once had anyone breached the camp without one of the scouts or tower guards spotting them.

The cries of newborn babies dominated as she entered the large room that extended all the way to the back of the dome. There were four other women assisting Caroline. Some with the toddlers, others with infants and the rest with the younger kids, playing games and keeping their minds occupied.

Caroline spotted her enter. "Allie?"

"We need to talk. It's about my father."

She was holding a young infant in her arms. Caroline was close to her father's age, early sixties, graying hair but with radiant skin. She was short in stature and was often found helping young mothers in the camp. Caroline passed off the child to another woman and followed Allie into one of the back rooms.

"What is it?"

"You're aware Andy Ford is in the cell units with my father."

"I knew Edison was there, not Andy. I thought he was released after his arrival."

She shook her head. "My father asked you to gather together the group. That now was the time." The color in her face washed out and she swallowed. "He said you would know what to do."

"That was a long time ago. So much time has passed, Allie."

"Were you aware that Jude was an ally of the raiders?"

Caroline shook her head and went to the door and looked out. "What you are asking me to do could get us all killed."

"I'm not asking. Andy and my father are. He will stand with you."

There was a look of reluctance on her face. She sighed and appeared torn.

"It's now or never," Allie said. "Jude won't release my

father. He's going to kill him."

Caroline frowned. "That would break the rule that the ten of us agreed upon in the beginning."

"I guess he no longer abides by that rule," Allie replied. Caroline wasn't easily convinced. It was clear that time had changed her views on Jude and what was important to her. People changed. That which people rallied behind in their early twenties often fell by the wayside when they reached the winter season of their life.

"Look, I told him I would tell you. You decide."

With that said, Allie turned and exited the room. She knew the guard carried the keys to the cellblock. Getting them wouldn't be easy. Although a large percentage of the camp was occupied by Tyler's arrival, the hulking guard stood by the doorway ensuring no one got in or out. She could see the keys hanging from his waistband overshadowed by his enormous frame. There was no chance in hell she could swipe them without raising the alarm. Allie stood near a dome and knew she could kill him with a single shot from her bow but he wasn't the enemy. She held no animosity for him. He was simply doing his duty, following orders. And forget flirting, that approach had got her in this mess in the first place. A distraction? She rifled through ideas but nothing came to mind.

She had no choice.

Allie scurried to collect her bow and returned minutes later. Eyeing for trouble, she removed an arrow from her quiver and lifted her bow preparing to take the shot. She knew the penalty for murder was death.

Forgive me, God, she muttered.

* * *

"It seems we are at a bit of stalemate," Tyler said. "You want Maddox here, and I want my family and friends back. What's more important to you, Jude?" He called him by his name because "father" just sounded too weird after all this time.

"What's important to me right now is you."

"Bullshit. Don't lie to me."

"Son, have I ever—"

"Stop calling me that." Tyler gritted his teeth.

Jude lifted two hands. "Look, I don't blame you, Tyler. You've been through a lot. Okay. There is a lot more at play here than you are aware of. But you don't want to squeeze that trigger. It will only end badly for you, Corey and Andy. You hear me?"

Tyler squinted. He wanted answers. As much as it was clear that Jude was involved with the raiders, in his time with him at the camp he didn't strike him as someone given to supporting causes that harmed others. Hell, he'd built a camp with Andy to provide protection for those who wanted it.

"I don't get it. Why? Why would you align yourself with them?"

Jude sighed. "I can't explain that. In time you will understand but there are things that need to happen first. Important things that affect all of us including you."

"Stop talking shit and just tell me the truth. I'm so goddamn tired of people lying to me."

"I'm sorry, I can't."

Tyler shrugged. "Then I guess I'll just put a bullet in Maddox's head. How about that, Maddox? Your father would rather you died than release a few people."

Some of Jude's men were waiting for the word to shoot him.

"Tyler, just wait!" he said extending a hand and trying to bridge the gap between them.

* * *

Allie felt the tension in the bow, and aimed for the heart. It would be a swift death. She'd make sure of that. As soon as he dropped, she would rush in, drag his body back, take the keys and release her father. Her fingers trembled. She was a split second away from releasing the arrow when she felt a hand on her shoulder.

"Allie," Caroline said. "Don't. Let me."

She lowered her bow and watched as Caroline stepped out into the main courtyard and crossed to the cellblock. The guard saw her coming. She stopped and spoke with him and glanced over at Allie. Caroline pointed to the gates but Allie couldn't hear what she was saying, however, she could see. Caroline lifted the keys off the guard's belt with all the skill of a pickpocket. She held them out and Allie knew instantly. She rushed in keeping her back to the dome and snatched the keys from her hand, pulling back into the space between the domes while the guard followed Caroline over to the gate. Her sway with those in charge was strong because she was one of the original ten who had established Camp Olney. Few argued with them. Their word was gold.

Allie moved in fast, unlocking the door and entering the cellblock.

"Allie," her father said rising from his bunk and gripping the bars.

"We don't have much time. Tyler is outside."

"Tyler?" Corey and Andy came forward and peppered her with questions.

"No time," she said, unlocking their cell.

As Markowitz passed her, he glanced but said nothing. She didn't expect a pat on the back or thanks. All that mattered now was arming them and turning back the tide before Tyler was swept away by the approaching storm of Jude's men. Would they kill him in order to save Maddox? She hoped to God not but Jude was a wild card given to do anything to survive.

* * *

As soon as they were out, one of the original ten met with them, leading them around the dome to an area where they had gathered together rifles. The rest of the core group that established the camp were waiting. He didn't need to explain what the situation was as Caroline had already briefed them. Andy had lived his life by rules and some of those were unbreakable. When he'd established the camp there were some that they all agreed upon if and when one or more of them were to lose their way. Jude had lost his way at least in the eyes of those he once called friends. They knew what needed to be done but whether they would do it was to be seen. Andy's greeting was short-lived as the sound of yelling outside the camp brought home the urgency of the present moment.

"Andy, follow me," Janson said leading him into a dome where another thirty people were waiting. Familiar faces that he hadn't seen in over twenty years stared back — those that he had brought into the midst of them — those he had helped, supported, laughed and even cried with. "Thank you for coming," he said. "I know I left you all with many questions. And in time I will provide answers but what I'm asking you to do now is for the longevity of this settlement. Will you stand with me?"

He knew his words might fall on deaf ears but he was surprised by their response.

"We never walked away," said one of them.

Their words cut him to the core as he knew that his decision many years ago hadn't just affected his son or Jude, but it had torn away at the friends he'd left behind. To hear that now brought home how much he'd missed them.

"Are you going to kill him?" Devlin asked referring to Jude.

"Not if I don't have to."

Marching out as one army, Andy felt a swell of pride marred by the harsh realization that he could be leading them to their deaths.

* * *

Tyler saw them before Jude did. A smile formed on his face.

"I need you to rethink what you are about to do," Jude said still concentrating on preventing Tyler from squeezing the trigger.

"I could say the same for you," he replied with a nod to the swarm of armed men and women now pointing their weapons at the rest of Jude's men. Jude turned, a look of shock on his face.

"It's over, Jude," Andy said eyeing the crowd. "No one needs to die."

Jude looked bewildered as he scanned the faces calling out names. "Janson? Caroline. Why?"

Caroline stepped forward. "You broke the rules."

"Rules? Everything I have done has been for you all," he said. "The only reason you are alive is because of me.

And now you turn and bite the hand that feeds you and choose to stand behind this man. The same man that left us? Who was there to pick up the pieces to keep this place going?"

"All of us," Janson replied. "It was never just you, Jude."

The tension was palpable.

"What, so you're now going to follow him?"

"They're not following anyone," Andy replied clarifying. "We built this place together; we'll move forward together."

Jude laughed. "Now you decide. Really? Now?" He shook his head and removed his rifle from his back.

"Disarm," Andy bellowed.

"Never," Jude replied. "And those of you who agree. Follow me."

Eyes darted between faces. Hesitation. Reluctance. Confusion. It was all there.

But like any who had given their lives to a cause, to a leader, there were those who still believed in what Jude was building. A large number of people from the camp stepped out, backing away with their fingers on triggers ready to engage. It would have been a slaughter fest if any one of them made the fatal decision to shoot.

Instead, Andy let them leave.

He extended the same courtesy to them that they had to him many years ago.

Untangling the shotgun from Maddox, Tyler did the same. Maddox looked at him, confused. "Go. I only give one free pass," he said using the same words Jude had with his father. Maddox hurried and caught up with Jude. They exchanged a glance and Tyler knew there was no going back. Over the comms he heard Bennington say, "Are you sure you don't want to change your mind? I've got him in the crosshair."

Tyler chuckled. "Come on down, old man," he replied.

As Jude and a large number of Camp Olney melted into the forest, Corey hurried over to his brother and grasped him. They hugged it out as Andy approached. He gave Tyler a strained smile and thanked him before turning to leave. "That's all I get?" Tyler said.

Andy cast a glance back and frowned. A moment of hesitation, perhaps confusion, then Andy did something he hadn't ever done, he extended a hand and said, "Good job." Tyler smiled. Andy was still Andy to him. It was hard to change the emotional and physical scars he bore but right then he glimpsed another side, a man that was equally damaged. Tyler stepped forward and they shook hands. It wasn't a hug but it was the beginning of healing, and by the looks on the faces of Camp Olney, that was exactly what was needed.

Epilogue

The sun was melting into the horizon, two days after Tyler had threatened to kill Maddox outside Camp Olney. In those first forty-eight hours they'd fully expected Jude to return, enraged by those who had turned coat and sided with Andy. He didn't. In that time emotions ran high and talk of the future, the raiders and Jude was on the lips of everyone. After being privy to the discussions between Andy and the original members of the settlement, Officer Ferris returned to Whitefish to get word of how the town was holding up, to give Nate the heads-up on where they were, and to see if Erika was out of the coma. Tyler couldn't say either one of them had been on his mind, and in some ways he felt bad about that. "Out of sight, out of mind," Corey had said. Though he could tell Corey was better at giving out advice than following it. The grief of losing Ella and their daughter was still raw.

Even though Allie didn't need to apologize, she did after giving a lengthy explanation and then apologizing again. Tyler understood. He couldn't fault her. All of them had made dangerous decisions. And, if placed in the same position he probably would have put Corey's life over the lives of strangers.

Still, she had redeemed herself in more ways than one. Not only had she taken the risk to release their group but her trip into the heart of Camp O'Brien hadn't been a total loss. Thomas had informed her to tell Jude when and where he would be meeting with the mysterious Morning Star, the raiders' apparent leader.

In light of recent events, they were taking a chance that Jude hadn't been in contact with Thomas and rescheduled. And, they were going out on a limb venturing out without informing Andy, but he figured it would only ignite an argument and strangely enough they seemed to be on good terms, at least for now. Besides, he wasn't planning on attacking, it was more surveillance, curiosity over who was able to rally so many people together. It wasn't like it was a hard thing to do under the circumstances. Higher-ups in organizations had been doing it for years. Religion used fear. Politics used propaganda. And the sex industry used porn to sucker in the desperate, gullible and needy. All they needed to do was wave a carrot out on a stick and there would always be ones who would chase after it, and justify their actions later.

"You sure it's near here?" Tyler asked.

"Positive. Madison accompanied Thomas in a Jeep up to the ridge. There's a lookout that had been used as an observation point for spotting forest fires since the early fifties. They always meet here."

They trudged through the darkening forest and up the steep, rocky incline, soaking in the breathtaking view of a salmon and red sunset stretched across the horizon. Tall pines rose like upstretched fingers silhouetted against the evening sky.

They soldiered on coming up over a rise.

"There it is," Allie said.

In the distance they saw the towering structure that overlooked the town of Troy and the Kootenai Valley. It was perched at the top of the ridge. The glow of flickering candles illuminated the inside making it clearly visible to the eye. Tyler glanced at his watch. "Well, someone is home." They clambered up over boulders so they could find a clear shot of the top. Tyler crouched and dug into his backpack to retrieve the high-powered binoculars. He brought them up and zoomed in on the wooden cabin at the top of what looked like a 45-foot railroad water tank tower. Multiple newly installed white windows wrapped around the four sides leaving a small catwalk encircling the building covered by the roof's lip. He squinted.

"What do you see?" Allie asked.

There was enough room inside for at least four or five people. He could make out a twin bed, a couple of mattresses, a fridge, lights, a table and chairs and a propane stove. There was no toilet by the looks of it but a quick scan of the landscape and he spotted an outhouse a short distance away. "Hold on. I can't see anyone."

He continued to scan and then he saw a cloud of dust behind a truck coming up the winding roadway. "We got some action." He adjusted the zoom and his lip curled. It was Jude, and he was alone. He parked at the foot of the lookout and got out. He looked around before making his way over to the staircase-style ladder that crisscrossed up to the top. There were no other vehicles visible but he was convinced that if Morning Star was already there, they must have camouflaged it. "Where are you?" he mumbled under his breath. It didn't take Jude long to reach the top. The river nearby could be heard rushing, and a flock of birds broke away from trees, probably scared off by a bear, wolf or mountain lion that frequented those parts.

"Let me take a look," Allie said.

"Hold on," Tyler said adjusting the focus from blurred to clear.

He watched Jude step inside the doorway, remove his rifle and set it down against the end of the bed. He shrugged off his jacket and tossed it on the back of a chair before crossing the room and proceeding to pour himself a drink. So focused on what Jude was doing, he didn't notice another vehicle arrive and they were too far away to hear it. It was only when Jude turned towards the door and it opened that he got his first glimpse at the new arrival. Cloaked in a long dark trench coat with a hood covering their face, they closed the door. *This was Morning Star. It had to be.* He felt his pulse speed up. Finally, he was going to find out who it was.

Jude handed the stranger a glass with what looked like two fingers of bourbon just as they pushed back their hood. *No. How? It was impossible. It couldn't be.*

Tyler's eyes widened, and his jaw went slack. "Mom?"

* * *

THANK YOU FOR READING

Rules of Engagement will be out in May
Please consider leaving a review. Even a few words is
really appreciated. Thanks kindly, Jack.

A Plea

Thank you for reading Rules of Darkness: A Post-Apocalyptic EMP Survival Thriller (Survival Rules Series Book 3). If you enjoyed the book, I would really appreciate it if you would consider leaving a review. Without reviews, an author's books are virtually invisible on the retail sites. It also lets me know what you liked. You can leave a review by visiting the book's page. I would greatly appreciate it. It only takes a couple of seconds.

Thank you — **Jack Hunt**

Newsletter

Thank you for buying Rules of Darkness: A Post-Apocalyptic EMP Survival Thriller (Survival Rules Series book 3), published by Direct Response Publishing.

Click here to receive special offers, bonus content, and news about new Jack Hunt's books. Sign up for the newsletter. http://www.jackhuntbooks.com/signup/

About the Author

Jack Hunt is the author of horror, sci-fi and post-apocalyptic novels. He currently has over thirty books published. Jack lives on the East coast of North America. If you haven't joined Jack Hunt's Private Facebook Group you can request to join by going here. https://www.facebook.com/groups/1620726054688731/ This gives readers a way to chat with Jack, see cover reveals, and stay updated on upcoming releases. There is also his main Facebook page if you want to browse that.

www.jackhuntbooks.com

jhuntauthor@gmail.com

Made in the USA
Columbia, SC
03 February 2020

87469739R00252